WALKING in the LIGHT

the LIGHT

A Soldier's Spiritual Journey

WALKING in the LIGHT

A Soldier's Spiritual Journey

By Lewis W. Halstead

Walking in the Light: A Soldier's Spiritual Journey

All Scripture quotations are from the Holy Bible, King James Version. Public domain.

ISBN 978-1-955295-38-3

 COURIER PUBLISHING

100 Manly Street
Greenville, South Carolina 29601
CourierPublishing.com

PUBLISHED IN THE UNITED STATES OF AMERICA

Acknowledgments

Special thanks to my brothers in Christ.

Thanks to Mom, Missy, and Mark.

To my late wife, "Every good gift and every perfect gift is from above … ."

Finally, thanks to my "little brother" for your continued support.

INTRODUCTION

Sergeant First Class Michael Logan had always read about the many journeys the apostle Paul had taken to further God's kingdom. He never thought he, too, would be given a journey as well. From the sands of Kuwait to the sandhills of North Carolina, Michael begins to understand God's purpose and reason in his life.

WALKING in the LIGHT

A Soldier's Spiritual Journey

CHAPTER 1

Sergeant First Class E-7, Michael Logan, awoke suddenly to the alarm on his ten-dollar wristwatch. "0400" flashed in a dull green light but did little to illuminate the nearly pitch-black surroundings of his tent. The useless orange chem light that hung from the top of the tent only served as a reminder to avoid walking into the pole. He tried to focus his eyes enough to find the button that would silence the alarm and flashing light. Finally, after several failed attempts, he succeeded. He drew a deep breath and sat up, kicking his feet over the side of his cot into the cool sand.

"Are we getting up?" a voice from across the tent asked.

"No, just me. Go back to sleep."

The voice belonged to Specialist E-4, Joey Dutton, SFC Logan's Humvee driver. He said no more and almost immediately went back to sleep.

Logan fumbled under his cot and found the flashlight and Bible he had strategically placed there the night before. He sat back, trying to stretch the stiffness out of his back, and opened the Bible to a marked passage — one that he read every morning, Isaiah 41:10–13:

Fear thou not; for I am with thee: be not dismayed; for I am thy God: I will strengthen thee; yea, I will help thee; yea, I will uphold thee with the right hand of my righteousness. Behold, all they that were incensed against thee shall be ashamed and confounded: they shall be as nothing; and they that strive with thee shall perish. Thou shalt seek them, and shalt not find them, even them that contended with thee: they that war against thee shall be as nothing, and as a thing of nought. For I the Lord thy God will uphold thy right hand, saying unto thee, fear not; I will help thee.

Logan closed the Bible and silently prayed. He began by thanking God for his mercy and grace. He thanked God for loving and saving him many years ago as a teenager. He also thanked God for the men who served in his platoon. He had always believed when praying that God should come first, before any other requests. Thank God first, then make your supplication.

He continued by asking for the safety of his men and a quick resolution to the battle that was only weeks away. Several men in the platoon did not know God, but he prayed that each one would turn from their sinful ways and accept Christ.

He had no more ended his prayer than the tent flap opened, and SPC Chris Boone, the .50 cal. gunner on his Humvee, stepped in.

"Sergeant Logan, are you up?"

"Yes, I'm up."

"I've always wondered why you tell me to get you up at four, but then you are already up."

"Got to have a backup plan. I've never put a lot of trust in this watch."

"Do I have time for a nap?"

"A short one. We will be moving out at 0530."

From the darkness, Dutton asked, "Are we getting up?"

"No, go back to sleep," Boone said, making his way to his cot. He had just finished a two-hour shift of guard duty.

Logan put on his socks and boots, walked out of the tent, and headed to the latrine. Logan was the Platoon Sergeant for the best scout platoon in the entire First Armored Division — at least, that's how he felt. He had been with the platoon for two years and had come to know each man well enough to know their strengths and weaknesses.

His men had few weaknesses regarding knowing their jobs as scouts.

However, in their personal life, that was another matter. They had deployed to Kuwait from Germany several weeks earlier and were now in the middle of Desert Shield. Preparations were being made by both sides for a battle that seemed imminent.

The remainder of his platoon — nine more Humvees and thirty-one soldiers that included the platoon leader, a first lieutenant, four staff sergeants, four sergeants, and the rest privates up to specialists — were several clicks north, spread out on a screen line observing the Iraqi forces. The number of Soviet tanks increased daily. T-55s, T-62s, and T-72s filled the valley under the scout's watchful eyes.

President Bush had given Saddam Hussein until mid-January to get out of Kuwait. It did not seem he would comply.

In the weeks ahead the war would begin, and the greatest tank battle since World War II would be fought. Of course, the lessons learned from WWII would not be repeated. Then, the United States used the underdog Sherman tank against the far superior German tanks, the Tigers and the Panthers. The only way a Sherman could take one of those out was to fire into the engine exhaust compartment. Many Shermans were destroyed, and many men died knowing the odds were against them. But that didn't stop them from fighting and trying.

This battle would be different. The United States had the best tank — the M-1 Abram. It was faster, better armored, lower profiled, and faster firing. In short, it was the best tank on the battlefield.

The assembly area that Logan's tent was in was part of the HQ's company for a tank battalion: medics, transportation, mechanics, cooks, supply, communication, and Cavalry scouts. Two companies of Abram's were on his left and two on his right. There was another battalion further left and another further right that made up their brigade. M-1 Abrams lay as far as one could see in either direction.

For now, the US and Iraqi forces were moving their chess pieces to the board, but neither side had made a move. The US was waiting for war to be declared in mid-January. During the preparation phase, a briefing on rules of engagement came almost daily: "Do not fire unless fired upon."

Logan entered the tent again, "Up and at 'em. Let's get moving."

Boone and Dutton both sat up and dressed.

"Are we doing Meals Ready to Eat for breakfast again?" Boone asked.

"I think they have something going down at the mess tent. I smelled sausage," Logan replied.

The hot meals had been slow in coming, and the two specialists hurried, eager to eat whatever was prepared — thankful they didn't have to choke down another ham slice or any of the less appetizing menus the MRE provided. They were cold, tasteless, and greasy. Hot sauce was included in about half the menus, and everyone cherished it. Even soldiers who did not use it saved it for those who did. At best, it added flavor and disguised the lack of it.

Logan added, "They may have some decent coffee, too. Let's take a marmite of whatever they got for the platoon. They will be glad to have it."

All three men walked to the mess tent in "full battle rattle": Kevlar helmet, flak vest, load bearing equipment, gas mask, and M-16 rifle. They prayed and then spent ten minutes consuming scrambled eggs, sausage, coffee, and an unexpected treat — sliced bread and fresh oranges. They went to the head cook, and he filled a marmite with the hot breakfast and a small beverage cooler with coffee. They carried the containers to the Humvee and loaded them around the cases of bottled water, MREs, and five-gallon jugs of water they had loaded the night before.

The Army Reserve units in the rear had done a fine job with water purification, but the demand had been high during the one-hundred-degree days. They had struggled to keep up. Bottled water had been shipped in to help with the shortage.

Boone took charge of the loading process. He wanted to make sure he had room to maneuver in the turret behind the gun, and he was also a neat freak and very organized.

"Do we have the mail?" Logan asked.

Sitting in the driver's seat and putting in the days new frequencies, Dutton replied, "I think Boone filed it under M for mail." The comment drew a laugh from everyone, including Boone.

Logan handed Boone his bag. He knew it was bound to be packed according to Boone's plan. Logan did not like to micromanage the small things. He enjoyed having soldiers that cared about keeping things neat and organized. John Wesley, the founder of the Methodist Church, had been credited with the phrase, "Cleanliness is next to godliness," and Logan reminded his crew jokingly that it worked for Baptists, too.

As Logan entered the Humvee, he noticed a yellow manila envelope sitting in his seat.

Dutton spoke up, "We thought you would enjoy that letter. It's from a church."

"Thanks, I'll check it out," Logan said.

The mail was mostly the "To Any Soldier" variety. Christmas was approaching, and cards, letters, and the occasional package offering thanks and prayers were common.

Logan examined the return address as he got into his seat. It had been sent by a Sunday school class in Tennessee. He laid it on the radio and picked up the hand mic. He looked at Dutton, who was holding the Signal/Standard Operating Instructions that contained all the sensitive information for the battalion. Challenge, passwords, and call signs were contained in the tiny book. Logan kept the book in his possession but rarely looked at it. He used the opportunity to train his crew how to read it. The book was coded and required a degree of knowledge and training to understand it.

"What's our call sign today?"

"Today, we are Dogs."

"What about HQ?"

"They are Joker."

Logan put the mic to his ear and squeezed the button. "Joker base, this is Dog 2. Radio check over."

"Dog 2, this is Joker base. Read you loud and clear."

"Copy Joker, Dog 2. SP time 0530."

"Dog 2, Joker base, good hunting."

"Dog 2 out."

The second radio, the platoon radio, came to life as the Humvee moved to the security gate made of concertina wire. A soldier pulled it open, and the crew began the trip north.

"Dog 2, Dog 1 over." The platoon leader, 1st Lt. David Samuels, said.

"Go ahead 1. This is 2."

Call signs changed daily for security, but the platoon leader was always one, and the platoon sergeant was always two.

"Two, are you bringing sunscreen?"

"Sorry, 1. They are out, but I have you a nice sun bonnet," Logan said.

Dutton smirked at Logan's attempt at humor. Logan had opened a can of worms, and the other scouts listening quickly replied to the bonnet joke.

"Is it a Me-Maw bonnet or a going-to-church bonnet?"

The caller didn't identify himself, but everyone knew who it was. Every platoon has a comedian, and Dog 4, the wing man for the senior scout Dog 3, was that man.

"Four, this is 3. Keep the chatter down and the lines open."

Logan knew Dog 4 was right but grinned at the picking and antics from a platoon that had endured blowing sand and dust, high temps, sparse shade, and little sleep for weeks. He was proud of his men.

His headcount of thirty-four was six men short of an entire platoon.

Only four crews were at full capacity. The three-man crews on the line had to pull two hours in an observation post forward of their Humvee, two hours behind a .50 cal., and then two hours in the back of the Humvee, trying to get some sleep. The process continued 24/7, day after day. Soldiers hoped a shower run didn't occur during their sleep cycle because they would lose it until the next go around.

"All Dog elements, we are en route to the dog pound. Dog 2 out."

Boone stood behind the .50 cal. in the turret, his eyes moving. He wore goggles over his eyes and a handkerchief over his nose and mouth to minimize the dust and sand intake that sometimes swirled at twenty knots. He had been oblivious to the radio chatter and instead focused on his job at hand. Logan tugged on his pant legs as Boone stood between him and Dutton. Boone bent down to hear his sergeant.

"Abraham's stomping grounds was right around here. The place called Ur."

"Might be why God had him move," Boone said.

The laughter was heard loudest from Dutton. "You got a point."

The Humvee continued to make its way toward the screen line as Logan reflected on his crew. Dutton and Boone had arrived in Germany as brand-new privates just out of Basic and Advanced Individual Training. Logan had only been there a few months before them and noticed something about each young man. They did not swear as many soldiers did. Nor did they go to the bars or associate with the constant barrage of young women in the barracks.

Logan had suggested a crew change for the platoon, and he selected both men to be on his crew. He brought both men into his office and laid out their responsibilities. He started by letting them know he was a man of faith and would not tolerate foul language and drunkenness. Both young men seemed relieved and assured Logan they were Christians, too. Logan had suspected it, and after the pep talk, the young men gave him some background on questions he had.

Boone was from North Carolina and had been raised in a Christian home without a father. He didn't share much about his dad, but Logan saw him seeking guidance. Occasionally, he would have to caution Boone and Dutton when temptation pulled them in the wrong direction. Still, Boone had a thirst for God. He was always seeking greater knowledge from the Bible and asking questions.

Boone and Dutton were not complainers but were hard workers and dependable. Their faith in God was the key ingredient for young men to mold their lives, and both were on the right track.

Dutton came from a family of men who served God and country. He was from a small country town in Kentucky, not far from Fort Knox, where he and Boone received their initial training. Dutton's father had served in Vietnam and instilled his values and ethics in his son as best he could. His grandfather had served in WW II and been all over Europe. Dutton had considered joining the Marines, but his dad reminded him that he came from a long line of army blood. He pleased everyone when he announced his plans to carry on the tradition.

The 1st Sgt., who assigned living quarters in the barracks, had made the two roommates, and the separation from the others in the platoon pleased Logan. Logan reminded them that the platoon was a team of different beliefs and backgrounds, but they should never compromise their beliefs. He even suggested not being afraid to minister to their teammates.

Logan reminded them that Jesus came to save the lost, and the two men would be living among the lost. Bringing a lost friend to Christ was the goal. Be an example, because when they stumbled, the lost would quickly point that out.

Logan has also shared that he was single. He was not against marriage but hadn't found a godly woman to put up with him. Both young men had girlfriends back home, young ladies they had grown up with in church and school. Logan warned that if he could be faithful to a woman he hadn't met, they could be faithful to their women. The talk sparked a deep respect between the three men — a friendship in a professional sense of the word. Logan was pleased with their spiritual growth. It reflected their maturity greater than many older men.

Dutton broke the silence as they neared the scouts on the screen line. "Are we starting on the west end today?"

"Sounds good. We don't want to get into a routine," Logan said.

Dutton turned the Humvee left and headed to the scouts, who were the farthest on the left. Dog 3 and 4 tied into the other battalion on their left.

As much as Logan's crew tried to avoid routine, the resupply they did daily was just that. The scouts had seen a blue and white vehicle, much like a VW bus, traveling at different points of the screen line and at different times of the day. They had given it the nickname "Hippie Van," feeling certain it was Saddam's version of a scout.

The platoon had preset targets registered with artillery and air support, and they did not doubt their locations were known by the Iraqis. The van could have pulled up to a scout Humvee, marked a precise location, and, with the ROE, pummeled the American scouts.

Fortunately, the van stayed about two hundred meters away. Its presence kept everyone on edge because they had nowhere to move that provided cover but still allowed them to see the tanks below. The battalion commander knew of the problem and decided the platoon should stay where they were. He had brought the company commanders out to see the terrain and massive Iraqi army growing by the day. He needed the reports to keep coming in.

The hippie van did not cause much concern to the scouts, nor did the enemy tanks that would soon be heading toward them. Instead, they feared being shot by their own tanks. An M-1 could fire and hit its target from such a great distance that the back of their Humvees might be mistaken for the bad guys.

When the firing started, they would most likely hold the line until the tanks passed unless the Iraqis got there first. A Humvee was an easy target for a tank round, and a .50 cal. would not destroy a tank. Their future was uncertain. How the scouts would affect the battle after both sides began moving was yet to be seen.

Logan's Humvee pulled up to the first scout on the screen line, Dog 3, and the crew handed out water, MREs, mail, and the hot breakfast that was now only warm. No one complained. All welcomed it, even if the eggs were probably powdered, the sausage was gray, the meat was turkey instead of pork, and the coffee was cold. Each scout smiled like a kid receiving a new bike at Christmas. They were happy to get a change from the MREs.

The Humvee kept moving east, resupplying each Humvee crew as it went until it came to the middle of the platoon and 1st Lt. Samuels' crew. Logan got out and talked to him while Boone and Dutton handed out the resupply.

"Where's my bonnet?" Samuels asked.

"Oh, that. Well, yeah, it blew out the window," Logan joked.

"We can send some of these guys back to get a shower if you can fill in at Dog 9 and 10."

Samuels dropped the joking and was now business as usual. Weeks on end of the task at hand dampened his mood for humor.

"We can do that. Have you seen the hippie van today?" Samuels asked.

"Not yet. It's probably too early for them."

"How's morale?" Samuels asked. "I haven't heard any complaints, but they usually complain to you instead of me."

Two men in the platoon were past their ETS date. With the war looming, all ETSs had been frozen. No one was getting out. Logan had served as a drill sergeant some years before going to Germany. The standard time was two years, but months after his Permanent Change of Station, he was notified he was being involuntarily extended a third year. Logan understood their frustration.

Soldiers were required to honor the contract, but the contract makers didn't have to. Yet, he didn't talk the army down, even if he disagreed. He had to keep morale up.

"I'll check on them as we head down the line," Logan said.

"All right. I'll see you tomorrow. Be safe."

"You, too. I'll bring some sunscreen as soon as we get it."

Morale was as well as could be expected from men who ate more sand than MREs, slept little, and showered twice a week if they were lucky.

The crew continued east down the line until reaching Dog 9. The resupply was done, and Logan told the crew to head in for showers. Dutton moved forward and replaced a scout in an observation post. Boone stayed behind the .50 cal., and Logan sat in his seat as the Dog 9 pulled away for a shower run. He picked up the envelope that was lying on top of the radio and opened it. There were several drawings and well wishes from a Sunday school class that looked to be around six to eight years of age.

On top was a note written by the teacher:

> Dear Soldier,
>
> We are praying for you. As Christmas approaches, and you cannot be home, do not be discouraged. You are not forgotten. We thank you for serving our country. May God bless you and keep you safe. The children wanted to send you a Christmas card, which has been enclosed.
>
> Mrs. Whitmore

Logan was thankful to know that people were praying for them. He felt a tear form as he looked at the first card, written in crayon, with a drawing of Santa Claus in a battle-dress uniform. The note was from Jenny and read, "We love you and Merry Christmas." Another was from Billy and was a drawing of soldiers feeding a reindeer. It read, "I hope you don't get killed."

Logan whispered, "I hope I don't let you down, Billy."

A third note was from Ann and was a nice drawing of the star of Bethlehem and the manger of the baby Christ. It simply read, "Merry Christmas."

There were a few more cards, and Logan read each one and smiled. Children being brought up in God's house comforted him. He looked at the return address again. Dickson, Tennessee. He had never heard of it but vowed to write back to them and thank each one.

He put the cards back in the envelope and laid it on the top of the radio just as Dutton called, "Dog 2, this is Dog 2 Delta."

Logan picked up the mic, "Go ahead, Dog 2 Delta."

"Dog 2, the hippie van is back, about half a click out moving east to west."

"Good. Copy, 2 Delta. All Dog units be advised."

"3, copy."

"4, copy."

Each of the scout crews answered until the last vehicle.

"10, copy."

"They are driving really slow 2," Dutton added.

"Keep your eyes on them, 2 Delta."

"Roger, 2 Delta. Out."

Logan handed Boone the mic. "I'm going up to Dutton and check this out."

"Okay," Boone said.

Logan grabbed his M-16 and slipped up behind Dutton, trying to keep a low silhouette.

"Where is it?" Logan asked.

"Five hundred meters out, behind that dune, and sitting still."

Dutton pointed in the direction of the vehicle slightly to the left and eleven o'clock from their position.

"Dog 1, I can go down there and pull him out by his turban and chin hairs," Dog 4 said over the radio.

"4 this is 1. Negative. Stay where you are."

Logan looked at Dutton. "I think the men are getting tired of this, don't you?"

"Hooah."

"I'd be happy to find out this is just an old goat farmer looking for strays."

"Sergeant Logan, I don't think we're that lucky."

"No, I don't think we are either."

The vehicle started moving again, continuing its journey west.

Dutton radioed, "Dog 8, you should see him now."

"Roger that. We have eyes on him."

The vehicle was soon out of sight of Dutton's OP, but they could still see the dust trail. Both men sat back, relieved that the vehicle had moved on.

"Sergeant Logan, why did you want to be a Cavalry scout?" asked Dutton.

"I always liked the old westerns. The Cavalry would ride in on horseback and save the day. They always had a scout who read the sign and checked everything out before they came charging in."

"I liked the old westerns, too."

"Which ones are your favorites?"

"Probably anything John Wayne did."

"Absolutely. *True Grit* is my favorite."

Logan nodded. "But you can't rule out Clint Eastwood."

"I liked Eastwood, but John Wayne is tops with me."

Logan changed the subject. "Saddam's got a boat load of tanks."

Dutton looked below at the dot-sized men moving around like ants in every direction.

"I wonder if any of them are Christian."

"I would say you might be surprised."

Logan grabbed his rifle and patted Dutton on the shoulder as he left. "9 will be back soon. Hold it down."

"Hooah."

Logan returned to the Humvee and found Boone scanning with binoculars in the direction the vehicle went. Boone put the binoculars down.

"I ain't seen nothing. Can't see nothing but sand back here."

"They went off to the west just a few minutes ago," Logan said.

"I don't see how Abraham was able to feed his herds in this dust bowl," Boone said.

"It probably had a little grass here and there years ago."

"And yet, here we are today, living in a tent just like Abraham."

"That's true, except for the rest of the platoon, who would cherish a tent to get out of the sun and dust," Logan said.

"I'm not complaining. I know we are blessed to get showers daily and have a tent with a roof over our heads at night."

"Yes, we are blessed. God has a plan for each of us. Do you know what God has planned for you in the future?" Logan asked.

"I feel the Lord leading me into ministry. Although, I don't know in what capacity," Boone said.

"I'm glad to hear that. He will reveal it to you in time. I'll pray that God will make it known to you."

"Thank you, Sergeant Logan," Boone said.

The 9-crew returned, and Logan's Humvee continued down the screen line and met with the 10-crew. Resupply was completed, and although the breakfast was cold, it was welcomed, as was the news of a shower run. Dutton took his place forward in the OP, Boone stood behind the .50 cal. scanning the desert sand, and Logan sat in his seat, monitoring the radio. The 10 crew headed back, and soon the only sounds heard were the whistling of the wind and the sand peppering the side of the Humvee.

Logan pulled out his small Gideon Bible that he carried in his pocket. It only contained the New Testament, but he took advantage of the time to open God's Word. He turned to the gospel of John and began reading. He spent the next hour undisturbed, deep in his worship. The events of the day and even where he was were forgotten. Only when he paused to shift in his seat did he realize, "Kuwait, that's right. We are in Kuwait."

Logan looked out the windshield of his Humvee, staring into the endless sand. Yet, he was deep in thought, not seeing anything. He wondered what God had in store for him. He knew God had put these two young men in his life for a reason.

"Sergeant Logan, can you relieve me for a few minutes?" Boone asked.

Boone climbed down, grabbed a small shovel, and hurried on his way. Logan stood behind the .50 cal., stretching his back and scanning the miles of emptiness. He studied the .50 cal. in front of him. He took hold of the back plate handles and traversed the weapon left and right and up and down, feeling the weight of it. He had been a gunner once, and he grinned when he recalled his years as a private. His gunner days were in an armored personnel carrier. He much preferred the Humvee.

He wondered if he would have to take a man's life. He pulled his hands off the weapon and hung his head. The thought of it did not appeal to him. He looked up again, hoping he would not have to do it but prepared if he must.

He thought about how many battles King David fought and how the Lord was always with him, directing and guiding him. David always spoke with God before he warred on any nation, and David never lost a battle.

"Dust cloud behind us. Must be 10 heading back," Boone said as he returned.

Logan turned around and lifted the binoculars to his eyes.

"Humvee."

The crews switched out. Logan's crew returned to prepare to do it again the next day. Dutton parked the Humvee, and the routine continued. Empty water cans were filled and loaded, as were MREs and bottled water. The marmite was returned to the mess sergeant, and Boone checked the guard duty roster. Neither he nor Dutton had duty that night. Dutton pulled the Humvee away to refuel with Boone in Logan's seat.

Logan put his bag in the tent and went to the HQ tent to meet with the 1st Sgt. The company commander, Captain Webster, was the only one in the tent.

"1SG Phillips had to step out, but can I help you, Sergeant Logan?"

"Yes sir. Just checking to see if there were any new instructions."

"As a matter of fact, there are. We got word today that the division commander for the Army Reserve units in the rear is coming tomorrow. He wants to visit your screen line and look at Saddam's hardware. You will be taking him up with you in the morning. Should be here by 0500."

"A general?"

"Brigadier General Thomas Davidson."

"So, I drew the short straw?"

"No, actually, the First Sergeant recommended you."

"Very good, sir. And when will the First Sergeant be back?"

"Not sure, but he was at the supply tent earlier, chewing on someone. I'm pretty sure Saddam heard him. You're welcome to talk with him. Might want to stand back out of arms reach, though. He was hot."

"I know the feeling."

Logan left the tent, steaming. He had always tried to avoid officers, and now he was getting a general dumped into his lap.

"Lord, give me the strength to hold my tongue."

Logan headed toward the supply tent and found the 1st Sgt. ready to leave.

First Sgt. Phillips put his hand on Logan's shoulder and steered him out of the tent.

"Just the man I wanted to see. Have you heard about your mission in the morning?"

"Exactly why I'm here, First Sergeant."

"Look, Sergeant Logan, I can't send anyone else but you. No one knows the layout like you. Do you want me to send the maintenance sergeant? He has not been out of that gate, and neither has any other choices. You are it. It makes sense for him to go with you."

Logan saw the obviousness of the 1st Sgt.'s statement, but that didn't ease his grief.

"How long will the general be nosing around?" Logan asked.

"He wants to see the Iraqi tanks, and then he'll be out of your hair. A couple of hours, tops."

"Well, I'm sure First Lieutenant Samuels will do most of the escorting. If all I must do is have him follow me out there, I guess it could be worse."

"Glad you see it my way."

The 1st Sgt. stepped off, having won the battle, leaving Logan void of his next sentence.

Logan headed back to his tent like some of the wind had been knocked out of his sails. Boone and Dutton were in the tent, readying for a shower.

"Do we have everything loaded for tomorrow?" Logan asked Dutton.

"Everything but the mail, and they won't give it to us."

"Okay. I'll head over and get that. I just got word that we will escort a general up to the line in the morning. Be on your toes."

"A general? Did you say a general?" Boone asked with a puzzled look and arms loaded with clean clothes.

"Yes, you heard me. I'm going down to check on chow. See you down there."

"A quick shower, and we will be right behind you, Sergeant," Boone said.

Boone and Dutton hurried out of the tent, talking amongst themselves.

Logan sat down to a bowl of chili mac and a cup of hot coffee. He gave thanks for the food and was glad to see hot chow after weeks of nothing but MREs. He felt guilty as he ate, knowing his men were on the line eating nothing but MREs. The old saying, "Rank has its privileges," didn't comfort him — even though he had been in their shoes many times as a young soldier.

Boone and Dutton sat across from him with one of everything offered on the menu. Both had a huge appetite and took full advantage of the hot meal. They each lowered their heads and prayed.

"This is the best chili mac I've ever seen."

Boone was trying to talk and eat at the same time, but he continued to shovel it in.

"It's better than another chicken ala king," Dutton said.

"Chicken ala king with hot sauce is not bad. Probably my favorite," Logan added.

Dutton spoke between bites that seemed nearly constant. "I know, Sergeant. It speaks volumes when you spend enough time in the field with someone else that you know their MRE preference, like Boone. He could care less about the other stuff. Just save him the candy."

Boone nodded as he focused on his food and the desire to conquer it as quickly as possible.

"You soldiers up for Bible study after I get a shower?" Logan asked.

"Sure, if you are leading the discussion," Dutton said.

"Negative. Thought you might lead tonight. Thanks for volunteering." Logan smiled as he got up from the table. "Meet you back at the tent."

Logan took his shower and got the mail. He walked into the tent to find the two young men thumbing through their Bibles, trying to find a message that spoke to them. He retrieved his primary Bible from under his cot. He did not carry it in the field for fear it might be damaged.

"I have been reading about David and the ark. Let's study there."

Again, David gathered together all the chosen men of Israel, thirty thousand. And David arose, and went with all the people that were with him from Baale of Judah, to bring up from thence the ark of God, whose name is called by the name of the Lord of hosts that dwelleth between the cherubims. And they set the ark of God upon a new cart, and brought it out of the house of Abinadab that was in Gibeah: and Uzza and Ahio, the sons of Abinadab, drave the new cart. And they brought it out of the house of Abinadab which was at Gibeah, accompanying the ark of God: and Ahio went before the ark. And David and all the house of Israel played before the Lord on all manner of instruments made of fir wood, even on harps, and on psalteries, and on timbrels, and on cornets, and on cymbals. And when they came to Nachon's threshing floor, Uzza put forth his hand to the ark of God, and took hold of it; for the oxen shook it. And the anger of the Lord was kindled against Uzza; and God smote him there for his error; and there he died by the ark of God (2 Samuel 6:1-7).

Logan looked at both young men, waiting for a response. He was trying to let Dutton lead the discussion and did not want to take over the conversation.

Dutton chose his words carefully. "I have read this Scripture repeatedly, and I can't help but think ... well ... Uzza was trying to do a good thing, but God struck him down."

Logan looked at Boone. "What about you, Boone? What's your understanding?"

"I feel like Dutton, but I know something was done wrong. God isn't going to strike a man down for doing the right thing."

Logan scanned the notes that had been written in his Bible. Some were written by him, and some by his father.

"You know my dad died a young man. This Bible belonged to him, and now that he is gone, it belongs to me. I have read many of the notes in the margin of this old Bible, and over the years, it caused me to do deeper research into your question. Dad is still teaching me things. I studied this passage because, at one time, like you, I questioned why God would do this. We have a problem understanding because we, like David, have forgotten things God has already covered. David got mad and left the ark until he figured it out. I'll give you a hint. David figures it out, and so will we, thanks to some help from Dad. Turn to 1 Chronicles 13:6–10, and let's read that."

All three men turned in their Bibles, and Dutton began to read.

And David went up, and all Israel, to Baalah, that is, to Kirjath-jearim, which belonged to Judah, to bring up thence the ark of God the Lord, that dwelleth between the cherubims, whose name is called on it. And they carried the ark of God in a new cart out of the house of Abinadab: and Uzza and Ahio drave the cart. And David and all Israel played before God with all their might, and with singing, and with harps, and with psalteries, and with timbrels, and with cymbals, and with trumpets. And when they came unto the threshing floor of Chidon, Uzza put forth his hand to hold the ark; for the oxen stumbled. And the anger of the Lord was kindled against Uzza, and he smote him, because he put his hand to the ark: and there he died before God.

Dutton quickly replied, "Okay, other than his name being spelled differently, it's almost word for word."

Logan said, "I did not intend to take over your study Dutton, so forgive me. We have many things in these two Scriptures that give us some understanding, but there are things found elsewhere that will tie it all up for us. First, let's look at what God has given us. Abinadab is mentioned here. David had a relative with that name. They were from the tribe of ..."

Logan pointed for the answer.

"Judah," both men simultaneously responded.

"And Saul had a relative with that name as well. Do you remember which tribe they were from?"

"Benjamin."

Once again, both men teamed the response.

"Turn to 1 Chronicles 15:2 and read that."

Dutton began reading again. "Then David said, none ought to carry the ark of God but the Levites: for them hath the Lord chosen to carry the ark of God, and to minister unto him for ever."

Logan added, "David figured it out. It was something God had told Moses years before. It was something forgotten."

"So that's why God killed Uzza?" Boone asked.

"Only part of the reason. What did the ark represent?" Logan asked.

"The presence of God."

"Right, and you are going to haul God around in a cart? The Philistines came up with that when they sent the ark back to Israel. We know the Levites were the ones who could move the ark. Look at Exodus 25:14 and 15. Boone, you read it."

Boone read, "And thou shalt put the staves into the rings by the sides of the ark, that the ark may be borne with them. The staves shall be in the rings of the ark: they shall not be taken from it."

Logan further explained, "The Levites were to carry the ark using the poles, not a cart. Are you seeing the wrong that was done here?"

Boone nodded, and Dutton said, "It makes sense now."

Logan warned, "Hang on. There is more. Turn to Numbers 4:15. Dutton, you read this one."

And when Aaron and his sons have made an end of covering the sanctuary, and all the vessels of the sanctuary, as the camp is to set forward; after that, the sons of Kohath shall come to bear it: but they shall not touch any holy things, lest they die. These things are the burden of the sons of Kohath in the tabernacle of the congregation.

"Does that help?" Logan asked. "So, God had said if you touch it, you die. That's why Uzza died. Not to mention, they forgot the poles, and only a Levite could carry it. And not just any Levite. It had to be someone from the clan of Kohath. Uzza should not have been anywhere near the ark. Joshua 3:4 tells the people to keep a space of 2000 cubits between them and the ark. I think Isaiah 6 will help you. Remember, he said, 'Woe is me, for I am a man of unclean lips, and I have seen the King.' Isaiah understood that sin cannot enter the presence of God. That's why no one could touch the ark because sin separated them from coming into His presence. But, when Jesus died on the cross, the sin debt was paid. The veil of the temple was rent in twain from top to bottom. The veil separated the ark from the people and their sin."

"Preach it, Sergeant," Boone said.

"Do you understand now?" Logan asked.

"Yes, now I understand," Dutton said.

"I see God's mercy when I read it," Logan said. "God could have killed Ahio, the musicians, and even David, but he only killed the one who touched the ark with sinful hands. This should teach us that when we encounter Scripture that causes us to lack understanding, God may have already covered it."

"I was struggling with that one," Dutton admitted.

Logan closed his Bible. "Good study, men. Boone can lead the next one. Maybe, I won't take over next time."

"No, I'm glad you did," Dutton said.

"Well, ladies, we have an interesting morning ahead of us, so I am turning in. Good night. God is good all the time."

Both men echoed his statement.

The 0400 alarm was soon blinking and buzzing. Logan fixed his eyes and felt around on the watch. He silenced it and sat up, kicking his feet into the sand floor. He thought he might never see the beach as a pleasurable experience again. He pulled his Bible and flashlight from under his cot, turned to his marked passage in Isaiah, and began to read.

Dutton sat up. "Are we getting up?"

"Just me. Go back to sleep."

The young soldier could be heard snoring within seconds.

Logan had chosen the Scripture in Isaiah as his devotional but did not understand why. It spoke to him, though. He felt close to God, as if God were speaking to him. He began to pray and thanked God for calling Boone and allowing him to be part of his life. He thanked God for Dutton and his desire to understand God's Word. He thanked God that He had put both young men in his life. He prayed for the safety and salvation of his entire platoon. He asked God to show Boone the path he should follow in the ministry. He ended by asking forgiveness for his anger and resentment toward the general he would escort shortly.

"Help me be more like Jesus in all I do. In Jesus' name I pray, amen."

Logan put on his socks and boots, grabbed his rifle, and stepped out for the latrine. He smiled, thinking how scouts avoid routine, but every day since they had been in Kuwait, it had become just that.

A few minutes later, as he headed back to the tent, he heard a diesel engine pull up to the security gate. He looked at his watch in disbelief. The general had arrived at 0430, early. He rushed to the tent.

"Up and at em. The general is here."

Dutton and Boone jumped up as if they were responding to a fire. Neither said anything as they rushed to get dressed, much like all soldiers had done in basic training. The "move with a purpose" attitude had worked. Five minutes later, they were getting in the Humvee. Dutton began putting in the new frequencies and getting the call signs ready. Boone climbed into the turret, and Logan handed the mail to him to be filed under "M." All three men were sitting in the Humvee when the general's Humvee pulled down to the HQ tent. Logan looked at his watch. It was 0445.

Two men got out and were met by the sergeant of the guard. He pointed towards Logan's tent, and each man began walking toward it. Logan got out of the Humvee and stepped into their path.

"General Davidson, sir?"

"Yes, and are you SFC Logan?"

Even in the darkness, Logan could tell the general was a giant of a man compared to himself — somewhere between 6' 6" and 6' 9" and weighing at least 250 pounds. Logan was a thin 5' 10" and tipped the scales at 190. The man beside the general looked like an adolescent beside a parent. He was closer to Logan's build than the general he accompanied.

Logan snapped to attention and rendered a hand salute that was quickly acknowledged by each man. "Yes sir, General. I am."

"Stand at ease, Sergeant. This is my driver, Captain Knight. We appreciate your taking us up this morning."

"Not a problem. Has the general had breakfast yet?"

"As a matter of fact, no. Are you buying? Lead the way, Sergeant Logan."

The general had a way with words that made Logan feel almost at home. Had he made too much of his task of escorting him?

Logan motioned for his men to join them. They followed behind at a distance, not wanting to bring attention to themselves. The five men entered the mess tent to find an aggravated mess sergeant who snapped at the group.

"Chow is not ready yet. Wait outside."

Logan did not move but instead made introductions.

"General, I'd like you to meet our mess sergeant, SFC Payne."

The general walked over to Sgt. Payne and began shaking his hand like a politician running for office. Sgt. Payne looked dumbfounded, as if he had stuck his foot in his mouth. The general greeted everyone in the tent and then turned back to Sgt. Payne.

"Sergeant, I apologize for intruding."

"No sir, General. You are not intruding. My mistake. Get some coffee, and we'll open this line in five minutes."

"That will be fine, Sergeant. We are running a little early this morning. Take your time."

Sgt. Payne began to bark orders to his cooks. "Let's go. Get on the line. We have a guest this morning."

Logan followed the general and Capt. Knight to the coffee. The general had not stopped smiling, and Capt. Knight did his best to conceal a smirk. Logan poured a cup as Boone and Dutton waited, still expecting to be thrown out.

Logan turned to them as he began to take a drink. "Come get you some coffee, men."

"General, this is my driver and gunner, SPC Boone and SPC Dutton."

The general leaned forward, almost bending down. "Glad to meet you, gentlemen. Don't be shy. There's plenty of coffee."

The general patted Dutton on the shoulder as he walked by, and both men responded with, "Glad to meet you, General."

It was the first time they had spoken to a general, but they quickly overcame their apprehension.

"General, chow is ready when you are. And I apologize for the delay," Sgt. Payne announced.

"Sounds good. Thank you, Sergeant." He sat his coffee on a table. "Is this table good with you, gentlemen?"

Every man affirmed their own way and followed the general through the line. Scrambled eggs, bacon, toast, and grits were on the menu. Oranges were also available, which Boone and Dutton slid into their pockets for later.

The group sat, and the two visitors picked up their forks, ready to dig in.

"General, may I give thanks?" Logan asked.

Both men laid down their forks, and the general said, "Oh, yes, please. I got in a hurry there, didn't I?"

"Father, we thank You for this food, and I ask for the safety of anyone who stands a post today. I pray for the lost that they may come to know You. We give You thanks and praise. In Jesus' name, amen."

"I was raised in a Christian home, but I admit, at times, I must be reminded. Thank you, Sergeant Logan," the general said.

"Yes sir, General. We all need reminding at times."

Dutton and Boone began conquering their breakfast. Capt. Knight took a more civilized approach, and the general took his time as he studied SFC Logan.

"So, are you a strong man of faith, Sergeant Logan?" Gen. Davidson asked between bites.

"Strong in my love for the Lord but a weak sinner not deserving God's grace."

"Interesting response, Sergeant. Humble but objective."

Logan prepared to respond as Capt. Webster came up behind him.

"General, I'm Captain Webster, the company commander here. We are glad to have you."

"Thanks for having us. We were just grabbing a bite before we hit the road."

"May I join you?"

"By all means, but we don't have much time."

The general looked at his watch and then at Logan. Logan interpreted the general's response as "Find a way out."

Logan got up and excused himself and his men.

"General, I must send a radio check. Excuse me, sirs."

"We are right behind you, Sergeant Logan."

Logan was glad to go. Three officers jawing it up was more than he could stomach. Although, the general did not seem too bad, and Captain Knight hardly spoke at all.

Logan and his crew got in the Humvee, then looked at Dutton.

"So, what's our call sign today?

"River."

"And HQ?"

"Cowboy."

Logan picked up the mic. "Cowboy base, this is River 2. Radio check over."

"River 2, Cowboy base. Read you loud and clear."

"Copy, Cowboy. River 2 out."

Logan picked up the second hand mike for the platoon radio. He looked at Boone and Dutton.

"Should I tell him?"

"May as well, Sergeant," Dutton answered for both men.

He squeezed the button, "River 1, this is River 2. Over."

"Go ahead 2. This is 1."

"1, we are having company for breakfast."

The pause was just long enough for Lt. Samuels to go through his list of possible guests in his head.

"Copy that 2. Anyone we know?"

"Negative, 1."

"Copy that, 2."

"1, this is 2. See you in a bit. River 2, out."

"Sergeant Logan, that's cold," Boone said.

"I gave him a heads up. Just didn't tell him who was coming."

"Yeah, that's what's cold."

"Just having a little fun with the lieutenant. Besides, you don't know who is listening. Can't say we are bringing a general to see you."

Logan laid the mic down and looked toward the mess tent. The general had not made his escape yet.

"Am I the only one that finds it strange that the general has no gunner?"

"Might be because he has no gun," Dutton said.

Logan reasoned that an Army Reserve general was just like any other general. They want to see the battlefield and what they are up against. Even though the reserve units were deeper in the rear, they still had to come forward to deliver fuel, supplies, tank rounds, water, and MREs.

Many regular army soldiers did not give the Army Reserve soldiers any respect. In their way of thinking, the reserve soldiers were less disciplined and trained. The battalion commander had not even come out to greet the general. Logan did not appreciate that. However, the Army Reserve soldiers taking care of Logan's battalion always needed items delivered on time. Logan did not share the negative view as many did. They were in harm's way and serving their country as well.

Two men exited the mess tent and walked toward SFC Logan's Humvee.

"Sergeant Logan, I'm sorry to hold you up this morning. Couldn't get away from your company commander."

"Yes sir, General. He is not a man short on words."

The general laughed. "My thoughts, exactly. Are we ready to go?"

"Yes, sir. How many radios do you have?"

"We have two."

"Would you like our platoon frequency? We may need to speak to each other on the way."

"I was going to ask you for that. Sure enough. My call sign is Saber 6."

"I am River 2."

"Sounds good. We will follow you when you are ready."

The men got into their Humvee, and Captain Knight began putting in the scout platoon frequency on the second radio. Logan picked up the HQ hand mic.

"Cowboy base? River 2 over."

"River 2, Cowboy base. Go ahead."

"Cowboy base, River 2, SP 0530."

"Good copy, River 2."

"River 2, out."

Despite the unexpected delays, Logan stayed on time and left when he was supposed to. He breathed easier as the Humvee approached the security gate.

"Stop here, Dutton."

Logan opened his window and spoke to the guard at the gate. "The Humvee behind us is with us."

"Hooah, Sergeant."

Both Humvees pulled through the gate and headed north. Logan tugged on Boone's pants leg.

"Weather report says we have a chance of rain today."

"Bring it on."

The scarce rain settled the dust. Boone much preferred the rain to the dust.

The radio turned Logan's attention from his conversation.

"River 2, Saber 6, radio check over."

"Saber 6, River 2, read you loud and clear."

"Copy 2, 6 out."

Logan knew that every scout on the line was now wondering who Saber 6 was. The general was from a different unit, so his SOI was different from the one used by the scouts. Saber was not in the scout's SOI for that day. The only clue they had about the identity of their guest was that he was not from their battalion.

The rattling of the diesel engines and squeaking of the shocks were the only sounds for several minutes.

"Let's head straight to the lieutenant. We will have to back track on the resupply, but I don't want to hold the general up," Logan said.

Dutton laughed. "You mean you don't want to baby sit the general any longer than you have to."

"No, I like it better the way I said it. Notice the use of tact? The more rank you gain in the army, the more tact you use. Before you know it, you're talking like a politician."

"Hooah."

First Lt. Samuels' Humvee came into view. Logan motioned Dutton to pull to the left corner of Samuels' Humvee. The general pulled up behind them in their left corner. Logan got out and walked around to Lt. Samuels. The general was on the radio and had not gotten out yet.

"Are you going to tell me who this is?" Samuels whispered.

"Brigadier General Davidson from the reserve units in the rear. He wants to see Saddam's tanks. I'll introduce him to you when he gets out."

Suddenly, Boone turned his turret ninety degrees to the left.

"Contact west, 300 meters and closing."

Dutton jumped out of the driver's seat and hurried to the vehicle's passenger side to take up cover.

"River 1, this is River 5. The hippie van is behind us and heading your way."

"Copy 5, we have eyes on it."

"Yes sir, but he is heading straight at us," Logan said.

Logan motioned to the general to get out of the vehicle but was given the "one-moment" signal as he continued his call. Suddenly, less than two hundred meters away, a man popped up from the cut-out roof and exposed an AK-47. He began spraying the Humvees. Logan took a rested position off the back of the Humvee and squeezed off one round. The AK-47 fell to the ground, and the man slid inside the vehicle.

Two more men stood up, each with AK-47s.

"Light 'em up, Boone, light 'em up!" Logan screamed.

Boone and Lt. Samuels' gunner, SPC Thomas, opened up their .50 cals. at a deafening pace. Tracer rounds went flying, marking their path. The glass in the van shattered, and tires popped. Quarter-sized holes chipped the paint away until the holes looked as big as a fist.

The men in the van fired nonstop until their magazines were empty. Bullets were flying everywhere into the sides of the Humvees. Logan glanced to the left just as Captain Knight fell forward into the steering wheel, and the general called out in pain. Logan ran from his Humvee to the general's, snatched open the door, and grabbed the general by his collar. He pulled the large man onto the ground in a seated position and then drug him to the rear tire and propped him up.

"Target destroyed," Boone called.

"Cease fire, cease fire," Samuels yelled.

The van was riddled with holes. Smoke poured out, and the hissing of steam could be heard one hundred yards away.

Logan grabbed the general's pressure dressing from his LBE and began opening it as he barked orders.

"Boone, get down here and check that driver! Lieutenant, we need a medivac ASAP!" He was wrapping the general's shoulder and reassuring him between orders. "You are fine, General. Not too bad. We'll get you wrapped up and out of here in a minute. Thomas, stay on that gun! Dutton, go down and check that van out! LT, we need that chopper!"

Boone came running around the vehicle. "Captain's dead."

Logan focused on the task. "Boone, give me a hand with this dressing. Hold pressure on his shoulder while I wrap it."

Dutton hurried to the group. "Four in the van are done. They had rocket-propelled grenades, too."

Lt. Samuels sprinted over to Logan. "Blackhawks on the way." He looked down and saw blood coming out of Logan's pant's leg. "Sergeant Logan, you are hit. Sit down."

Logan stared in disbelief at his leg. He hadn't felt anything, but now the pain shot through him. He tensed his fists and stuck a hand to his mouth, biting down on a finger. Dutton and the lieutenant tore his pants leg to expose the wound and quickly applied a pressure dressing to stop the bleeding.

Dutton reassured his sergeant with a shaky voice. "You're okay, Sergeant. You're okay."

"Well, I don't feel okay," Logan said.

The general had his mouth wide open, head leaned back, and eyes rolling back. He was going into shock.

"Captain Knight?" Logan asked, half knowing the answer.

"He's gone, sir."

Lt. Samuels loosened the general's clothing and laid him on his back as the sounds of two Blackhawks could be heard in the distance.

"Those choppers will kick up a lot of sand and dust. Better cover these wounds up," Dutton said.

Dutton sprinted to the Humvee and grabbed two rain jackets, then hurried back as the Blackhawks began to land. He tossed one jacket to Boone, who wrapped the general's shoulder. Dutton covered Logan's leg just in time to close his eyes and mouth as the chopper blades caused a gale-force wind. The sand hit each man so hard that they froze until it eased some.

"What do we have?" a crew member from the chopper asked.

Samuels opened his eyes. "Shoulder and leg injury here. Killed in action in the driver's seat."

The crewman motioned to another soldier who rushed up with a stretcher.

"Load these two on our chopper."

Dutton and Boone helped pick up the general and put him on a stretcher as a second stretcher and body bag arrived. Then, they lifted Logan onto the stretcher and carried him to the chopper.

"Don't worry about me. God is good all the time," Logan said.

"All the time, God is good," they responded.

The crewmen motioned them back as Captain Knight's body bag was loaded on the second chopper. Dutton and Boone turned and shielded their eyes as both Blackhawks lifted off, turned south, and began to gain altitude and speed. They turned back to watch the choppers getting smaller and smaller in the distance. They both felt a wide range of emotions. Neither spoke.

Everything had happened so quickly. Logan was there one moment, and he was flying away the next. They wondered if he would be okay and if they would ever see him again. Only the sound of the wind and the sand peppering the Humvees broke the eerie silence.

CHAPTER 2

Logan opened his eyes slowly. The bright, white lights hurt his eyes as he tried to focus. He was confused. Was he in heaven? He opened his eyes more and looked around. Monitors beeped, and an IV tube was in each arm. He began to squirm around as a shot of pain reminded him not to move.

"Hold on there, Sergeant. Just lie still. I'm Captain Davis. I will be attending to you. You're on a hospital ship in the Persian Gulf."

The doctor checked Logan's pupils with a pen light. "Can you speak?"

Logan gave a thumbs up to the question but said nothing. The doctor leaned closer to his face. Even over his pain, Logan smelled the scent of coffee on the doctor's breath.

"Coffee," Logan muttered.

"Well, you may have to wait a little while for that, but we will take care of you. On a scale of one to ten, how's your pain?"

Logan tried to speak, but his throat seemed too dry. He extended a finger on each hand.

"Are you saying two? Your pain is a two?"

Logan slowly brought his hands together, a finger on each hand pointing out.

"Ahh, an eleven. I don't doubt you, Sergeant. You have lost a little blood and have some damage to your knee, so we are going to pump you back up and give you something for your pain. You rest now."

Logan soon felt a warm sensation move through his body. He felt his eye lids get heavy, and soon he drifted back to sleep. Hours later, he opened his eyes, curious about the voices he heard. Two women in blue smocks surrounded him. One woman seemed to instruct the other as they looked at a chart. The same woman noticed Logan opening his eyes.

"Go get the doctor. He's waking up."

The second woman left the room, and, in a few minutes, Captain Davis followed her back in.

"They tell me you are waking up. How are you feeling?"

Logan spoke in a gurgled whisper. "Like I was hit by a Mack truck."

"How's your pain?"

"My teeth hurt."

"How about your leg?"

"Everything hurts, including my teeth."

He felt nauseous, dizzy, and exhausted. He looked at the captain with a "Please hold your questions until a more suitable time" expression.

"We have you stable, but you will need some work on your knee. We will get you ready here in a bit and send you to Walter Reed. They have some fine orthopedic doctors."

"Walter Reed?"

"Yes, that's right. The bullet struck your patella and …"

"Patella?"

"Sorry, the knee cap. You will need an implant to replace what was damaged."

"Will I walk?"

"I am not an orthopedic surgeon, but I feel certain you will. None of your arteries, tendons, or ligaments were damaged. The end of the femur only had slight contact."

"How's the general?"

"He's fine. We are going to send both of you back together."

Logan tried to process most of what he had been told, but with his pain, nausea, and distaste for officers, he had filtered most of the conversation. He lay there for several minutes until he drifted back to sleep again. His sleep was the most peaceful he could remember. He didn't dream about anything. He would partially awaken occasionally and hear the rustling of someone in the room with him but then drift back to sleep.

"Hello there, Sergeant."

Logan opened his eyes more fully and noticed his surroundings had changed. The people standing around him were not familiar. The way the room was set up was also different.

"Where am I?" he whispered.

"You are at Walter Reed Hospital. I am Lieutenant Commander Jackson. I will be the attending surgeon for you today. Your X-rays look good. You rest easy, and we'll talk more later."

Once again, he drifted back to sleep. He thought he heard people talking but could only see light around him as he slept. The place where there were usually dreams was replaced by bright light, as if he were lying in a field of light. It was peaceful and calming. He felt relaxed. The sleep seemed only minutes when he heard someone speak in his ear.

"Sergeant Logan, can you hear me?"

The voice reminded him of someone, but he could not recall.

Logan opened his eyes and looked around. He was unsure once again where he was. A few seconds passed as he tried to focus and look for something familiar to explain his confusion. He felt as if he could throw up.

"Feel as if I'm going to get sick," he whispered.

"That's just the effects of the anesthesia. That will improve. Your surgery went well. I am going to give you some time to come around, and then I'll be back."

The doctor walked out, and a nurse approached his bed. She checked his IV and hung another bag of saline. As he lay there, he noticed his leg's pain seemed more centralized.

"That's some pretty good pain medicine," he said.

"Most people say that," the nurse said, smiling.

"I apologize for being so grumpy."

"I never thought you were grumpy. We do get some of that in here, but I never thought that of you."

"Well, I mean, I wasn't myself."

"You are fine, Sergeant — nothing to apologize for. You were shot in the knee. I take that into account."

"Well, thanks for all you have done."

"Not a problem. Do you mind if I ask how you got shot?"

"Some people just got to poke the bear."

"I don't follow you."

"Think of it as a bear in a cage at the zoo. Lots of people walk by day after day and look at the bear. The bear pays them no mind. Occasionally, someone with a mean streak pokes at the bear with a stick to get his attention."

"Okay, and then what happens?"

"The bear eats them, of course."

"I will have to remember that. Just rest for a bit, and I'll be back in to check on you. Your nausea should improve in the next hour or so. Do you want me to turn the TV on for you?"

"No, thanks. I prefer the quiet."

"Okay, just rest. I'll be back. Ring the button if you need me."

The nurse left the room, and Logan whispered a prayer. "Thank You, Lord, for bringing me through this ordeal."

His door opened slightly, and a man stuck his head in.

"Hey there, are you up for a visit?"

Logan did not know the man but said, "Come on in."

The man walked in and stood by his bed.

"I am Lieutenant Anthony Campbell, one of the chaplains here. Just wanted to meet with you and see if I could do anything for you."

"Pull up a chair, sir."

"How are you feeling?" the chaplain asked.

"Better than I was. Still got some pain and nausea, but nothing like before."

"Well, that's something to be thankful for. Are you a man of faith, Sergeant?"

"Yes sir, I am."

"I thought so."

"If you can't pick out the Christian in the group, then the Christian is failing in his calling."

"I agree with you. How we interact should be a testimony to our faith."

Logan nodded his approval and then paused as he shifted the conversation.

"I have not been in church for a long time. In Kuwait, we would receive an occasional visit from the chaplain. In Germany, I would go if we weren't in the field, but we were in the field a lot. I study the Bible and pray, but I miss gathering with other believers."

"Yes, Hebrews 10 says we should not forsake the assembling of ourselves together. We should lift each other up. Church attendance should be important to a Christian. I can see where you would miss that. We have a service in the chapel every Sunday. You are welcome to attend."

"I'll be there as soon as they let me out of this bed."

"You have been through a lot these past few days, Sergeant. Is there anything you want to discuss that brought you to this point?"

"I haven't had time to reflect on what happened. They have had me knocked out a lot."

"I understand. I'll check back on you. Is there anything I can get you?" the chaplain said, standing and stepping toward the bed.

"I'd like a Bible. I had a Gideon Bible in my clothes, but I don't know where it is. My regular Bible is still in Kuwait."

"That's an easy one."

The lieutenant opened the drawer on the nightstand beside the bed.

"They usually keep one in every room. Here it is."

He laid the Bible beside Logan on the bed. "Anything else?"

"No, I'm good. I would appreciate you dropping by when you are in the area."

"I look forward to it. May I pray with you?"

The chaplain bowed his head and held Logan's shoulder.

"Father, I thank You for this soldier for Christ. I ask that You heal and comfort him. I pray he can get out of this bed soon and worship in Your house, Lord. He has a desire to be there. Give him the strength. I ask in Jesus' name, amen."

"Amen, and thank you, sir."

As the chaplain left, a man opened the door and brought a food tray.

"Enjoy your meal. I'll check in on you later," the chaplain said.

After both men left, Logan stared at the food on the tray: meatloaf, green beans, mashed potatoes, applesauce, milk, and iced tea.

"Thank You, Lord."

He picked up a fork and began to eat. His nausea had diminished enough that he felt a little hungry. He thought about his last meal — the breakfast with Boone, Dutton, the general, and Captain Knight. He shook his head in remorse when he thought of the captain. He remembered seeing him hit. His head fell forward on the steering wheel, blood running down his face and dripping off his nose.

He paused his chewing and felt a tear form in his eyes. "Lord, I pray for the captain's family. Give them comfort as they deal with their loss."

He continued to eat and reflect. He wondered how Boone and Dutton were. He missed them. He wondered how the general was. No one had told him much, or maybe they did, and he just didn't recall it in his medicated state.

Lt. Cmdr. Jackson stepped into the room. "Glad to see you are eating. How do you feel?"

Logan finished swallowing a bite and replied, "Sore, but my pain is only in my knee now."

"That's normal. Are you feeling well enough for a little talk? You can keep eating."

"Yes sir."

The doctor was holding a strange-looking piece of metal in his hand. "This is a prosthetic implant, just like the one we put in you. Normally, older patients receive this when they have arthritis, degeneration of cartilage, or bone on bone. We do arthroplasty or a total knee replacement. Most patients are up and walking at least by the next day. Your surgery was a little more complex. You had most of your kneecap removed by a bullet. You had tissue damage where the bullet entered and exited. Fortunately, you had no real damage to anything else. Your tendons and arteries were intact."

The doctor pulled the sheet off Logan's feet.

"Can you wiggle your toes?"

Logan complied.

"Can you rotate your ankles?"

Once again, he could perform the task, but some pain was involved.

"That one hurts a little."

"You will have a little discomfort for a few days, but I need you to do rotating and stretching exercises every thirty minutes while lying in bed. Also, I need you to use this."

The doctor set a clear plastic container with colored balls on his table beside Logan's food.

"This is called a spirometer. You need to exhale. Blow as hard as possible and get all the balls to the top. This helps to keep you from getting pneumonia. Do this five times every thirty minutes."

A nurse walked in with a pitcher of water and a cup of ice.

The doctor added, "And drink plenty of water."

Logan removed the lid from the pitcher and drank over half of it in a few gulps.

"Not a problem. I've been wanting some water."

The doctor laughed. "Good, you are not the first to drink from the pitcher."

The nurse picked it up and went to refill it.

"So, do you have any questions for me?" the doctor asked.

Logan continued eating but asked, "Are there any limitations with this new knee?"

"Yes, I'm glad you brought that up. You cannot do any high-impact activities. That means no running, jogging, trampolines, football, baseball, etc."

"No running? How will I do my Army Physical Fitness Test?"

"There are instances where soldiers receive a waiver, but in most cases, this results in medical retirement, the doctor said.

"Medical retirement? I'm not ready to retire. I'm only thirty-five. The army is all I've ever done."

"That decision has not been made, and I am not the one who makes it. I just want you to be aware of it."

"So, they aren't sending me back to my unit, are they?"

"Probably not. I hate to be the one to tell you this news, but you need to prepare yourself. I will check on you in a little while. Do those exercises and use the spirometer. Lots of fluids, too."

The doctor left, and the nurse returned with his water. Logan sat there with a perplexed look and deep in thought.

"They may put me out of the army. Eighteen years of service gone," he said.

"I'm sorry, Sergeant," she said.

Logan pushed his tray back and felt his mood take him to a dark place, full of pain and regret. He did not take the news well.

The door of his room opened again, and two men in business casual attire stepped in.

"SFC Logan, I am Major William Stevens. This is Captain Riley. We are with the Criminal Investigation Division. We're here to ask you a few questions about the shooting."

This is turning out to be a humdinger of a day, Logan thought.

Major Stevens pulled out a pen and notepad.

"Sergeant, can you brief us on the events?"

Logan felt anger start to swell in him. He breathed deeply to regain his composure.

"We were engaged by a shooter. I returned fire. More individuals began firing at us. I ordered my gunner to return fire. I believe at that point, everyone was firing. Four aggressors were taken out. Two of us were hit, and one killed."

"Who were the other men involved?"

"First Lieutenant Samuels, SPC Boone, SPC Thomas, SPC Dutton, Captain Knight, and BG Davidson."

"Did you confirm the identity of the shooters?"

"I did not personally. I sent Dutton to check their status."

"So, you do not know if they were soldiers or a family out for a drive?"

"They were soldiers. They had AK-47s and RPGs, for Pete's sake."

"Sergeant, could you have done anything to have avoided this confrontation?"

"Look, sir. The ROE said don't fire unless fired upon. We were fired upon," Logan said, raising his voice.

"Why are you getting upset, Sergeant? We are just trying to get the details straight."

"Seems to me you're trying to cook my goose. I've told you all I know. Pardon me for not getting the door for you."

Major Stevens closed his notepad. "Well, we still have to question the general. We may be back and ask you a few more questions."

Both men left the room, and Logan felt like throwing something. The only thing in his reach was his tray, water, and Bible. He chose the Bible. He didn't throw it but instead opened it to Isaiah 41:10: "Fear thou not; for I am with thee: be not dismayed; for I am thy God:"

Then, he closed the Bible and whispered, "Thank You, Lord. I needed reminding."

He began doing his foot and breathing exercises and felt some of his stress relieved. He picked the Bible back up and opened it again. This time he turned to Psalm 88:

O Lord God of my salvation, I have cried day and night before thee:
Let my prayer come before thee: incline thine ear unto my cry; For
my soul is full of troubles: and my life draweth nigh unto the grave.
I am counted with them that go down into the pit: I am a man that
hath no strength.

His reading was suddenly interrupted by the man in the next room. He closed his Bible and tried to listen … tried to understand what was being said. He knew it was a man but could not understand what he was saying. He only knew the man was not happy. He was yelling at the top of his lungs. Then just as quickly as it started, it ended.

The door to his room opened.

"Are you SFC Logan?" a woman asked.

"Yes ma'am."

The woman stepped into the room and hurried to his bed. She began crying and bent down, wrapping an arm around his neck. Two younger women walked in and stood just inside the door. Neither said anything. The first woman continued to sob as Logan patted her on the back, confused as to what was happening. The woman stood up and wiped her tears.

"Thank you, Sergeant Logan."

"You're welcome, but I don't think I understand. Who are you?"

"My fault. I am an emotional wreck right now. I am Sarah Davidson, Thomas's wife."

Logan's confused look had not changed. "Thomas?"

"The general. I am the general's wife."

"Oh, sorry, I will blame that on the medicine. I'm glad to meet you, Mrs. Davidson. Who are these two lovely ladies?"

She placed a hand on the first woman. "This is our firstborn, Rachel." She reached out for the second woman, who stood her ground. "And this is our youngest daughter, Monica."

"I'm glad to meet you both."

Rachel answered for herself and her sister. "We are glad to meet you."

She came to the bed and shook his hand, followed by Monica, who only said, "Thanks."

Sarah pulled out a tissue to wipe her eyes. "I thank you for being there for Tom. Thank you for saving him."

He did not know what to say. What he had done, he would have done for anyone. He felt the Lord lead him to grab the general. He didn't have time to think about it. He just reacted.

"You are welcome, but I'm sure your husband would have done the same for me. How is the general?"

"You mean you didn't hear him? He gave an ear full to a couple of unfortunate men just minutes ago."

"The CID investigators?"

"Yes. You met them, too?"

"Yes ma'am."

Just then, they heard a tapping at the door. It opened, and Gen. Davidson stepped in.

"I must be in the right place. Sergeant Logan, how are you doing?"

"I am good, sir. How are you?"

"Fine, fine. The navy doctors wanted me to get up and walk, so I decided to visit you."

"I had no idea we were roomed beside each other, General."

"I was just made aware of that fact myself. You have met my family then?"

"Yes sir."

The general turned to his wife, Sarah.

"Darling, would you all give me a moment with SFC Logan?"

The ladies began filing out the door, and Sarah added, "We'll go see what they have at the cafeteria. Nice to meet you, Sergeant Logan."

Logan threw up his hand. "Nice to meet you all as well."

The general pulled up a chair and gingerly sat, careful not to disturb his left arm.

"How's that shoulder?" Logan asked.

"Sore as a toothache, but I guess I'm pretty fortunate to have use of it. They had to replace the ball and socket. My golf days may be fewer, so I may have to take up fishing."

"Fishing is a fine sport. Even if you don't catch anything, you still win."

"Well, I at least want a bite now and then. How is your leg?"

"Sore as well. They replaced my knee. The doctor told me I would be limited and to avoid high-impact activities."

"Well, you may have to take up fishing, too."

"Not a problem. I love to fish."

Logan took advantage of the lull in the conversation.

"General, was that you yelling earlier?"

"You heard that, did you? I apologize. That's not my normal demeanor. Those CID fellows got me riled up, though."

"Yes sir, I know the feeling. They were in here first."

"Don't you worry about them. I told them to take their investigation, roll it up, stick it in their pipe, and smoke it."

Logan laughed. "I wish I had thought of that. That's a good one."

"No, seriously, don't worry about that. You were completely in the right. I fear things would have turned out far worse had you not reacted as you did."

"I feel I was justified."

The general patted Logan on the arm. "You were, son. You were. I regret we lost Captain Knight. He was not just my driver but a good friend as well."

Both men paused to reflect on the events and thought of Captain Knight.

The general finally broke the silence. "Have they told you when you will be out of here?"

"No sir. They did tell me I may be medically retired, though."

"What? That's preposterous. You will be able to walk, won't you?"

"I haven't gotten out of bed and proven that fact, but they tell me I should."

"I'm guessing retirement doesn't fit into your plans?"

"No sir. I wanted to make E-8 and retire on my terms. I've been in the army since I was seventeen. It's all I've ever done. Mom and Dad signed for me, and I was in basic right after I graduated high school."

"Sergeant Logan, what did you say your first name was?"

"Michael."

"Well, Michael, would you mind if I tried to pull some strings?"

"I'd appreciate that, General. They haven't made a final decision yet."

"Let me ask around and see what I come up with."

"Very well, sir."

"You can call me Tom when we are alone."

"No sir, I can't. I would feel awkward and most likely call you by your first name when I shouldn't. I'll stick with general if you don't mind."

"Suit yourself. Let me get out of here and dig around some. I'll let you know what I find out. I owe you that."

"General, you don't owe me anything."

"Then, it's what I want to do, okay?"

The general stood and stepped toward the door. He paused, then turned back to Logan.

"I want you to know I appreciate what you did for me. Thank you."

"General, I have to give thanks to God for that."

"Truer words were never spoken."

The general walked out, leaving Logan with a feeling of hopefulness. He knew the general would bring good news if it were God's will.

Logan lay in his bed, undisturbed for nearly thirty minutes. Before, the door had been almost constantly opening with people coming in and out. He enjoyed the chance for silence. He did a few foot/ankle exercises, used his spirometer, and finished his water. He looked out the window and saw the snow begin to fall. It seemed as big and light as feathers. It made him think of home in West Virginia, where he was born. The snow was a regular occurrence in the mountain state. Logan missed it.

Just then, the phone rang. He pulled the nightstand on its wheels closer to make it easier to access the phone.

"Joe's pool hall. Eight Ball speaking."

"Well, you sound like you're in a good mood," his mother, Janis, said.

"Hey, Mom. I was thinking about home."

"So, how are you doing?"

Her voice began to crack. Logan knew she had been crying.

"Oh, I'm fine."

"The Red Cross called me yesterday but could not update me. All they told me was you had been injured and were on your way to the hospital. Then, I got a hold of them today, and they told me where you were."

"Yeah, I'm good. Should have zigged instead of zagged."

"Are you sure? I saw you in my dream last night. You were lying in the sand."

"I'm fine. Should be up and around shortly."

"Missy and I are going to come up and see you."

"How is my sis doing?"

"She's fine. Worried about you like the rest of us. She told me she would drive me to see you."

"I would like to see you both but hold off on that. It's snowing pretty good here, and they may let me go home in a few days."

"Are you coming here?"

"Yes, I said home. Only home I have."

"Okay, I'll tell her. Everyone at church is praying for you. I called the preacher and told him."

"I appreciate that. Tell them all I thank them."

"I will. I'll call you tomorrow. It's good to hear your voice and know you are doing well. Get some rest. I love you, son."

"I love you, too, Mom. Tell Missy I love her, too."

Logan hung up. He knew his mom was now crying, thankful he was safe. He tried to keep the details of his injury to himself. He did not want to worry anyone. His mother didn't need to know everything right now. He would talk more about that in the next conversation.

He closed his eyes and bowed his head. Until now, he hadn't had much opportunity to speak with the Lord.

"Father, I thank You for being my God. Thank You for sparing me and the general. Thank You for your mercy. Thank You for these fine doctors and nurses. Most of all, I thank You for Jesus, who died for my sins, so I can be counted as a child of God. Father, I don't understand everything or why You have set me on this path, but I will follow wherever You lead me. I will follow the example of Job. Through all the trials, I will worship You. Use me that I may bring glory and honor to You. In Jesus' name, amen."

He felt a tear slip from his eye. His chest felt as big as his bed, filled with God's love. He loved the Lord. He knew God had a purpose for what had happened and trusted the Lord would guide him on the journey.

Lt. Cmdr. Jackson walked into the room.

"How are you feeling, Sergeant?"

"Just a little sore, sir."

"Well, a therapist is coming by in a minute to get you up and walking. We may get rid of some of that soreness."

"Sounds good. I would love to get out of this bed."

"I spoke with the general. He told me how you saved him. I hope you don't mind me saying so, but I don't see how it was possible."

The nurse walked in and brought him a new pitcher of water and more ice.

Logan nodded his thanks and replied to the doctor. "How was what possible?"

"You were hit in the knee. You shouldn't have been able to stand, much less pull someone the size of the general out of a vehicle."

"With God, all things are possible."

"I understand that. I'm saying you couldn't do that physically."

"Wasn't me in my strength, but God who gave me the strength. I did not even know I had been hit. God guided me, and I followed."

He assumed the doctor was not a man of faith, so he added, "If God can make a donkey talk, He can make a man stand on a bum leg."

"A donkey talk? God did that?" the doctor asked.

"There are countless times in the Bible where God did things that we would say are impossible. He parted the waters for Moses to pass, tore down the walls of Jericho for Joshua, and, yes, made a donkey speak."

He thumbed through his Bible and turned to Numbers 22. He laid the marker in place, shut it, and handed it to the doctor.

"Sir, you can read about it, and then you will have a better understanding of what God is capable of."

The doctor took the Bible.

"I would like to read that. Thank you."

The therapist came in and approached the bed. He and the nurse began putting down the rails.

"Are you ready for a little walk, Sergeant?"

"Sounds good to me."

"I want you to use a walker today until we see how you do."

The nurse brought the walker to the side of the bed. Logan sat up. The therapist instructed him on how to swing his legs over the side, which he did. He grabbed the walker's handles and stood up, expecting to feel pain. Surprisingly, there was little. He placed more weight on his leg and found that everything seemed normal.

The doctor opened the door. "You are doing fine."

"Let's see if we can walk out of the room and down the hall," the therapist said.

"What's this we stuff? If you can't walk, I can't carry you," Logan said.

Logan took his first step and felt a little stiff, but much of that had passed before he reached the door. He paused to tighten his gown to avoid baring his backside to the public. He turned out the door and began walking down the hall with the therapist following closely.

The doctor called, "I will check in on you tomorrow."

"Okay. I'll be here."

Logan took his time but continued to walk past the nurse's station.

"We can turn around and head back now. You did very well," the therapist said.

"Well, I've been practicing for thirty-five years. Do I have to lie in that bed?" Logan asked when they reached the room.

"No. You can get up on your own and move around. Short walks. Stay on this floor. If you hurt, lie down and rest."

"I can do that. Wanted to sit over here by the window and watch the snow falling."

"Sure, that's fine. Probably be a mess on the roads by the time I leave. I will be back tomorrow, and we will work on climbing stairs. Study up."

"I will. Thanks."

The therapist left Logan to stare out the window. The snow was over two inches thick on the limb of a nearby tree and still coming down. Quite a bit different than the weather he had just left in Kuwait.

He reached for the nightstand and pulled it closer. He opened the drawer and pulled out a pen and stationery. He decided to write a letter to Dutton and Boone and update them on the fears they may have had.

Dutton and Boone,

I wanted to let you know I am well. They sent me to Walter Reed to have surgery. My knee was replaced with a bionic one. I should be able to leap tall buildings shortly. I am sitting here watching it snow. That may be hard to believe with the weather you are having there. The general is roomed right next to me, and he is also doing fine. He walked in earlier and visited for a few minutes. I met his wife and two daughters. Nice folks. I hope you both are doing well and staying safe. Remember that God loves you and stay on the path He directs for you. I pray that whoever took over for me will not hinder your walk with God. Ask the 1st Sgt. to send my personal items, especially my Bible, to my mother's address. I apologize for not writing more, but I am not much on writing. Stay in touch, stay safe, and know I am praying for you both.

SFC Logan

He tore the note from the pad and got up on his walker. He walked down the hall to the nurse's station.

"Do any of you ladies have an envelope?"

"As a matter of fact, we do," answered one nurse.

The nurse reached into a drawer and handed it to him. He addressed it, stuck the note inside, and returned it to the nurse.

"Can you mail that for me?"

She looked at the address and said, "Sure can. And you don't even need postage for that one."

Logan smelled fresh coffee and suddenly had a craving that made his mouth water.

"Which way is the coffee?"

She turned and pointed behind her. "Keep going down the hall, and it will be on your right."

"Thank you, ladies."

As he walked past the station, the nurse called, "Sergeant Logan, you forgot to tie your gown."

He blushed and secured the gown.

"Bet you could have gone all day without seeing that?"

"We see it all the time. No harm."

He continued down the hall, and the nurses returned to their business. He followed the smell until he came to a small waiting room. He walked to the pot and poured the coffee into a cup. He took a small sip to test how hot it was, then took a longer drink.

"They just made that. It may be hot," a voice from behind him said.

Logan turned, startled to see Rachel sitting in the back corner of the room.

"Hi there. I didn't know you were there."

"I'm sorry. Didn't mean to."

"That's okay. My ninja-like reflexes are probably dulled because of the meds. Or I was just zoned in on the smell of coffee."

Rachel giggled as she stood and walked toward him. She poured herself a cup as well.

"Mind if I join you?"

"Not at all. This is my one true vice. I dearly enjoy coffee. Haven't had any since I left the sandbox," Logan said.

"Me, too. However, I like a little cream and sugar. I noticed you drink it black. I can't do that," Rachel said.

"I like the taste undisturbed. Don't care for these coffee shops that are popping up, offering weirdly named drinks they call coffee."

"I know. Some people are even drinking it on ice now."

"What is this world coming to?"

Rachel was close enough that he could smell her subtle perfume. It was as pleasing as the coffee in his hand. She turned and walked back to a closer chair.

"Would you like to sit, Michael?"

"You remembered my name."

Michael made his way to a chair beside Rachel, his coffee in one hand and his walker in the other. He eased into the chair.

"I would have dressed more appropriately if I'd known I would run into company."

Rachel giggled again. "You are fine."

They both took a moment to drink a sip, perhaps an opportunity to think about what should be said next.

"So, how long have you known Dad?" Rachel asked.

"I met him for the first time on the morning we got hit."

"Really. Dad won't tell me a lot about what happened, other than that you saved him. Can you shed light on the subject?"

"There's not much to tell."

"So, you mean you won't tell me?"

"I guess. If your dad won't tell you, I should not be the one who you hear it from. Give him time. He may tell you."

"I suppose you are right. It's just … we got the call he had been hurt, flew here … actually got here before you guys. Then, we had to sit and wait while he was in surgery. It's a lot of idle time, wondering with unanswered questions."

"Yeah, my mom said something similar."

"They called your mom? No wife?"

"No ma'am. I am single and have been for thirty-five years."

"Well, I've only been single for thirty-two years." She giggled and sipped on her coffee.

Michael got up and poured another cup of coffee.

"Would you like some more?"

"No, thank you. I may not sleep tonight with what I've already drunk."

"You may be right. This will have to be my last one as well." He sat back down and took a long sip. "So, were you in here getting some quiet time?"

"Yes, in a way. I was looking for a place where I could quietly pray. No one bothered me other than the nurse who made the coffee and you coming to drink it."

"I apologize for intruding," Michael said.

"No, not at all. That was what I call dry humor. You were supposed to laugh."

He smiled, and she did as well.

"Okay, we can work on your laugh," Rachel said.

He changed the subject. "So, are you a Christian?"

"I am."

"That's wonderful."

"You are as well?"

"I are," he joked.

"I was praying for Dad's recovery and the whole family's salvation, much like I've prayed for years."

"Your dad mentioned he was raised in a Christian home. I assumed he was a Christian."

"He was saved as a teen, but I guess you could say he is a backslider. He doesn't attend church, pray, or live for the Lord. Mom and Monica are not saved. They don't listen to any of my pleadings."

"Rachel, how would you feel if we prayed for them?"

"You would do that?"

"Of course."

He bowed his head and felt Rachel lay her hand on his.

"Father, we come to You today, thanking You for the Davidson family. Thank You for Rachel, who has prayed so long that each of her family members would come to know You. We ask that You speak to the hearts of Thomas, Sarah, and Monica. We pray that each of them will accept You as their Savior. We ask these things and give You praise in Jesus' name. Amen."

Rachel pulled her hand away and wiped a tear from her eye. "Thank you so much."

"You are welcome. Remember, Jesus said, 'Where two or three are gathered, there I am.'"

Rachel looked at Michael Logan. "You are a special man. Thank you. I hate to pray and run, but I need to check in on Dad before I head back to my room."

Michael stood up and extended his hand. "It has been good talking to you."

Rachel leaned in over the walker. "Nope, you get a hug. It's been nice talking to you, too. I will check on you tomorrow if you like?"

"That will be fine. Looking forward to it."

Rachel walked away, and Logan sat back down, his mind processing several thoughts. He enjoyed talking to Rachel and praying with her for her family. She seemed like a likable person, not to mention a godly woman. Was this the one God had guided him to? Did he wind up in the hospital to meet her? Did God send him here to minister to the general? So many questions and so much he did not understand.

He finished his coffee, got up, and walked back to his room. When he entered the door, he found his supper sitting on his table, along with a surprise: a new black leather-bound Bible, still in the plastic wrap. He assumed it was from Chaplain Campbell.

Logan sat on the side of his bed and pulled his table in front of him. He gave thanks and began eating while he looked out the window and watched it snow. He smiled. God had given him much to be thankful for.

The following morning, he opened the new Bible and turned to Isaiah 41:10–13. He read the Scripture as he had so many times before. This time, though, God revealed something to him. "I will strengthen thee; yea, I will help thee; yea, I will uphold thee with the right hand of my righteousness."

He stopped reading and reflected. That's exactly what God had done for him. God had given him the strength and help to pull the general from the Humvee. Even with a bullet in his knee, God had held him up. He felt no pain until the task was completed and the general was moved to safety.

Logan read, "They shall be as nothing; and they that strive with thee shall perish . ... They that war against thee shall be as nothing, and as a thing of nought."

He remembered the four men who had attacked them. He began to understand his devotion choice a little more. God had said these things to Isaiah about Israel, but as he lay in his bed, he could see how God was using His Word to speak to him.

God had been speaking to him for weeks when he read his devotion, but it was only now that he heard. He closed the Bible and silently prayed, tears in his eyes. He felt so close to God that he wanted to shout His praise.

Just then, the door opened, and a man brought in his breakfast. Coffee was included, and he thanked the man. Once again, the door opened, and Chaplain Campbell stepped in as the dietician left.

"Good morning, Sergeant Logan. Looks like I'm in time for breakfast."

"Good morning, sir. Come on in and grab a chair. Have you had breakfast?"

"Oh, yes, thank you. I ate before I left the house this morning."

"How are the roads? Looks like we got a lot of snow."

"They are not too bad. The road crews worked through the night, taking care of it. We probably got eight inches, though."

The chaplain changed the subject. "So, I had a doctor talk to me yesterday. Seemed he was interested in a talking donkey."

"Oh, yes. That would be Lieutenant Commander Jackson."

"I thought he heard it from you. How did that topic come up?"

"He is having a hard time understanding God can do all things. He told me it should not have been possible to stand on my feet, much less pull someone out of a vehicle."

"I see. I think God is speaking to his heart. I also think God has chosen you to minister to him," the chaplain said.

"I got that feeling as well. By the way, thanks for the Bible."

"You are welcome. You had mentioned yours was still overseas. That's my gift to you."

"I used it this morning during my devotion."

"I dropped by to see you before I went home yesterday, but you were not in your room."

"They had me up and walking yesterday, so I tried to stay out of bed as much as possible."

"I understand that. Have they said when you are going home?"

"Not yet. I plan to ask that question today."

Logan continued to eat his meal as Lt. Campbell shifted in his seat.

"I spoke with the general briefly."

"How did that go?"

"Let's just say he is not as receptive as you when it comes to the Lord."

"Yes, his oldest daughter, Rachel, told me the whole family needs our prayers."

"So, is Rachel a Christian?"

"Yes sir. The general is also, but I believe he has gotten away from the Lord."

"Well, that helps. I just need to change my approach."

"How's that?"

"You can't walk everyone to Christ the same way. A backslider knows God but has turned his back on Him. They are sometimes the hardest eggs to break."

"I will have to take your word on that. I don't believe I have ever led a backslider back to God," Logan said.

Logan pushed his table away from him and threw back his sheets.

"Don't mind me. Just going to get up before they come in here and start fussing."

"Do you need any help?"

Logan swung his legs off the bed and stood with one hand on the walker.

"No sir. That went well. I had to get up several times last night. Too much coffee, I suppose." Then he added, "I am convinced if you need somewhere to rest, you should avoid hospitals. All I have heard since I've been here is, 'Get some rest.' But last night, they must have awakened me four or five times, drawing blood and giving me medicine. I believe they woke me once to ask if I was asleep."

"Well, it seems you are doing much better."

"I am, thanks to God. Would you like to take a walk?"

"Certainly."

They headed out the door and down the hall toward the nurse's station. Several nurses turned their attention to the approaching men.

"Good morning, Sergeant Logan. Chaplain."

They each nodded, then continued to the waiting room. Logan walked to the coffee pot.

"Sir, let me pour you a cup of coffee."

"Yes, black, please."

Logan smiled. "I figured you navy men were not much different than army men when it comes to coffee."

A familiar voice called out.

"Sergeant Logan, just the man I wanted to see." The general walked up. "Mind if I join you, gentlemen?" He poured a cup and nodded to the lieutenant. "Good morning, Chaplain."

"Good morning, General. Sergeant Logan, I had best be on my way and let you gentlemen talk."

"Okay, sir. If I'm not in my room, you might find me here."

"Very well, General."

After the chaplain left, the general spoke in a lower voice. "Let's grab a seat. I've got some news for you."

The general took a long drink as he gathered his thoughts. Logan sat there with eager anticipation, waiting for him to swallow.

"I have good news, and I have bad news. Which do you want first?" the general asked.

"I'll take the bad news, General," Logan said.

"They are going to put you out, and there's nothing I can do about it. I talked to the top dog of the hospital. The reason is mostly your age and job. Scouts are too physically active to get a lifetime out of your new knee. Changing your Military Occupational Specialty is an option, but with your rank and time in service, it seems more appropriate to let you retire."

"Was that last part the good news?"

"No. I think I have a solution to your problem. The regular Army plans to retire you and start paying you. That would continue for the rest of your life, regardless of how you choose to supplement it. You said you wished to remain in the military, make E-8, and retire on your own terms, correct?"

"Yes sir."

"Well, I can get you switched over to the Army Reserve. You would work in a full-time role in an E-8 position. You would be on my staff at Division Headquarters. You would make E-7 pay, just as you are now. After a year, if you decide it's not for you, you can apply for your medical retirement and go that route. Of course, then you will have nineteen years."

"What would I be doing at HQ, sir?"

"Well, it's not as glamorous as being a scout. It's administrative. You would be overseeing the enlisted personnel. I have a Command Sergeant Major. He spends most of his time at our Drill Sergeant school. I believe I noticed you wear a Drill Sergeant badge on your uniform?"

"Yes sir. I spent three years on the trail as a drill sergeant."

"The position would be for a Master Sergeant E-8, but with your qualifications as a Drill Sergeant, you could qualify for First Sergeant E-8 if you choose to lead one of the companies. You would still be full-time and second in command on the enlisted side."

"Where is Division located?"

"We are in Charlotte, North Carolina. You would work Monday through Friday and then one weekend a month. We cover what we call the 'summer surge' at Fort Jackson. If you are in a First Sergeant position, you will do two weeks there."

"That's something to think about. Sounds like a pretty good gig. Why are you doing this for me, sir?"

"Well, Logan, I think I am a fairly good judge of character. Even though I have only known you briefly, I have been impressed. And let's not forget that the events that brought us here bond us together as well. Also, I feel I am being pulled in the direction that keeps you around."

"Can I pray on it and get back to you, General?"

"Of course, take your time. They said I will be released tomorrow. If you haven't decided by then, I will give you my number, and we can talk more about any questions you may have."

"Sounds good, sir."

The general got up and patted Logan on the shoulder.

"It's your choice. Myself, I hope you stick around."

With that, the general turned and walked away, leaving Logan to his thoughts and a cold cup of coffee. He had been given a lot to think about. Later, as he returned to his room, he saw Rachel and Monica standing in the hallway outside their fathers' door.

"Good morning, ladies. How are you both today?"

"We are well. Hope you are," Rachel said.

"Yes, thank you for asking," Monica said.

"Nice seeing you both, and, yes, I'm feeling pretty good today. You will have to excuse me, though. I think I've drunk too much coffee again."

Logan stepped inside his room and shut the door. Twenty minutes later, he heard a light knock on the door, and Monica opened it slightly.

"Is it okay if I come in?"

Logan sat in a chair with his feet reclined. "Of course, come on in."

She walked into the room, and he motioned to a vacant chair, which she accepted. She seemed nervous, wringing her hands.

"Sergeant Logan, I want to apologize for my rude behavior. Not to make excuses, but I am an R.N. at a hospital back home. I don't care much for the way things are done here."

"I have no complaints. They all seem pretty efficient to me."

"Well, they should be glad they don't work for me. Also, I wanted to thank you for what you did for Dad. It means a lot."

"Thank you. I enjoyed getting to meet his family. God has blessed him."

Monica stood rather quickly with a change in her expression. Logan understood from her actions that God-talk was her kryptonite. She reassumed the scowled look he had been familiar with and stepped toward the door.

"Well, all the same, thank you."

Logan sat there thinking how different the two sisters were. How was it that one was such a strong woman for God and the other the opposite? Dare he think Monica was even a little disturbed? He decided he was willing to give her a chance but not many.

He took the family to prayer and prayed for God's will. He was unsure of the general's choice for him, but as the general had admitted, Logan also felt himself being led to stay with him. As a man of faith, he recognized when God was doing the leading. He had started his prayer with a question but concluded knowing God wanted him to go to North Carolina.

The door opened as Lt. Cmdr. Jackson entered the room, Bible in hand.

"Good morning, Sergeant Logan. I had an early surgery this morning, and I'm just now getting around to checking in on you."

"Not a problem, sir. Just got back from a walk anyway."

"Good, good. Is your knee giving you any problems? Does it hurt more if you sit or lie too long?"

"A little stiff when I woke up this morning, but it worked itself out."

"Sounds good. We will have you work with the therapist today, and if he gives me a good report, we will probably discharge you on Thursday. You will be home for Christmas."

"Today is Tuesday, so two more days?"

"I want to ensure we don't have any infection surprise us. History reveals that when we have been involved in war, the enemy goes to great lengths to inflict as much misery as possible. Poison-tipped bullets, feces, or even liquid chemical hazards. Your blood test was negative, but we need to monitor you a little more to be sure."

"I understand. By all means, let's be sure."

The doctor handed the Bible back to Logan. "That is an interesting story about the talking donkey. Still, there is quite a bit I don't understand."

"I will admit, I don't understand everything, but I will help you with what I can."

"Well, for starters, I don't understand why this Balaam fellow had caused God to want to take him out."

"Balaam was a wizard or sorcerer. He used his powers to turn on Israel. God does not condone magic or being mixed in with false gods. He let Balaam know that when the angel appeared to him. Balaam could not see the angel because his eyes were closed to God, but the donkey did see the judgment to come, and he tried to turn away and save his master. For his troubles, Balaam beat the donkey. That's when God had the donkey speak. Balaam then understood the donkey had tried to save him. God opened his eyes. He understood he had sinned against God."

"I see."

"I had mentioned what God had done that people say is impossible. The greatest thing Jesus ever did, though, was die on the cross for the world's sins. Three days later, He defeated death and rose from the grave. The story of Balaam and the donkey is like Jesus and the cross. Jesus was beaten and flogged for trying to save people just as the donkey tried to save Balaam."

"Why would Jesus die if He was the Son of God?"

"He died so we can be saved. He didn't stay dead. He lives. He didn't have to die for us. He chose to die for us. God sent His only Son so whoever believes in Him would not perish but have everlasting life."

"I think I understand that better now."

"Sir, you may understand it better, but do you believe God raised Jesus from the dead?"

"I don't know. I want to believe it."

"When you told me it was not possible for me to stand, but I stood anyway, that was by the power of the same Jesus that rose from the grave. I did not do that on my own. I agree with you. It is not physically possible for someone to do that. It is possible for God to do it, though."

"You've given me a lot to think about. I must get on with my rounds. Can we speak again later?"

"Absolutely. You know where I'll be." Logan turned to Romans 10, placed the marker in the Bible, and handed it back to the doctor. "You might as well keep this. It belongs to the hospital anyway. Read chapter ten, and we can discuss it on your next visit."

"I will. Thank you, and I'll check in on you later."

The doctor left the room, and Logan bowed his head. "Father, thank You for sending me here and allowing me to witness to the doctor. I pray that You will continue to speak to his heart. Let him see the error of his ways that he may come to know You. In Jesus' name, amen."

CHAPTER 3

Michael Logan spent a more intensive afternoon with the therapist than on the first day. He did several squats, walked up and down stairs with a handrail, and walked with a cane back and forth on his entire floor. Rachel stood in the hallway outside her dad's room, watching him comply with the many instructions given him. Eventually, he was released, and the therapist left.

He walked back toward his room but stopped in front of Rachel, who leaned against the wall, arms folded in front of her.

"Got rid of that walker, at least," he said, holding up his cane.

"Yeah, that walker kind of made you look old."

"I thought so myself."

"Are you finished with your therapy?"

"Therapy? That was medieval torture. I'm ready to sit for a few minutes. Would you like to come in for a while?"

"Sure, for a few minutes. Although, a woman in a man's room alone is grounds for marriage in some cultures."

Logan pushed the door open, sat in one of the chairs, and reclined.

"I believe our culture was one of them many years ago."

Rachel took the remaining chair. "So, how are you feeling today?" she asked.

"Like I'm ready to get out of this place."

"Dad said the same thing."

"The general told me he was busting out tomorrow."

"Yes, we will be heading back as soon as they release him. Should be able to catch an afternoon flight. What about you? Have they said when you will be released?"

"Well, if I didn't flunk that therapy session, I am supposed to leave Thursday."

"Good, that's not too bad."

"No. I need to work on my patience, though. It's easy for me to get off track and forget the good God has done for me."

"That's all of us at some point, I believe."

Logan looked out the window and noticed the sun shining brightly on the new snow.

"You mean the airport is still operating with all this snow?"

"They have several cancellations and delays, but some flights are still going out. I need to get back to work."

"What do you do?"

"Real estate. I stay pretty busy."

"Do you enjoy it?" Michael asked.

"Oh, yes. I am my own boss and work my own schedule, which, right now, is nearly every day. Charlotte is booming."

"Speaking of Charlotte. Do you deal with rental properties?"

"No, I stay busy without dealing with that. Why do you ask?"

"Well, I haven't told the general yet, but he made me an offer to work for him. I've decided to move to Charlotte."

"That's great. I can tell you where to stay away from."

"Hold that news to yourself, please. I want the general to hear it from me."

"Sure, I will act surprised when Dad tells us."

"Well, I am going to go and let you rest. I can drop by in the morning and say goodbye."

"Yes, I would like to see all of you before you leave."

Rachel left, and Michael closed his eyes. In a few minutes, he had fallen asleep.

An hour later, he was awakened by a nurse who had come in to check on him. When she left, he got up and walked into the hall. He knocked on the general's door and, for a second, heard nothing. Then after a short silence, "Come in."

Logan found the general alone, rubbing his eyes.

"Did I wake you, sir?"

"I guess I dozed off when the girls left."

"I took a power nap earlier myself."

"What can I do for you?"

"General, I will take you up on your offer."

The general smiled from ear to ear. "That's great. You will not regret it. And I know the girls will be thrilled."

"Girls thrilled?"

"Oh, yes. Monica and Rachel have been asking me all day about you. Of course, I do not know that much about you, but that didn't slow down the questions."

"I have enjoyed meeting them."

"And Sarah thinks you are the best thing since sliced bread."

Logan laughed, and the general went on. "She said we will have the boathouse ready for you if you decide to come."

"Boathouse?"

"Yes, it has a small room for changing. There's a bathroom and shower. It's not big, but yours until you find a place."

"I couldn't do that."

"Yes, you can. I insist. No one is using it right now. It's too cold to go out in the boat, so it's perfect for you."

The general seemed almost excited about the news. Logan accepted the offer reluctantly. He was thankful for the general's kindness. He had already gone out of his way to show his gratitude. Logan had learned as a young man not to refuse another's blessing. Instead, to accept it so both people can be blessed.

As he returned to his room or cell, as he thought of it sometimes, he heard his phone.

"Hello, Mom."

"How did you know it was me?"

"You are the only one who calls me."

"How are you doing?"

"I'm good. Been up walking around a lot today."

"Did you find out when you will be coming home?"

"Looks like Thursday. You and Missy going to be able to drive up?"

"We sure will. I'm glad you will be home for Christmas."

"Me, too. I've missed a few over the years."

"You couldn't help it, son. You must go when Uncle Sam says go. Well, I just wanted to check in on you. We are looking forward to seeing you."

"I am looking forward to it as well. And I'm looking forward to getting out of here."

"I love you, son. I'll give you a call tomorrow evening."

Logan hung up and decided to break the news to his mom and sister on the trip back. It was more appropriate for a face-to-face conversation. His mom was still dealing with the loss of his dad. It had been a few years, but something in her had changed. Part of her died, too. He was careful not to mention anything that would add to her grief. He was not sure if the Red Cross had even mentioned he had been shot. He remembered his mom saying he had been injured. He decided, for now, that was sufficient.

The evening meal was delivered, and Logan wondered where his doctor was. The chaplain had not stopped in before heading home, either. He hoped he had not pushed the doctor away with too much information to digest. He felt confident that God was leading him to speak. He decided he would not apologize for speaking the truth of God's Word. Lt. Cmdr. Jackson needed to hear it. Maybe the doctor had a medical emergency or just needed more time to process what he had heard.

Logan got up and walked around his floor several times. He stopped in at the waiting room and rested. He looked at the coffee pot and decided against it. He sat there alone, deep in thought. He'd had a wonderful conversation with Rachel just two seats over. The general had sat in the seat to his left. He had a fondness for the room.

On Wednesday morning, Logan woke up thinking, *The general and his family are leaving today.*

Logan spent time in prayer and God's Word until his meal arrived. He quickly sat up in bed and ate his breakfast. He kicked his legs over the side, ready to stand.

Then, the door opened, and Chaplain Campbell walked in. "Good morning, Sergeant Logan."

"Good morning, sir. I thought you might drop in yesterday evening."

"No, I did not get to. Your doctor was talking with me for quite a while. I just wanted to give you a heads up before he comes in to check on you."

"Is everything all right?"

"Oh, yes. I see God working with him."

"He didn't come by as he mentioned he would. I was concerned."

"That's my fault. We talked about Jesus for nearly an hour. He probably left after that. He mentioned an early surgery."

"I'm glad he is opening up to God."

Chaplain Campbell walked toward the door. "I just wanted you to know. I must be somewhere this morning, so I'll check back on you later."

"Sounds good, sir. I was about to check on the general. He's leaving today."

"Have you found out when you are leaving?"

"Probably Thursday. Guess I won't be here for your Sunday chapel service."

"I'm sure you will be in a service Sunday. Probably at your home church, right?"

"I hadn't thought that far ahead, but I suppose I will."

"That's great."

Logan got up as the chaplain left. He grabbed his cane and headed next door. He knocked, and Monica greeted him.

"Good morning, Sergeant Logan. Come on in."

A doctor was standing at the foot of the bed, giving the general instructions for his recovery. The general nodded while rolling his eyes at Logan, signaling his patience was wearing thin with the doctor. He was focused on getting dressed as quickly as possible. Sarah tried to help while Rachel and Monica stood back out of the way with Logan.

The general started to stand as the doctor finished his speech and walked out. A nurse came in with a wheelchair.

"I am not riding in that, am I?"

"Yes sir, policy," the nurse said.

"Very well." He sat down in the chair and handed Michael a folded piece of paper. "Michael, here is my number. Call me in a few weeks, and we can get the ball rolling. They tell me you will recover at home for six weeks. We will have everything ready for you by then."

The general stuck out his hand. Logan shook it.

"Sounds good, sir, and thank you."

Rachel nudged Michael. "Yes, Dad tells us you are moving to Charlotte."

He looked at her, knowing the nudge meant she hadn't spilled the beans.

"Yes, I am. I will be working for your father."

The general corrected him. "You will be working with me. Everyone, say your goodbyes. We have a plane to catch."

Sarah hugged Michael and followed the nurse out the door. Monica hugged him as well.

"See you around," Monica said.

Rachel walked toward him. "You know what they say, leave the best for last." She hugged him and whispered, "I'm glad you decided to stick around."

"I am, too."

They walked into the hallway to see the general shaking hands with the nurses at their station as he continued down the hall.

"We'll see you soon, son."

"Yes sir."

Logan waved. Monica was walking away with her arms folded in front of her.

Rachel looked at Michael one last time. "Promise me you'll go to church with me?"

"As long as they don't pass rattlesnakes around, I'll be there."

"Nobody uses rattlesnakes anymore. We switched to copperheads a long time ago," Rachel said.

Logan liked her sense of humor. He watched them leave until they got on the elevator. For a moment, he felt alone. He smiled as he walked toward the waiting room.

I am never alone. God is with me, he thought.

The Christmas decorations were on nearly every wall of the hallway. He stopped to read a few cards pinned to a corkboard. Suddenly, he remembered he had not written those kids in Tennessee. He could not remember the address, and the manila envelope was back in Kuwait. He scolded himself for not taking care of it sooner. He hoped it would arrive with his personal items in the next few weeks.

As he sat in the waiting room enjoying his coffee, Lt. Cmdr. Jackson walked up.

"When I went out to play, my mom always threatened to tie a bell around my neck to know where I was."

"I wasn't that hard to find, was I?"

"Actually, the nurses told me you were here."

The doctor changed the subject. He opened the Bible he was holding to Romans 10.

"Sergeant Logan, I have read this chapter you marked several times."

His voice began to crack, and he sobbed.

"Sit here beside me," Logan said.

The doctor sat, holding his hand over his eyes to conceal his tears.

"You need not worry about your tears. God is speaking to your heart. I have seen it these past few days. Your tears are evidence that your eyes are being opened to your sin. Remember how Balaam's eyes were opened?"

"How can I be saved?" the lieutenant asked. "God may not want me if he knows the things I've done."

"Jesus came to save the sinners. He died so that our sins could be forgiven and we could come into His presence. Paul said none are righteous. We are all sinners. We were born sinners, and we will die sinners."

"But you seem to be a good man. You seem to know a great deal about the Bible."

"Being good and knowing the Bible won't save us. The devil can quote Scripture. Jesus said, 'I am the way, the truth, and the life: no man cometh unto the Father, but by me.' You see, there is only one way to be saved, and that is through Jesus. The answer is right there in the Bible. Look at that chapter again, verse nine."

The doctor read the verse. "That if thou shalt confess with thy mouth the Lord Jesus, and shalt believe in thine heart that God hath raised him from the dead, thou shalt be saved."

"Do you believe in Jesus? Do you believe God raised Him from the grave?" Logan asked.

"Yes, I do." His sobbing became louder and more frequent.

Logan placed a hand on his shoulder.

"Close your eyes. Tell God you know you are a sinner and believe Jesus died for your sins and was resurrected. Ask Him to forgive you and to come into your life and save you."

The doctor prayed through his tears. When he had finished, he looked up at Logan. "Now, what do I do?"

"You live the rest of your life for Jesus. You are saved. You are now a child of God." Logan patted him on the back, and Jackson smiled, wiping away his last tears. Logan felt his joy.

"Congratulations, sir. From here, I would get into a church. Let them know you have just been saved and then ask to be baptized. Church attendance and baptism do not save you. Church attendance is for worship. It is also to lift each other up — believers gathering and sharing their worship. Baptism is professing your faith. In the New Testament, believers were baptized right after accepting Christ."

The two talked for a few more minutes. The doctor was overjoyed that Jesus had come into his heart. He had a new look in his eyes. They almost seemed to sparkle and shine. He left to finish his rounds. Logan prayed, giving thanks to God that the doctor had accepted Christ. He got up to return to his room but not before whispering one final prayer: "Lord, I like this waiting room."

Logan endured another round of therapy. He was surprised to find that for a man in excellent physical condition being wounded had taken a lot out of him. Still, he complied with the therapist and stubbornly accepted each challenge they offered. Soldiers are taught never to give up, and he was not about to start now, even if it hurt a little.

He was relieved to spend a few hours afterward in his room with his feet reclined. His right knee was throbbing, but he kept the pain to himself. He knew he had overdone it. No need to whine about it.

Later in the afternoon, the chaplain walked in. "Sergeant Logan, I trust you are well? How did it go with your doctor?"

"He accepted Jesus."

"Praise God. After speaking to him, I felt certain he was close to making a commitment."

"I think it clears up some questions about why God sent me to this place. I suppose it was to lead him to Christ."

"I feel certain of it. I am so happy. Isn't God good?" the chaplain said.

"All the time."

A light knock turned both men's attention. Two familiar faces stepped into the room. It was Logan's mother, Janis, and his younger sister, Missy.

"Hello there, stranger," his mother squealed, rushing to the chair for a hug.

"Hey, ladies. I was not expecting you until tomorrow."

"We decided to come up today, so we don't have to drive up and back all in the same day. It took about five hours," Logan's mother said.

"Hey there, big brother," Missy said as she hugged him.

"This is Lieutenant Anthony Campbell. He is a chaplain here at the hospital." Then, motioning toward his family, Logan said, "Sir, this is my mom, Janis, and my baby sister, Missy."

"It is wonderful to meet you both. Sergeant, I will get out of here and let you visit with your family. I'll be back by in the morning to see you off."

"Okay." The chaplain shook hands and nodded, "Ladies."

Logan's mom watched the chaplain leave, then pointed to the white bandage on her son's knee.

"Okay, Michael. Are you going to tell us about this?"

Logan knew the inquisition had begun. He delayed his speech, trying to think of a way to avoid telling them but decided against it.

He pulled his gown over the bandage. "I got shot in the knee."

Janis quickly cupped a hand over her mouth. "Oh, my goodness."

"I didn't think the fighting had started yet?" Missy asked.

"It hasn't. This was just some fellows who lacked patience."

"Lacked, as in past tense?" Missy asked.

"Correct."

"So, your knee is okay?" Missy asked.

"Yeah, it's fine now. They replaced it."

Janis turned and began crying. Michael motioned to his sister by swiping his fingers across his throat. She knew to stop the questions for now.

He stood up and hugged his mom.

"It's okay. See, I can walk. Look at the bright side. I will never get arthritis in my right knee, no matter how long I live."

His mother laughed through her sobbing. She walked to a chair and sat.

"We were worried about you, son. It brought back when I sat at home and worried about your dad in Vietnam."

"I remember. I was in middle school." He looked at Missy, trying to change the subject. "So, how were the roads?"

"They are fine. No problems. And fortunately, we are not supposed to have more snow for a few days."

"Have you checked in at a hotel yet?"

"Yes. That's our hotel right there," Missy said, pointing out the window.

Just then, Michael's doctor walked into the room. "I see you have some company." He walked toward the women and stuck out his hand. "I am Lieutenant Commander Jackson."

"Did you do the surgery?" Janis asked.

"Yes, I did."

"Is he going to be all right?"

The doctor recognized Logan's mother was unsure and fearful of his condition.

"Oh, yes, he is fine. He wore out the therapist today. He will have to recover about six weeks, but after that, you won't be able to tell anything different."

"Well, that's good news."

Michael had reassured her, but knowing he was probably not telling the whole story, the doctor's statement eased her discomfort.

"So, where do you recommend I start reading in the Bible?" the doctor asked.

Michael began to answer but was beaten to it by his mother.

"The Gospel of John, without a doubt."

Michael smiled and nodded his approval.

"Sounds good. I am heading home and just wanted to drop by. We will get you out of here in the morning."

Michael spoke up with enthusiasm. "Sounds great."

"New Christian?" Janis asked after the doctor left the room.

"Yes, I led him to the Lord just this morning. I suppose that's why God led me here. I haven't understood why I had to get shot, though."

"It was to slow you down."

Logan did not comment but only weighed her statement. She was most likely correct. She was a woman close to God, and Michael had sought her counsel many times. Even after his family left for the night, he studied her words. In time, perhaps God would reveal the answer to him.

Logan woke at four in the morning without needing an alarm. He turned on his lights and spent time in God's Word and prayer. He prayed for his men still in Kuwait and all service men and women in harm's way. He missed all of them. He missed being part of a team and contributing. He thought how his days as a scout were now over. Another chapter in his life was being written. The general had told him his new job would be administrative, much the same as when he served as a drill sergeant. He did not regret his decision because he felt certain God was leading him to do it.

Breakfast was served for the final time, and shortly after, his family came back in. Missy led the way.

"I know we are here early, but we were already awake around five."

"No problem. Have you eaten?"

"They had doughnuts and coffee, so we are good," Missy said.

"I can share my breakfast with you. We have to get some tacos before we make it home. I have been craving them since I was in Germany."

"That sounds doable," Janis replied.

"Did you happen to bring me some clothes? They probably cut mine off me," Michael asked.

Janis handed him two grocery bags. He stopped eating long enough to pull the items out. The first had a pair of leather work boots. Logan froze and hung his head. He sobbed until Missy and his mom came to his side to console him.

"Dad's boots. I would recognize them anywhere." He wiped a tear and opened the second bag. Pants and a shirt belonging to his dad completed the inventory. "Thanks, Mom."

Missy and his mother were both now trying to conceal their tears.

"We will have to wait and see if you look as good in them as Dad," Missy said.

"Only if you brought his favorite tractor hat."

Missy pulled out the hat she had hidden behind her back and handed it to him. He couldn't hold back the tears any longer.

A nurse entered to find all three embracing each other, tears rolling.

"Should I come back?" she asked.

"No, come on in," Michael said.

"I need to change your dressing and make sure you can reapply a fresh one."

Missy picked up the clothes, and she and Janis stepped to the opposite side of the room. Logan moved his tray table and pulled up his gown above his knee. The nurse removed the bandage, and his mother and sister shook their heads. His knee looked like a head of cauliflower. The lacerations that were sewn up veered in several directions.

"If you like that, you ought to see the back side," Michael said.

"Your knee looks horrible," his mother said.

Michael looked at the nurse. "Tell her it looks better than before my surgery."

"That is true." She cleaned it and said, "I would wear a bandage for a few more days. You still have a little drainage. Here is the stuff you need. Let's see if you can do it yourself."

He accomplished the task in minutes.

"I had a good teacher. Been watching you do it all week."

The nurse left, and Michael asked his mom and sister to leave while he dressed.

"They haven't told you to dress yet," his mother asked.

"Nope. I'm making a command decision. That's what we call that in the army."

A few minutes later, Michael called, "I'm decent."

"Well, that's yet to be seen," Missy said jokingly.

Michael laced up the boots and stepped toward the door with cane in hand.

"Come with me, ladies."

They followed behind. As Michael passed the nurses' desk, he joked with the three sitting there.

"Hold all my calls. I'll be in my office."

He continued to walk until he came to the waiting room. He poured his mother and sister a cup of coffee, then one for himself.

"You all can doctor it up how you like."

They began the cream and sugar routine and searched for something to stir it.

"See, if you drank it black, you wouldn't have to worry about that."

"When we were walking down the hall, I thought we were leaving," his mother said.

"No, just waiting here. Hard to tell how long it may be. Everybody knows where to find me."

The three had no more than sat before the chaplain walked in.

"Good morning, Sergeant Logan. I almost didn't recognize you with civilian clothes on."

"It's me. Ready to go when they say so."

Chaplain Campbell laughed and walked to the coffee pot. As he poured a cup, he looked at Janis.

"Mrs. Logan, did your son tell you he led his doctor to the Lord?"

"Yes, he mentioned it."

"Did he tell you how?"

"No, he didn't tell us that."

"He told him about a talking donkey. I have never heard of anyone accepting Christ by hearing about Balaam and the talking donkey."

"My son has always surprised me, too."

Janis looked at Michael and smiled, as though she could write a book about him.

Lt. Cmdr. Jackson walked up to the group.

"Did you ever threaten to tie a bell around his neck?" he asked.

"I probably did. He's never been one to sit still long."

"I can believe that." He turned to Michael. "So, the moment you've waited for has arrived. Next week is Christmas, so you may not get ahold of anyone, but when you do, make an appointment with a local ortho-pedic doctor. He may want to see you back again. Take it easy for the next six weeks. No driving during that time. After that, remember to go easy on the activities. I think we have already discussed what you should avoid. The knee will last longer if you avoid those high-impact activities."

Logan nodded.

"The nurses are getting all your items. You must meet the adminis-trator in your room, and the nurses will bring your stuff. Other than that, you are released. They will wheel you out when you are ready."

Logan got up to walk back to his room, and the chaplain held out his hand to stop him.

"Hang on there. Let's pray before you leave."

All five bowed their heads. "Father, as we come to You today, we come with gladness in our hearts. We thank You for Sergeant Logan and his family. We ask Your protection and mercy on them as they travel home. We thank You for Lieutenant Commander Jackson. We thank You for choosing him to be a child of God. We ask that You would strengthen Sergeant Logan physically and the doctor spiritually. In Jesus' name, amen."

As Michael returned to his room and gathered his belongings, the administrator walked in. She didn't tell him anything he hadn't already heard from the general. Michael listened to the news that would have crushed him without the general. He smiled politely and thanked her.

"I already have a plan. I'm ready when you are, nurse."

Logan got into the back seat of the car, assuming he might need to stretch his leg out occasionally. As the vehicle pulled away, he had mixed emotions. He was thrilled to be freed from the solitude of the environment but saddened to leave the people who had touched his life.

Chaplain Campbell had proven to be a strong man of faith who genuinely cared. Their talks reminded him how much he missed church and talking to the pastor. He thought how, in just three days, he would return to church where he had grown up. His extended family and childhood friends would be there. It would be much like a reunion. He thought about how he had missed many opportunities to worship in God's house by serving in the military.

He thought about Lt. Cmdr. Jackson and how he had accepted Jesus. Logan knew God had sent him there to witness to him. He smiled when he realized he had been used to bring glory to God. He would never have been at the hospital for that opportunity if things hadn't happened as they did. He understood it was God's plan. He thanked God for allowing him to be a part of it.

He also thought about his mother's statement. He felt as though she might be on to something.

"Mom, what did you mean when you said, 'God slowed me down'?"

She thought for a moment, staring out the window as the scenery passed by.

"Well, sometimes we miss opportunities God has set before us. The reason we miss them could be any of a hundred things."

"Name a few, please."

"We can get involved with work or family, and it's our only focus. Others may lack a spiritual connection. They may not understand what God is saying because they don't spend time speaking with Him and listening to Him when He speaks."

"I am probably guilty of all that."

"I have always told you to get quiet and listen to God. That's usually where most of us fail. We want to do most of the talking and less of the listening."

Michael thought about what she said. He knew she was right. He was not a good listener. He lacked patience many times. With people, he would find a way out of lengthy conversations. Several times, he had gone with his gut while seeking God's wisdom.

"Remember Paul?" his mother asked. "God gave him a thorn in his side and didn't remove it. In Paul's case, it was to keep him grounded in his faith. It was to keep him from getting a big head."

"I know God had a reason for my being shot, and I'm not whining about it, but I would like to understand it."

"God may tell you, or you may have to figure it out yourself. James said, 'The trying of your faith worketh patience. But let patience have her perfect work, that ye may be perfect and entire, wanting nothing.'"

Michael took out his Bible and read the passage his mother mentioned. He stared out the window in deep thought. Suddenly, he saw a familiar logo.

"Missy, hit my favorite taco place. I'm buying."

"Okay, but I think you just proved the point."

Having relieved his craving and feeling disappointed that he had made such a big deal about it, they journeyed on. He realized the tacos didn't matter. It was simply that he hadn't had them for the last few years. He had craved what he didn't have. Once he satisfied his craving, he understood his disappointment.

They pulled into his childhood home as the sun descended behind the trees. Michael sat up, peering over the seat as if seeing it for the first time. So many memories were stored away about the place. The house was older, with white-painted wooden ship-lap siding. It had a wraparound porch with several chairs and a swing. When Michael's dad returned from Vietnam, he started a carpentry business. Michael could see his work in the renovation. The windows and roof had been updated. His dad chose to leave the siding. He liked the lived-in look.

"Michael, you are in your old room," his mother said.

She went in and started scurrying about in the kitchen to prepare a light supper. Missy decided to stay for the night, exhausted from the five-hour trip.

The following day at 0400, Michael spent time in his devotion. About thirty minutes later, he quietly made his way to the kitchen and started the coffee. While it brewed, he stepped onto the front porch, cane in hand. He paused to look around in the darkness at how much things had changed. Small trees that had been planted during his youth were now giants.

He eased down the steps and into the crusty snow, then walked around back and headed to the barn. He used his cane to break the snow and ice mixture against the door. Michael opened it and stepped in. He turned on a light and stood there momentarily, looking around at the once active but now empty enclosure. There were a few bales of hay beside a wall. He walked over, sat on one, and closed his eyes as the memories flooded back.

Ten minutes later, the door opened, and Missy walked in with two cups of coffee.

"I see you found me."

"Well, I'm not a scout, but it was pretty easy to track you in the snow."

The two laughed and drank their coffee in silence. After several minutes, Missy wiped a tear. Michael put an arm around her.

"I miss him, too."

A few years earlier, their dad had died from a heart attack in the middle of the barn. He had gone out to give the cattle some hay and never returned. Their mom found him, fingers still in the strings of a bale, slumped over, as if he were kneeling. He never saw sixty.

They remembered the good times with their dad — each having their own personal memories. Their dad had been the rock of the family. They both quietly sobbed and reflected until Michael finally spoke.

"Guess we better get back in before we freeze."

The two walked into the house to find their mother busy preparing breakfast. Missy jumped in to help.

"What's on the menu this morning?" Michael asked.

"Biscuits and gravy. I may fry you an egg, too."

"Sounds good. I have not had biscuits and gravy since the last time I was here."

He filled his coffee cup again and eased over to his sister.

"Can you run me to the store tomorrow?"

"Christmas shopping? Four days before Christmas? I would rather take a beating. But for you, I'll do it."

"You don't need to worry about that. You have done enough already," his mother said.

Michael had sent his mother a little money every payday to help with bills. His dad had always provided for the family, but things got tight for his mom when he died. His dad had a small insurance policy and a little in savings, but his mom couldn't keep the farm up and running. She had to sell all the cattle.

His dad was a carpenter by trade and a farmer by the grace of God. He had always kept ten or twelve head of cattle to keep the forty-acre farm under control. He didn't want it to grow and become a problem. He did it more as a hobby. There were always chickens for eggs and a hog for butchering.

"Are these fresh eggs?" he asked.

"No. The chickens aren't laying much this winter. They are store-bought."

Janis continued to stir the gravy as Missy pulled the biscuits from the oven. The pleasant, familiar smell filled the room.

"Man, it's good to be home."

Sunday morning finally came, and Michael sang an old hymn as he dressed. He paused his singing to put on his shoes. He sat up, listening as his mother, in her room, finished the verse. They both sang the chorus together.

Missy and her husband, Mark, came by to pick them up. Michael was grateful that Missy was only thirty minutes away since his mom didn't drive. They pulled into the church to find the lot nearly full.

"Looks like a good crowd," Michael said.

He walked up the steps as he had so many times as a child. As they neared the door, he could hear the piano playing. The door opened, and they were greeted by a few of the deacons. Michael had known them for years. Greetings and hugs were exchanged as they walked in. People he had not seen for years were there. He thought about how the reunion in heaven, although far grander, would be like the one today.

He saw aunts and uncles, cousins, and childhood friends. The pastor was a man he had gone to school with. The pastor's uncle had been the pastor when Michael was younger, but he had passed away. The reunion continued for several minutes. Everyone was greeting Michael, patting him on the back, or hugging him. He was happy to see them all.

The pastor stepped to the pulpit. "Let's all stand and sing, 'Oh, How I Love Jesus.' Turn around and greet your neighbor."

The singing and greeting continued throughout the whole song. Michael was overjoyed to be back in God's house. As the congregation settled down and took a seat, the pastor continued.

"It is good to see everyone this morning. This will be our Christmas service today. In a few days, it will be Christmas, but we will celebrate Christ's birth today.

"We have a special guest with us, a man I grew up with. Michael and I sat on the back row. If you don't believe me, you can still see our names where we carved them with our pocketknives." The congregation laughed. "I'm serious. We were rascals back then."

Michael nodded in agreement.

"We are glad to have you home, Michael. We hear you have been through a lot in the last week," the pastor said. "We have all been praying for you, and as you see, God answers prayers."

The message was from Luke 2:8–12. Michael listened as if he were hearing it for the first time.

"And there were in the same country shepherds abiding in the field, keeping watch over their flock by night. And, lo, the angel of the Lord came upon them, and the glory of the Lord shone round about them: and they were sore afraid. And the angel said unto

them, Fear not: for, behold, I bring you good tidings of great joy, which shall be to all people. For unto you is born this day in the city of David a Saviour, which is Christ the Lord. And this shall be a sign unto you; Ye shall find the babe wrapped in swaddling clothes, lying in a manger."

Michael felt a tear form. He reflected on the birth of Jesus. God had sent His only Son to be born of a virgin. He came to earth to live among us. Jesus had come to take away the sins of the whole world. He offered salvation for those that believed. Sadly, many did not. Jesus was despised and rejected and hung on the cross to die.

Hundreds of years earlier, Isaiah had prophesied about the birth of Christ: "Therefore the Lord himself shall give you a sign; Behold, a virgin shall conceive, and bear a son, and shall call his name Immanuel [which means, God with us]" (Isaiah 7:14).

And Micah had told about the place of Jesus' birth: "But thou, Bethlehem Ephratah, though thou be little among the thousands of Judah, yet out of thee shall he come forth unto me that is to be ruler in Israel; whose goings forth have been from of old, from everlasting" (5:2).

As Michael sat there, he thought of the many Christmases he had missed with friends and family. He recalled how his duty had minimized God. Countless times, he had gone about training his men while the birth of Christ was in the back of his mind, not the front.

He looked at his mother and smiled. God had slowed him down, as she had said. It brought him home on Christmas. He was thankful.

The service concluded, and a few of his relatives gathered around him.

"We will be over Christmas day to help with the meal."

Michael hadn't heard anything about it.

His mother explained as they walked out of the church.

"Your aunts — Margie, Wanda, and Annie — are coming over to help fix Christmas dinner. I thought it would be nice to get everyone together."

On Christmas morning, Mark and Missy arrived as Michael and his mom sipped their coffee at the table. The turkey was already in the oven. Mark carried in a ham they had prepared at home.

As the four gathered in the living room around the Christmas tree, Michael felt God's goodness. He had been spared and was now with his family for Christmas. During his years in the service, he had not been home much.

They all exchanged gifts, and finally, his mother handed him a small package not much bigger than a jewelry box. He opened it as all three looked on in eager anticipation. He pulled out a key ring with four keys on it. Michael studied the keys and noticed two of them were for a Ford.

"I want you to have your dad's truck," his mother said.

He held back his tears and hugged his mom. "Thank you. That means a lot to me."

As the ladies entered the kitchen to begin the all-day task of cooking, Michael and Mark walked outside.

The red and white 1982 F-150 pickup sat on the side of the house. It has been undisturbed for some time. Michael climbed into the back and used a key to open the toolbox. He began pulling out the contents: a circular saw, levels, a reciprocating saw, several extension cords, a square, a sledgehammer, various boxes of nails, two tool belts, hammers, nail pullers, chalk boxes, and measuring tapes.

He could tell one of the tool belts had been used more. It belonged to his dad. The other was his. Michael had worked with his dad every summer during school break, building projects. He remembered the addition to the local restaurant, the new bank on Main Street, and the countless houses, garages, and storage buildings completed for county neighbors.

His dad always seemed to have work and never had to look for it.

People would find him on a project and find out when he could get to them. He was a craftsman who never cut corners and built everything as if it were for himself. People knew he would do it right.

Early in life, Michael had gotten used to rising early and laying his head down late. His dad took advantage of every minute of daylight. He would go all day, slowing long enough only to eat a sandwich, and then, he would get right back at it. The smell of sawdust was something Michael and his dad seemed to enjoy.

Michael had learned many life lessons during his summer months. His dad always said, "If it isn't worth doing right, it isn't worth doing." Michael had adopted that philosophy in his own life. He found the military thought the same way.

Michael laid all the tools on the truck's tailgate but stuck the two tool belts back in the toolbox, shut it, and locked it.

"Mark, you may as well take these tools. I may never get any use out of them."

"You sure? They belonged to your dad."

"I'm sure. He would want them used, not sitting around getting rusty. I kept his tool belt and the one he got for me."

Michael noticed a large dent in the side of the truck bed.

"What happened here?" he asked.

"Your dad was feeding hay to the cows, and a big black Angus bull charged him. He jumped into the truck's bed just as the bull smashed into the side."

"I can guess how that went."

"Your dad laughed and said, 'It'll buff out.' Of course, he got the last laugh. He loaded up the bull and took him to market that week."

"Yep, Dad always got the last word."

Michael unlocked the truck door and slid into the driver's seat. He inserted the key into the ignition and turned it. The truck fired up and idled with a low roar. It almost seemed ready to go, anxious to begin an adventure. He turned the ignition off and looked at Mark.

"I see you have kept it up."

"No, your dad kept it up. I just cranked it up and moved it around some."

"I appreciate that, and I know Dad would have, too."

The pair picked up the tools and carried them to the car.

"How's that knee doing?" Mark asked.

"It's fine. The cold weather makes it uncomfortable, though. 'Course, with a hunk of metal in there, I expect that."

Mark had not said anything about Michael's injury since Michael had been home. Michael decided to tell him. Mark listened intently to the details.

"You are the only one I have told the whole story. Don't say anything, please."

"I won't." Mark looked down at the ground, replaying the events in his head. "Is the general doing okay? Did he make it?"

"That is another story. Let's head in, and I'll tell Mom and Missy, too."

As Michael and Mark entered the house, the aroma from the kitchen made their mouths water. Michael walked to the coffee pot and offered Mark a cup.

"Tell me if I'm right. Do I smell potato salad?" Michael asked.

"You do," his mom replied. "Of course, I don't know how you reached that conclusion with only potatoes boiling."

Michael walked to his mom, wrapped an arm around her, and kissed her cheek.

"This isn't my first rodeo."

He moved to a portion of the kitchen counter that was not being used and sipped his coffee. He glanced up at Mark. Without saying a word, Michael said he was preparing to tell the ladies what the two men had discussed earlier, minus the details. Mark made eye contact, shrugged his shoulders, and nodded to indicate he understood.

"So, I want to tell you all what the administrator had to say," Michael said.

Missy and his mom suddenly stopped and turned their full attention to Michael. They wanted to ask but decided to wait.

He continued, "I was told this injury would result in medical retirement. However, I have been offered a job in the Army Reserve. I won't have to retire right now."

"So, you won't be going back to Kuwait?" Janis asked.

"No."

She put her forearm to her face, still holding a knife.

"Thank You, Jesus."

Missy patted her on the back. The two had discussed their fears, and Michael had just removed much of the worry.

"Where will you be stationed?" Missy asked.

"Charlotte, North Carolina."

"God has answered my prayers," his mother said.

"That's good. Charlotte's only three hours away," Missy said.

"Yep. I can visit more often."

He hated to break the rest of the news but added, "Well, there's no easy way to say this, but I am under investigation for the shooting."

Both women drew back as if they had smelled something rotten. Missy's expression changed to disgust.

"Investigation? Are they serious?" Missy asked.

"War has not been declared, and men were killed on each side. Don't worry about it, though. We were in the right. We were fired on first."

His sister and mom took a moment to think. The conversation had turned to unfamiliar territory, the area they had been shielded from. Michael could tell they still had questions but were still processing the information.

"There was a brigadier general who was also injured in this incident. He has told me I need not worry about it. He agrees we were justified in firing."

Michael could tell they wanted to ask more but didn't know where to begin.

"I may never hear another word about it, but I wanted you to know. Just know, regardless of what is said, I did nothing wrong."

"Son, we know that," Janis said.

Michael's mother turned back to the counter, picked up the knife, and began chopping her frustration on a head of cabbage.

"Government for you. They want you to dance to their music."

"Well, I think it's more local than the whole government. Probably, more like my battalion commander. He hasn't ever given me a reason to think he had my back."

Mark had quietly sipped his coffee during the conversation.

"What will you be doing in the reserve?" Mark asked.

"Supervising soldiers."

"So, nothing different than what you've always done?"

"This will be in an office."

"For someone who likes to be outside, is that going to work for you?" Janis asked.

"It's either that or get out. I don't see it being too many years before I hang it up. I'll be all right."

"I think the cavalry has arrived," Michael said, seeing a vehicle pull into the driveway.

Michael and Mark helped his aunts bring in the items they had already prepared for the Christmas meal. Michael quietly observed as the five women divided up duties and moved around each other with several conversations at once. He compared it to a beehive. Each bee knows what to do, but it looks like chaos when you step back and look at the big picture.

Michael and Mark retreated to the living room to watch television. Michael reclined in a chair with a glass of iced tea as the news began updating the war to come in Iraq. He remained silent as he thought about his men still there on Christmas day. Reporters from all the major news stations were in Iraq, and many went to great lengths to report something big. Michael became disgusted at the misinformation they were speaking about.

"You can turn that anytime," Michael said.

Mark settled on a football pregame show. Michael paid no mind but only looked out the window. He missed his men and hoped they would remain safe. Kuwait seemed so far away. Michael knew they were most likely still observing the growing army of tanks that Saddam had. War would begin in just a few weeks.

Michael closed his eyes and quietly prayed for every serviceman and woman in harm's way. The voices and laughter coming from the kitchen caught his attention. It was good to be home and see family he hadn't seen in years. Still, his sense of duty made him wish he were in Kuwait with his men. He decided he would not disclose that. He closed his eyes and drifted off to sleep.

CHAPTER 4

The following week a letter arrived from Kuwait, along with a notice of a package at the post office. Michael picked up the boxes, under protest from his mother. He carried the boxes in and laughed as he looked at them. First Sgt. Phillips had sent his belongings in three MRE boxes. The joke was received.

He opened each of them as his mother looked on, hoping at least to find his dad's Bible. The first contained his BDU uniforms. The second had boots, socks, T-shirts, and underwear. The third held a poncho liner, his leader's book that contained all the personal info for his platoon, the manila envelope from the kids in Tennessee, his dad's Bible, a chicken-ala-king meal (a joke from his men), and a note from the 1st Sgt.:

> SFC Logan,
> I hope this note finds you well. Boone and Dutton helped me pack these boxes, so I feel sure we got everything. You must send me a special power of attorney so I can clear your room in Germany. I will update you when your remaining items ship.

Michael picked up the Bible and examined it for damage.

"Looks like Dad's Bible made the trip in good order."

"That's good news. I was worried you would never see it again," his mother said.

Michael put all the clothes in the washer. He opened the letter sent from Boone and Dutton. They were happy to hear that he was alive and well. Things had changed a little, as most things do when new management takes over. The senior scout had taken his position. He was efficient but lacked personality. The platoon had received a few brand-new privates to help fill in the void with some of the crews. The pair ended their letter by sending their continued prayers. There was no mention of the investigation.

As Michael picked up the boxes to clean up, he noticed each contained a few tablespoons of sand.

"Mom, take a look at this."

He poured the contents into an empty jar. Holding it up, he explained, "The way the sand blows in Kuwait, they couldn't help but send some back."

"What are you going to do with that?"

"I don't know. Keep it for now, I guess."

At the end of the week, Michael called the general as he had promised.

"Davidson residence."

Michael recognized Sarah's voice.

"Mrs. Davidson, it's Michael Logan. How are you all doing?"

"Michael, it's good to hear from you. We have been wondering when you would call. Hang on a minute, and I'll get Tom."

After several minutes of silence, the general picked up the phone.

"Michael, hello there. It's good to hear from you."

"Good to hear from you, General."

"So, how's the rehab going?"

"Good. I don't need the cane anymore. How's your shoulder?"

"It's doing much better. I may sneak into work in a few weeks. Starting to get cabin fever."

"I know the feeling, sir."

"We have everything ready for you whenever you decide to come. Just tell us when to expect you so someone can let you in the gate."

Michael imagined the security measures the general had. He saw a concertina wire gate with a few .50 cal. manned Humvees. Maybe a minefield, too.

"So, you are not going back to Kuwait?" Michael asked.

"No, my superiors feel I should sit it out and let my replacement have the duty. I'll reassume my position at division headquarters."

The two concluded their discussion, and Michael sat in a recliner to form a plan. He knew he did not want to sit in the house for three to four more weeks. His knee hadn't given him much trouble, so he debated whether to head to North Carolina early.

Michael picked up the manila envelope lying on an end table by his chair. He reread the address and thought how he had vowed to write them. Weeks had passed, and he still hadn't got around to it. Maybe his mom was right. Perhaps he needed to slow down to honor his commitments.

"How long do you think it would take to drive to Tennessee?" Michael asked his mom.

"Probably six or seven hours. But you know the doctors said you don't need to be driving for six weeks."

"Yes, but I broke that rule when I went to the post office."

"The post office isn't seven hours away."

Michael said no more. His mind was made up. He would drive to Tennessee and thank Mrs. Whitmore and her Sunday school class personally.

On Saturday morning, he picked up a suitcase he had packed the night before and hugged his mom.

"See you in a few days."

"You are going to miss church tomorrow," she said.

"I'll be in church, Lord willing."

He loaded his things in the pickup and started out the driveway. He glanced in the rearview mirror and noticed his mom standing on the porch crying. She had cried for him many times in his eighteen years of service. He thought how, in the past, he was always leaving, never sticking roots in one place very long. He reasoned with himself that this was only a short trip. He would be back in a few days.

Michael realized after a few hours that the trip would probably take more than seven hours. His knee began to ache, and he pulled over to get out and stretch it. The weather was cold enough that much of the snow from the previous weeks was still on the ground. However, the roads were clear, and nothing was in the forecast for the next few days.

He smiled and muttered to himself. "I'm in no hurry. If God wants to slow me down, so be it."

He climbed back into the truck and continued the journey, stopping occasionally for gas and a snack but mainly to stretch. He had the heat as low as he could stand it without fogging the windows, but the heat in the truck seemed to make the aching worse.

After nearly ten hours, he pulled into the church's parking lot. The sun was down enough that the lights on the sign in front were on. He exited the truck and walked up to the sign to find the service times: Sunday School 9:30 a.m. Worship Service 11:00 a.m. Pastor Rick Jordan.

As he turned to get back into the truck, a man exited the church and began locking the door.

"Can I help you?"

"I was just checking your service times."

"I'm Rick Jordan, the pastor, and you are?" the man asked, walking up to Michael.

"Michael Logan. Good to meet you, sir."

Michael reached for the dash and retrieved the manila envelope.

"I got this Christmas card from Mrs. Whitmore's class while I was in Kuwait, and I just wanted them to know it was appreciated."

"You received that? Well, we love our soldiers, and Mrs. Whitmore is not shy about it. That's great. I'm glad to hear about God's work touching people's lives."

"I was planning on meeting them tomorrow and thanking them,

but I guess I need to find a hotel for the night. Do you have any recommendations?"

"Hotel? How far have you traveled?"

"From West Virginia."

"That is a drive. How about you park here and walk to the parsonage with me for supper."

"I couldn't impose on you."

"Nonsense. I was finishing my study for tomorrow and heading in myself."

Michael was reminded of Paul's missionary trips and how he stayed and ate with different people on his journey. Christian hospitality was still alive in Dickson.

"Very well. I thank you."

The pastor entered the house and told his wife they would have company.

"Something smells good," Michael said.

The pastor's wife shook hands with him. "Well, that's yet to be seen. Welcome …?"

She turned to her husband for the answer.

"Michael Logan. I'm sorry, I need to do introductions," the pastor said. "Michael, this is my wife, Jackie. He's driven to us from West Virginia."

"You have probably been driving most of the day?"

"Yes ma'am, a great deal of it."

They washed up, and Mrs. Jordan seated everyone. The pastor asked the blessing and thanked God for sending their visitor. She began filling bowls and passing them to each of the men.

"Tonight is chili night. I hope you like it, Mr. Logan."

He smiled. "You can call me Michael or Logan, ma'am. I'll answer to either one."

"Michael, then."

"Michael is a soldier. He got a Christmas card from us while he was in Kuwait."

"Really? That's wonderful. We pray for our military and are glad to hear that our labors have blessed someone."

Michael explained that he had received the card before Christmas but was injured and unable to respond as planned.

"I'm on medical leave right now, so I thought I would visit rather than write."

"How were you injured, son?" Pastor Jordan asked.

Michael looked at Jackie, hesitating to reveal the answer. He had been brought up not to worry women with disturbing details or to speak of such things at the supper table.

He looked back at the pastor and whispered, "I got shot."

"Well, bless your heart. I hope everything is better now."

"Yes sir. Thank you."

Michael didn't disclose the details but explained that his knee was on the mend. The trip had proven to be a challenge, though.

After the meal, the three talked for a while. Mrs. Jordan brought out a blackberry cobbler and coffee for dessert. Michael enjoyed the company and the food. Her recipe was a strong contender with his mom's.

Later, Michael thanked the couple for the wonderful meal and fellowship but said he needed to get checked in at the hotel.

"Michael, you can stay with us tonight. We have a couple of extra rooms," the pastor said.

"I appreciate that, but I couldn't do that."

"Sure you can. We'd be glad to have you."

Since the pastor's wife agreed, Michael accepted their blessing.

The following day after a wonderful breakfast, the three went to the church.

"Michael, I must do a few last-minute things before the congregation arrives. How would you feel about addressing everyone during the worship service?" the pastor asked.

"I suppose I could do that."

"Good. I'll cue you when to speak. We usually meet first thing in our classes. I'll take you to Mrs. Whitmore's room when everyone gets in."

"Sounds good."

Michael sat in the sanctuary alone. In a few minutes, people began arriving, and several greeted him and moved on to their room. Pastor Jordan came out and walked toward Michael as a lovely silver-haired lady entered the church.

"Good morning, Mrs. Whitmore," the pastor said. "We have a surprise for you today."

"I like surprises," she said.

"This is Michael Logan. He came to us from Kuwait, where he received one of your Christmas cards."

The little woman was moved to tears as she extended a hand to Michael.

"We are glad to have you. Thank you for your service."

"Thank you for the card, and I'm glad to meet you."

"Would you mind if Michael and I sat in on your class this morning?" Pastor Jordan asked.

"Not at all. The more, the merrier."

The three walked to her classroom, and Michael and the pastor sat against the back wall and out of the way. Mrs. Whitmore prepared as the children began filing in. They all became very quiet when they noticed a stranger sitting with the preacher.

One little boy walked up to Michael, unafraid, and spoke. "Hi. I'm Billy. What's your name?"

Michael stuck out a hand. "I'm Michael. Nice to meet you, Billy."

The boy smiled and took his seat as the remainder of the children turned in their chairs to get a look at the visitor.

"Children, let's turn around and get started."

Mrs. Whitmore opened with a prayer that was spoken by each child.

"Children, we have a guest with us today. This is Michael. He is a soldier. He got your Christmas cards and wanted to thank you."

The children returned to their seats to look at the pair in the back. Michael pulled the cards from the envelope and stood.

"Yes, thank you all. You are all such talented artists. I have one here from Jenny."

A small, shy girl lowered her head to avoid being seen.

"And I got one from Billy and Ann. Thank you all. It means a lot to our soldiers to get mail and to know we have children being brought up in God's house."

Michael sat back down, and the pastor smiled. The class continued as Mrs. Whitmore told the story of Jonah and the big fish. The children seemed more at ease and even asked questions. At the conclusion, Billy flew by, mimicking a race car.

"He is just as I imagined him," Michael whispered to the pastor.

"Yes. Billy is Billy," the pastor chuckled.

Everyone began gathering in the sanctuary as the Sunday school classes finished. Numerous conversations were going on. Greetings and hugs were exchanged throughout. Michael felt as if he had walked into his home church. Nothing was that different from what he had grown up around.

The pastor took his place at the podium as Michael settled into a seat. They sang a few hymns, greeted each other, and received the offering.

"We have a special guest today. Michael is a soldier, and he's come from Kuwait to see us this morning."

The congregation applauded as Michael stood, surprised at the welcome.

Michael held up the manila envelope and began to speak. "While in the desert, I received this envelope containing several Christmas cards from Mrs. Whitmore's Sunday school class. I was able to sit in with them this morning, and I thank you for that."

He looked around and found Mrs. Whitmore seated only a few rows from himself.

"For some soldiers, the letters addressed 'To Any Soldier' is the only mail they receive. It meant a lot to me to receive this and see how our children are raised in God's house. However, I want to challenge Mrs. Whitmore and all of you not to stop with Christmas cards. Keep it going throughout the year. We all know where this thing is headed. Our soldiers may be there for a while. Send them your thoughts and prayers at every opportunity you get. It's a wonderful step into reality when you get one of these. Thank you."

Michael sat as the entire congregation stood and applauded. Those near him shook his hand or hugged him. He briefly felt like a politician.

After the service, he was greeted again by several people who crowded around him. Billy pushed his way through until he came to Michael. He stuck out his hand.

"Thanks, army man."

"Thank you, Billy."

On the drive home, Michael kept thinking about the kindness of the pastor and his wife. He was glad to finally meet Mrs. Whitmore and her class of children. Mostly though, he was glad he followed through with his commitment to contact them.

I see why God slowed me down, he thought.

After arriving home, Michael spent most of the following morning in the recliner with his feet up. His mother didn't say anything, but Michael knew she would have been correct if she had. He had overdone it. The trip to Tennessee had cured his cabin fever, and he was thankful to be home once again.

"Michael, would you like to have lunch with me?" his mother called.

"I believe I would."

They sat at the table, and Janis asked the blessing.

"Father, I thank You for bringing my son home safely. I thank You for the time we have spent together. We thank You for this food and give You praise. In Jesus' name, amen."

Michael poured a glass of iced tea as his mother passed him the bowl with homemade chicken salad.

As he made a sandwich, his mother said, "You are leaving soon, aren't you?"

"I haven't decided when, but yes, soon. I can't sit too long. You said that yourself."

His mother nodded as she continued chewing. She wasn't the kind to say, "I told you so."

"So, I guess you will rent an apartment or house?"

"Yes. I have to see what is available."

"You don't have any furniture, do you?"

"No ma'am. The military has always provided that. I can probably get all my possessions in the cab of the truck."

"Have you thought about what you will do when you retire?"

"Not a lot. I might end up staying thirty years. Never know."

"I asked because you and Missy will get this place when I'm gone."

Michael had heard that statement before. He was not ready for the-last-will-and-testament conversation.

"Mom, we will deal with that when the time comes. For now, let's not worry about it."

Michael got up from the table and walked into the living room. He knew his mom meant well, but he was unprepared to deal with losing another parent. The conversation confirmed that he needed to move on. He and his mom needed a break.

Later that week, Mark and Missy stopped by to have supper with the family.

"I am going to head down tomorrow," Michael announced as everyone enjoyed their meal.

"We all figured you were close to a decision," Missy said.

Mark and Janis dug in their pockets. Each pulled out a dollar bill, and handed it to Missy.

"I had Saturday," Missy explained, revealing she had won the bet.

Michael called the general and got directions, then packed his belongings in a suitcase, a small duffel bag, and three MRE boxes. He was right. Everything would fit in the cab.

Saturday morning, after coffee, Michael put his things into the truck. He hugged his mom and promised her he would try to visit more often now that he would be closer to home. He pulled out of the driveway and noticed his mother standing on the porch. She waved goodbye. He knew she was crying.

About halfway through the trip, the snow began to disappear. It was cold but sunny as he neared the general's gated community. He saw no snow anywhere. He had missed the snow, but now, he was glad to be out of it.

He pushed the call button at the gate.

"Welcome, Michael," the general answered.

The gate opened, and he pulled through. As he drove along the road, he glanced at the large houses and beautiful yards. Even in the dead of winter, they were something to see. He noticed they all bordered a lake. Each house had a boat dock. Several had elaborate boathouses.

About halfway around the lake, he came to the Davidsons' driveway. He turned in to see rows of Bradford pear trees on each side of the drive. It split off in front of a large ranch-style house and circled around to the front yard, then joined back.

Large oak trees and shrubbery were everywhere. Michael took in the view as he got out of the truck. The general walked around the side of the house.

"Glad to see you made it safely."

Michael walked toward the general to shake his hand.

"Yes sir. No problems."

"Come on back. Bring your bag, and I'll show you to your quarters."

Michael retrieved one of his bags and followed. The back yard was just as impressive as the front. The large yard rolled into the lake about fifty yards from the house. There was a covered picnic table and a beautiful rock-built grill. Outside the shelter was a fire pit with several chairs around it. There were oaks, maples, and even a weeping willow for shade. Even though the trees had no leaves, Michael imagined the beauty of the summertime.

"You have a beautiful place here, General."

"Well, it's quiet most of the time. The people on the lake get a little rowdy in the summer, but it's not too bad."

They neared the boathouse, and Michael was amazed. It was nothing like he had imagined. The dock was eight feet wide and probably fifty feet long. On the left at the end was a large sitting area. On the right was the boathouse. A pontoon boat was hanging out of the water under the covered enclosure.

The general unlocked the door and handed Michael the key.

"After you, Michael."

They walked into the land side of the enclosure. There was a bed and chest of drawers on one wall, a small table with two chairs on the opposite wall, and a refrigerator. Another wall had a sink with counters on each side and cupboards above and below. In the corner was a door that opened into the bathroom, which contained a shower stall, toilet, and sink.

"It's got everything you need except a closet," the general said.

"You were right. It's perfect."

He sat his bag down and continued looking around. The general sat down in one of the chairs.

"Sarah is preparing something special tonight. The girls will be over in a while to eat with us. They usually come by every weekend."

"So, the girls don't live here?"

"No. They both have their places not too far from here."

Michael sat in the remaining chair.

"General, I appreciate what you are doing for me. I did not expect anything like this. This is very nice."

"Well, thank you, Michael. I'm glad to help you out. You can stay as long as you like or until you find something. It's up to you."

"I will probably start looking Monday morning after I get updated on where I should be looking."

"Sure. Rachel knows that stuff. She can help you with that."

Michael had a wide-eyed expression as he continued to look around in amazement. Then, the general's expression changed to a more somber tone as he cleared his throat and looked at the floor.

"Michael, if I tell you something, will you promise me it will stay between us?"

"Of course."

The general reached into his pocket and pulled out his keys. There was a metal pill case attached that he unscrewed and held in his opposite hand.

"Hold out your hand, Michael."

The general poured the contents into his open hand. Initially, Michael was not sure what he was looking at. He studied the two objects. The first was a piece of metal — a mushroomed bullet — the outcome of a round striking an object. The second was the top of a tooth without the roots.

Michael glanced up at the general, almost knowing what he would say.

"That is the bullet they pulled out of my arm. The tooth belonged to Captain Knight." He took a moment to regain his composure. "That's the bullet that killed him. It went through him and lodged in me, along with one of his teeth. We wouldn't be having this conversation if I was six inches shorter. It would have hit me in the neck or head."

"General, God has other plans for you."

"Michael, I have not spoken with God for several years. I don't know what He has planned for me or why He spared me."

"Most of the time, I have a hard time understanding God's reason for things, too," Michael said.

The general got up and walked to the door. "It's good to have you here, Michael. Please keep that between us. Even Sarah doesn't know about it. Only you and I."

"It will go no further."

"You can get settled in, and we will see you after a while."

The general left, and Michael remembered Chaplain Campbell's statement: "Back sliders are sometimes hard eggs to crack." It seemed the general was not comfortable speaking about God. He had reacted just like Monica: by running.

Michael got the rest of his things out of the truck and started unpacking. He took a moment to rest and heard a knock at the door. He opened it to find Monica standing in her nurse smock and holding a bottle of wine.

"Hey there, Sergeant Logan. May I come in?"

"Sure, good to see you."

"It is good to see you, too. We have been wondering when we would see you again."

Michael noticed the quiet hard-shelled woman was replaced with a more talkative, easy-going Monica. He assumed the wine was the reason.

Monica walked in and sat at the table. Michael joined her.

"Where are my manners? Would you like some wine?" Monica asked.

"No, thank you. I don't drink."

"Not even a little wine. Is it because you are religious?"

"It's a personal choice."

"Suit yourself." She poured her glass full and took a long sip. "After the day I've had, I need a drink."

"You mentioned you are an R.N.?"

"Yes, that's right. I work in the recovery wing of the hospital."

"Do you like it?"

"I love it. Helping people is something I enjoy. The doctors and other nurses cause my stress. Some of them need to find another job."

"Working with people who don't share the same passion can be difficult."

"Egg-zackly."

Monica spoke with a slight lisp. The alcohol was taking effect. Michael remained silent and let Monica vent, but she said no more. She sipped her wine and stared into a place where she kept her pain.

He wanted her to leave but didn't want to be rude. The Davidsons had gone out of their way to accommodate him. He purposely brought God into the conversation, expecting her to escape.

"Do you ever go to church with Rachel?"

Monica smiled a sheepish smile. "No. I have gone with her, but I don't go much."

Michael was surprised she hadn't gotten up to leave. He thought he should take it more seriously and witness to her instead of trying to drive her out.

"Would you like to go with me tomorrow?"

Monica got up, shaking her finger from side to side. "No, no, no. I am off tomorrow, and I am sleeping in."

"Well, maybe some other time then?"

Monica stepped to the door and tried to open it without dropping her glass or bottle. Michael got up and opened it for her.

"Yeah, sure. Some other time," she said.

After Monica left, Michael wondered what he had gotten himself into. Monica had surprised him with her drinking, but it explained a lot. He had been there less than a few hours and had already driven the general and Monica away. He walked outside the boathouse and sat on the pier overlooking the lake. The winter breeze off the water seemed to be coming right at him.

"Hey there, stranger."

Michael turned to see Rachel walking toward him. He was glad to see her and needed a conversation with someone who knew where he stood.

"Hello."

Rachel sat beside him, hands in her coat pocket to stay warm.

"What are you doing out here? You're going to freeze."

"I just drove from West Virginia. It's about ten degrees colder there."

"Well, if you don't mind, let's go inside."

They walked into the boathouse, relieved to escape the cold air. Rachel sat in a chair and rubbed her hands together to warm them. Michael sat next to her.

"Are we going to church tomorrow?" he asked.

"Yes. I was going to ask you about that."

"Your sister was here earlier, and I invited her. I don't think that went so well."

"I can imagine. Did she have her bottle with her?"

"Yes. I didn't know she was a drinker."

"You wouldn't have come if I told you about all the skeletons. I pray for them. Sometimes, I feel that's all I can do," Rachel said.

"I know sometimes we view prayer as a last resort, but we would fair better to begin with prayer."

"I know you are right, but understand how long I have been dealing with a family that hears none of my pleadings."

"I ran the general off within the first thirty minutes I was here."

"Dad takes it in spurts. Somedays, he will listen and even comment. On other days, he will walk away."

"Today was a walk-away day," Michael said.

"It's okay. I'm glad that you are here. You may make more progress than I have."

Michael changed the subject as Rachel removed her coat.

"Did you have to work today?" he asked.

"Yes, Saturday is a popular day to show houses. It works with most people's schedule."

"So, where do you recommend I look for a place?"

"Well, after church tomorrow, I can show you if you like?"

"Sounds good to me."

Michael listened to Rachel talk for nearly an hour. He shared in the conversation, but mostly he was thinking to himself. He wondered if she was the one — the one he had waited for God to send. She met all his criteria. She was extremely attractive, had a wonderful sense of humor, and was a godly woman. He wondered why she had not been snatched up. Perhaps she had a skeleton, too.

Rachel got up and put her coat on. "We can head to the house. I'll give you the grand tour." She giggled as she sang *Grand Tour,* like the George Jones song. "By then, dinner should be ready."

"Yes, I'd like to see the house."

"How would you like to come over to my place tomorrow evening? I'll pop some corn, and we can watch the best John Wayne movie ever made," Rachel asked.

"You have *True Grit?*"

"Not hardly. I was talking about *The Cowboys.*"

Michael accepted the challenge. She had entered his area of expertise.

"*The Cowboys* is in the top ten at best. *True Grit* is the greatest John Wayne movie ever made."

"Okay, I agree, *The Cowboys* is all I have."

"I would be delighted to share a movie with you. Just let me know when and how to get there."

"I'll show you after church."

The next morning, Rachel knocked on the door of the boathouse. Michael followed her back to her car. She wanted him to ride with her so she could show him around. The church was only minutes away.

"I may have told the pastor about you … some. He is looking forward to meeting you. We better get in, or the best snakes will be taken," Rachel confessed as they pulled into the parking lot.

Michael laughed, remembering their joking in the hospital. They walked inside, and Rachel stopped to greet several people and introduce him. They made their way to a seat as a man approached and stuck out his hand.

"You must be Michael?"

"Yes sir, Michael Logan."

"I am Tommy Hatcher, the pastor here. Rachel has told us so much about you."

Michael smiled and glanced at Rachel, who turned her head away sheepishly.

"Well, there's not a lot to tell."

"She told us you had been injured in Kuwait. That's a lot where I come from."

Michael was curious how much Rachel had disclosed. He knew she did not know the whole story unless the general had told her.

Michael and Rachel settled into a seat. He enjoyed being with her in God's house. She smiled the whole time.

After the service, Pastor Hatcher put a hand on Michael's shoulder. "I hear you are just settling in, but I'd like us to grab lunch together when you do."

"I would like that."

Rachel had not stopped smiling. She could not hide her happiness and joy. After they left the church, she drove by her house to let Michael know where it was. Then, she drove him to the division headquarters building. The gate was closed, but she sat at the entrance just off the road.

"This is where you will be working. All along this road are decent places to live. Do you want an apartment or a house?"

"Probably an apartment. I don't need anything large."

"There are nice apartments about three blocks down."

They pulled into the driveway of the apartment complex and stopped in front of the office. No one was there, but there was a sign out front advertising several availabilities. Michael felt fortunate to find something within walking distance from work.

"I think I will check with them Monday morning. This doesn't look bad," he said.

"Do you want to see some more?"

"No, I think these are fine."

"There is a grocery store within walking distance the other way."

Rachel drove him back to the boathouse.

"If you see Mom or Dad, tell them I had to run errands. Also, come by at six. I'm altering our movie night to include dinner."

"I'll be there. Should I bring anything?"

"Just you."

Michael walked through the back yard and headed to the boathouse. He reflected on the day as he opened the door and walked in. He had enjoyed going to church with Rachel. They all seemed to be wonderful people. And finding an apartment and grocery store within walking distance of work was a bonus.

He looked forward to dinner and a movie later that evening. He wondered if this was an official date or just friends getting together. It did not concern him if they enjoyed each other's company, and so far, it seemed they did.

On the way to Rachel's, Michael stopped at the grocery store and bought a small bouquet. He was unsure if she liked flowers but felt compelled to bring something to show his appreciation.

He walked up her sidewalk, but it opened before he reached the door.

"I heard you pull in. Come on in."

She had flour on her apron, and her hair was pulled back to do some serious cooking. She still looked beautiful. Michael offered the flowers as he walked in.

"I got you some flowers. I hope you like them."

"What girl doesn't like flowers? Thank you," she said. "Grab you a seat in the living room, and I'll put these in water. Dinner is almost ready."

"Take your time. I'm in no hurry."

Rachel brought him a glass of iced tea. "I hope you like homemade chicken and dumplings?"

"I sure do."

"Good. Give me a few minutes to clean up, and I'll be right back."

Michael sat, sipping his tea and smelling the aroma of the meal she had prepared. He smiled when he thought about how finding a woman who could cook was an additional bonus.

Rachel walked back in and sat next to him. She had removed the apron and let her hair down.

"You look very nice," Michael said.

"Thank you. Are you ready to eat?"

They spent the evening talking and enjoying the meal. Afterward, they watched the movie. They remained silent during the movie, but Rachel didn't pull her hand away when he held it.

On Monday morning, Michael awoke and spent time praying and reading God's Word. He couldn't help but think of Rachel. She was everything he had wanted in a woman. He thanked God for bringing them together.

A few hours later, he made the trip to the apartment complex, found someone in the office, and was given several choices. He settled on a studio apartment. It was a little bigger than the boathouse and had a closet. After living in a tent, Michael was not picky. It was plenty big enough for him.

He did the paperwork, paid what was due, and got the key. A huge weight was lifted off him. Finding a place had concerned him, but, thanks to Rachel, it was painless.

The apartment had no furniture. He was going to need to make a few purchases. He bought cleaning supplies, toiletries, washcloths and towels, and a small vacuum. Eventually, he would buy a bedroom suit, but for now, he stopped at a sporting goods store and bought a cot.

He spent the day cleaning and unpacking. He set the cot up and placed his Bible under it, just as he had in Kuwait. He sat the jar of sand on a counter and thought how blessed he was to have such a comfortable dwelling. Boone and Dutton came to mind as he looked at the jar. They were still dealing with the heat, blowing sand, and cramped space of the tent.

Later, he headed out again to purchase a few groceries. His apartment was on the second floor. As he started down the steps, he noticed an older woman, perhaps in her eighties, walking up the steps. She was short and portly with a dress that almost covered her swollen ankles. She grasped the handrail with one hand and held a large pocketbook with the other. She clutched a small bag of groceries. She was taking the climb, one step at a time. She stopped to rest as Michael approached.

"Good day, ma'am," Michael said.

"Good day, young man."

No sooner had they spoken than she dropped her bag of groceries. A half gallon of milk bounced down the steps and erupted at the bottom.

"Well, fiddle sticks," the woman said.

"Let me help you with that."

Michael began picking up the remaining items and placing them back in the bag.

"I can carry this up for you."

"Thank you. I have the dropsies today."

Michael extended a hand. "I am Michael Logan. I just moved in. What's your name?"

"I am Violet Thompson. Nice to meet you."

She took her bag from Michael as they neared the top of the steps. "I can get it from here."

"I was going to the grocery store myself. I can get you some more milk if you like."

"No, no. I'll get some later. Where do you live?"

"Right across from you. I'll be working down the street at the Army Reserve Center."

"An army boy? My Walter was in the army."

"If you need anything, don't hesitate to ask," Michael said.

Violet smiled as she opened the door and stepped in.

"I thank you, but Myrtle and I get along pretty well."

She closed the door, and Michael made his way to the store. Later, he went by the general's, retrieved the last of his belongings, and notified him where he would be living.

"You are always welcome here, Michael," the general reminded him. "Come by Saturday, and we'll grill out."

As he left, he thought, *It must never get too cold for the general to grill.*

Michael settled into his apartment, scheduled to have a phone hooked up, and made several other trips to the store to get things he had overlooked. Around the middle of that week, he got his first visitor.

"Come on in, sir," Michael said, seeing the general at his door. "What brings you this way?"

"I just got word that the war has begun. We are now in the Desert Storm phase. Bombing of strategic targets has already happened."

Michael felt as if he had been kicked in the chest. "I knew we were getting close to taking action, but with the move, it slipped up on me."

"I will update you more when you come over Saturday, but I will probably return to work on Monday."

"Me, too. I'm with you."

During the remainder of the week, Michael felt as if he were in a fog. The news of the war had sobered his illusions. The comforts of the states had concealed the reality he had left weeks earlier. Now, his thoughts and concern for his men were constantly with him.

Michael wrote Boone and Dutton and let them know he was still praying for them. He did not expect an immediate response since he felt certain the fighting occupied their every minute. He had seen both young soldiers develop into fine men. Although they were less than fifteen years apart, he likened his relationship with them to a father and his sons. They had made him proud.

He got his uniforms ready for Monday. BDUs were ironed and starched with a crisp seam. Boots were spit-shined until they glimmered like glass. Michael was ready to return to work — ready to put the uniform back on and continue what he had started eighteen years earlier.

Michael drove to the Davidsons' home on Saturday for a winter cookout. He noticed Monica's car in the driveway and chose to avoid her by walking around the side to the back yard rather than going through the house. The general was already at the grill cleaning it.

"Afternoon, General."

"Good afternoon, Michael. You are just in time to hear me fussing. There needs to be an easier way to clean these things."

"Have you tried foaming it with oven cleaner and then spraying it with the water hose?"

"I may try that next time. I love to grill, just despise the cleanup."

"I'll burn the rest off." He set the heat up, closed the lid, and looked at Michael. "So, you feel up to heading back Monday?"

"Yes sir. I'm ready."

"I feel the same way. I'm tired of waiting." He took a chair under the shelter and offered Michael one. "I have a master sergeant in the slot you will fill, but he is retiring soon. Once we get you switched over and official, you can shadow him. He can show you the ropes."

"I appreciate that, sir."

"I have asked the sergeant major to be there so you can meet him. Like I told you, though, he stays down at the Drill Sergeant School in Fort Jackson most of the time. He will be your boss. The reserve and national guard soldiers servicing your unit in Kuwait were a mixed group of units. We have several people who work at division filling roles there. You won't have a full house."

"I understand."

Monica approached with a glass of iced tea in each hand. She handed the first to her father.

"Thank you, darling," the general said.

She handed the second glass to Michael. "We didn't even know you were out here, Michael."

"I used the code and snuck in. And thank you for the tea."

Monica was still in her nurse smock, and he assumed she had just gotten off work. She turned to head back to the house.

"You are welcome. I'm helping Mom, so please excuse me."

"What do you think of my daughters, Michael?" the general asked.

"I have enjoyed meeting them. I believe Rachel and I have more in common, though."

"Yes, I heard she fixed you dinner the other night."

"She is a fine cook. I enjoyed the meal."

"I'm not trying to be nosey, Michael. It's none of my business, but they both like you."

"Both of them? I never thought that. Monica and I have had only short conversations."

The general went in to get the meat. Rachel walked out, made her way to the grill, and sat in a vacant chair.

"I have a bone to pick with you," she said, doing her best to conceal a smile and trying to look serious and menacing.

"Today is Saturday. I have not heard from you since our dinner last Sunday," she said.

"Well, I had to move this week. I wanted to come by but didn't want to drop in uninvited."

The general opened the back door, and Michael could tell he needed help with the numerous things he was carrying.

As the general loaded the grill, Rachel leaned over to Michael and whispered, "You don't need an invitation."

"Sir, would you like to attend church with Rachel and me tomorrow?" Michael asked.

The general did not turn around but continued arranging the meat on the grill.

"Not tomorrow, but I may go with you sometime."

Rachel grabbed Michael's forearm and smiled. Michael had just made more progress than she had in the years past. She was hopeful and thankful.

On Sunday morning, Michael walked out his door and turned to lock it. He heard Violet exiting her door.

"Good morning, Mrs. Thompson."

She turned to answer, and Michael noticed a Bible in her hand.

"Good morning, Mr. Logan."

She noticed Michael also held a Bible.

"You are heading to church, too, I see."

"Yes ma'am."

"I ride with Heather. She's a young lady who lives above you. She's a schoolteacher down the road."

"I'd like to meet her."

"You will. She should be down in a minute."

"Is Myrtle not feeling well this morning?"

Violet stopped and gave Michael a puzzled look.

"Myrtle? Oh, no, she doesn't go to church."

"Well, I'll pray for her."

As they reached the bottom of the steps, Violet laughed.

"I'm afraid prayer won't help Myrtle."

A young lady started down the stairs.

"Sorry, I am running late, Mrs. Thompson."

"Nonsense. We just walked out ourselves."

Violet turned to Michael.

"Heather, I'd like you to meet Michael Logan. Mr. Logan just moved in across from me."

Heather smiled and shook his hand as she rushed to get going.

"Nice to meet you, Mr. Logan. Welcome to the neighborhood." She turned to Violet. "We had best be going, or we'll be late."

Michael turned to head to his truck. Heather had not taken two steps when she froze and turned back to Michael.

"Did you say your name was Michael Logan?"

He stopped and turned back to face Heather. "Yes ma'am."

"Sergeant Logan from Kuwait?"

"Yes ma'am. I was in Kuwait."

"Were you wounded?"

"Yes, but how did you know?"

Heather ran to him and wrapped her arms around his neck.

"Chris Boone is my boyfriend. I have heard everything about you."

"It's a small world, isn't it? How is Boone?"

"He is fine. He misses you; I can tell you that. He thinks a lot of you."

"I think a lot of him, too."

"I feel like I already know you. All the letters he has written describe you so well."

"Well, it's good to meet you, ma'am."

"Heather. Call me Heather."

"Okay. Heather then."

She looked at her watch as though she had lost track of time.

"Yikes. We are going to be late."

The ladies departed for church, and Michael did as well. Following them, he noticed they pulled into the same church as him.

Michael went to where Rachel was seated and exhaled deeply as he sat beside her.

"Sorry I'm late. I ran into a neighbor."

"No problem. We still have a few minutes."

"Before I forget, would you like to dine with me this evening?"

She smiled, almost relieved. "Of course. I was wondering if we would get back together again."

"We are together now."

"You know what I mean," Rachel said, lightly punching Michael on the arm.

Pastor Hatcher approached the podium, and everyone took their seats. He began greeting everyone and opened in prayer.

"I'll be right back," Rachel whispered.

When the pastor concluded praying and Michael opened his eyes, he saw Rachel and Heather standing on the stage with microphones. The piano began to play, and the two ladies sang a duet of "He Lives." Their voices complimented each other as Heather sang the lead and Rachel the backup. They both joined in for the chorus.

Michael smiled as he thought of God's goodness. God had taken him from Kuwait and introduced him to the general, which led him to meet Rachel. He had no idea that Boone's girlfriend was a close friend of the general's daughter. God was revealing some of His plan. Michael was amazed as he understood a little more of it.

As the ladies concluded their song and everyone stood to applaud, Michael whispered a prayer: "Thank You, Lord. Thank You."

Chapter 5

On the Monday morning before Michael headed to work, he spent devotional time. He prayed:

Father, I thank You for this journey You have set me on. I thank You for the many people You have introduced me to. They have blessed my life. Help me to bless them through You. I pray for the safety of the servicemen and women as we enter a time of war. Continue to work in the lives of Dutton and Boone. I pray for the salvation of the Davidson family. Help me to witness to them. Father, be with me as I start this new job today. I know this is all part of Your plan. Help me to bring glory and honor to You. In Jesus' name I pray, amen.

The general had given him the code to the security gate at the reserve center. The two had planned to meet in the parking lot at 0800 before too many others arrived. Michael pulled in at 0730, parked, and sipped his coffee while waiting.

He observed the large flag that flew just outside the entrance. Many men had died to keep that flag there. He was glad to do his part as well. It felt good to be back in uniform and serve his country. This new job would be no different. He would no longer be a scout, but the new role would not diminish his sense of duty and honor.

He spent the morning meeting and talking with Sgt. Major Samson and Master Sgt. Hill. Afterward, he did all the in-processing paperwork to get him switched over. That afternoon, he began meeting all the soldiers under his leadership.

Before he realized it, the first day had flown by, and at 1700, everyone started leaving. The general approached Michael on his way out.

"What do you think so far, Sergeant Logan?"

"I like it, sir. The hardest thing for me is the 9-to-5 schedule, but I can get used to that."

"Good. Glad to have you."

When Michael got home, he noticed Violet climbing the steps.

"Good evening, Mrs. Thompson," he called.

"Good evening, Michael."

Michael took her small bag of groceries and walked with her up the steps.

"Mrs. Thompson, wouldn't you like an apartment on the ground floor so you don't have to deal with these steps?" he asked.

"No. The doctors say I need to get exercise, and this is exercise."

Michael laughed as he glanced down at the bag he carried. The contents were the same as the groceries he had picked up off the ground just a few days earlier: bread, bologna, and a half gallon of milk. He felt confident Violet was not getting much to eat.

Violet stopped the climb to rest. "You look handsome in your uniform, Michael. Reminds me of my Walter. He was in the Army, too."

"Yes ma'am, I remember you mentioned that."

"Walter served in World War II. He was on the beaches of Normandy."

"That's wonderful. That battle turned the outcome of the war."

"I miss him. I lost him a few years ago. That's why I'm living here. Had to sell our place."

They neared the top of the steps, and Violet retrieved her bag.

"Thank you, Michael. You need to let me cook for you sometimes to pay you back. I love to cook."

Michael thought for a moment that her statement might be the answer to her getting more to eat. He assumed she was on a limited income, and with her independence, she wouldn't accept a handout.

"If you let me buy the groceries, I would be honored to share your cooking."

She agreed, and they settled on a day to eat together. Michael picked up a few groceries and dropped them off with Violet. She was excited to cook for him. Michael was glad to know she was going to eat well. His plan had worked.

On Wednesday evening, when Michael got home, Violet opened her door as he started in his apartment.

"Supper will be ready in thirty minutes."

"Sounds great. I'll grab a quick shower and be right over."

Twenty minutes later, Michael knocked on Violet's door, and she opened it with a smile he had not seen before. She seemed to shine. Cooking again had given her joy.

She sat Michael at the table around a wonderful aroma of serving bowls. She had prepared baked chicken in a mushroom sauce, asparagus, mashed potatoes, and homemade biscuits.

She asked Michael to say the blessing.

"Father, I thank You for Mrs. Thompson. I thank You that she is my neighbor and for the meal she has prepared. We give You thanks in Jesus' name, amen."

"Amen."

Violet had not stopped smiling as she handed Michael a glass of iced tea. She served him and then herself.

"Dig in, Michael."

"Yes ma'am. Everything looks and smells so good."

"Is Myrtle going to join us?" Michael asked.

"You need to meet Myrtle," Violet said laughingly.

She got up, opened a drawer in the china cabinet, and pulled out a .357 mag revolver.

"This is Myrtle."

"Mrs. Thompson, have you ever shot that thing?"

She put it back in the drawer and sat down.

"No, and I hope I never have to."

"That thing has got some kick. It might break your wrist. Wouldn't you like a smaller gun?"

"No, that was Walter's. I'll keep it."

"You were right. Prayer won't help Myrtle."

The two laughed, and then Violet explained.

"I didn't know if I could trust you. A woman living by herself is dangerous sometimes."

"I understand."

"Is everything to your liking?"

"Yes ma'am. Makes me homesick for Mom's cooking."

"I fixed an apple pie for dessert."

"Sounds good." Michael thought momentarily about how to ensure Violet would not have to worry about eating.

"We need to do this again sometime."

"Of course. Anytime."

Michael developed a plan in his head as he ate. He would suggest that Violet cook for the two of them on Mondays, Wednesdays, and Fridays. He assumed she would have leftovers to eat herself on the remaining days.

The idea thrilled Violet. She gave him a weekly shopping list, and he bought a few extra things to ensure she had plenty. The arrangement had been a blessing, and Violet didn't have to accept a handout.

The week continued, and he became more comfortable in his new role. Sgt. Hill began stepping back and letting him solve the problems and interact with the soldiers more. He preferred that. He was eager to understand as much as he could. The soldiers seemed receptive to his leadership style and wanted him to succeed. By the end of the week, he felt sure he had made the right choice. He gave God the glory for bringing him there.

On Saturday, he arrived at the Davidson residence for dinner. The general had invited him again for their family dinner. Michael felt humbled that the Davidsons considered him in that elite group.

Rachel met him at the door. "Don't I know you? You look like the man who took me to dinner the other night."

Michael walked in with a serious look on his face. "I know I should have stopped in to see you, but the truth is, I had dinner with my neighbor a few times this week."

Rachel's expression changed. Michael could tell he needed to explain quickly.

"You know Mrs. Thompson, right?"

"Yes, she goes to our church."

"Well, I will be eating some with her. I wanted to ensure she is provided for."

Rachel smiled and hugged him. "That is so sweet. You keep on surprising me."

They walked into the living room and found the general reading a newspaper.

"Michael, glad to see you made it."

After greeting the general, Michael stepped into the kitchen to say hello to the remaining ladies.

"Mrs. Davidson, Monica, how is everyone?"

Sarah turned from her task of cooking. "We are fine. Hope you are as well."

Monica said nothing but looked at him and waved.

Rachel joined them in their preparations, and Michael stepped back into the living room and sat near the general, who folded his paper and prepared for a conversation. Gen. Davidson seemed he had something to ask but made small talk about the new job.

"I think you are coming along fine, Michael. I have been pleased with your progress."

"Thank you, sir. I'll get the hang of it."

The general nodded, then cleared his throat.

"Michael, I have been thinking a lot about the morning we had breakfast in Kuwait. I had never met you, but within five minutes, I knew you were a man with a close relationship with God."

Michael's heart began to beat faster. He liked where the conversation was heading.

"As you sat at that table and bowed your head to pray, I saw a man who was serious about that relationship. I remembered my half-hearted attempts at having that same relationship."

Michael felt he should not speak but only nodded and let the general continue.

"As I said before, I was raised in a Christian home and always knew what was expected of me, but I rebelled. I chose my own pleasures and work. I have not spoken with God for many years, but I think He spoke to me the day I offered you a job."

The general sat upright in his chair and cleared his throat several times.

"I felt as if I needed to keep you around. I'm convinced God had something to do with that."

"God gave me the same message. I felt led to come here," Michael said.

"Do you know why God led you here?"

"General, I am sure God wants me to lead you back to Him."

"I thought so, too. I would like to go to church with you tomorrow."

"That would be wonderful. Rachel and I would be thrilled to have you go with us."

The general began to sob as Rachel walked in with two glasses of iced tea. She froze when she saw her father crying. Michael turned to her and placed his finger on his mouth, letting her know to remain silent.

"I am thankful for Rachel. Bless her heart, she has tried for years to reach me, and I have shut her out."

Michael glanced at Rachel, who bit her lip to hide her emotion and tears. She was so thankful. God was speaking to her father's heart, and he was listening. The general looked up and saw his daughter standing there. He stood and walked over to hug her. She handed Michael both glasses, and the father and daughter wept tears of joy. Rachel cried loudly, and Sarah and Monica entered the room to investigate.

"I love you, Rachel," the general said, stroking her hair.

"I love you, Daddy."

"Can someone tell us what just happened here?" Monica asked.

"We are going to church tomorrow," the general said.

Sarah hugged the two, but Monica held her ground.

The general, Sarah, and Monica walked into church on Sunday morning with Michael and Rachel. The general seemed excited to be there — as if he had received tickets to the world series.

Pastor Hatcher preached, and the general listened intently. As the service closed, the pastor invited anyone seeking salvation and a personal relationship with Jesus to come forward. The general did not hesitate. He stood and walked to the front. Sarah walked with him. Rachel put her head against Michael's shoulder and cried. The pastor met with the general and Sarah as they knelt at the altar. Monica tried to stubbornly hold back a tear but could not.

After a few minutes of silence, Pastor Hatcher stood and prayed to close the service. He invited everyone to come and welcome the two new children of God. Rachel quickly rushed to greet them, followed by Michael. Monica remained at her seat.

Michael shook hands with the general and Sarah, and they hugged each other. He recalled how God had introduced him to Gen. Davidson and the events that had happened since. They had both been taken to the hospital in Maryland, where they got to know each other. Their journey had continued all the way to Charlotte, where Michael had accepted a job, working with the general. He could see God's plan becoming a reality. He was overjoyed that the general had recommitted his life to Christ and that Sarah had trusted Christ as her Savior. He was also humbled that God had used him.

"When are we having lunch?" the pastor asked Michael.

"How about this week?"

They settled on Tuesday at the sandwich shop down the street. That evening, Rachel and Michael had dinner again. She couldn't hide her excitement that both her parents had received Jesus as their Savior.

As they sat at a table in a restaurant, she reached over and grabbed Michael by the wrist.

"I am so thankful you came along. I thought I would never see this day."

"Jesus said if we pray believing, we shall receive."

"So, you think my doubt was why my prayers went unanswered?"

Michael felt she might be on to something but wanted to spare her feelings.

"God works in His own time."

"I suppose you are right. I can't get over it, though."

"I'm happy for both of them as well. I didn't know how to witness to your dad if he kept walking away."

"You just had to be an example for Christ with Dad. Monica, I'm afraid, will take some thought."

"We never spend more than ten minutes talking before she leaves," Michael said.

"Maybe you should ask her to dinner. She might be less likely to leave."

"You wouldn't be jealous?"

"Jealous? You and I are just friends. I wouldn't mind. You may get through to her."

Michael thought perhaps he was trying too hard with Rachel. Maybe their relationship was going to take longer than he had hoped. He felt sure she was the one. He wasn't going to give up on her.

Michael left work Tuesday to meet Pastor Hatcher for lunch. He was glad to finally meet him since Michael had been so busy with other things. He walked into the sandwich shop, and Pastor Hatcher waved to him. He sat across from him in the booth and stuck out his hand.

"How are you today, Pastor?"

"I'm getting along pretty well."

The waitress approached and took their order. When she left, Pastor Hatcher asked, "So, Rachel has told me a lot about you. I wanted to meet you and welcome you to church."

"I grew up in West Virginia in a Christian home and joined the army when I was seventeen. I was in Kuwait just a few weeks ago when I met the general. I met Rachel while the general and I were recovering in the hospital."

"She told me you had both been wounded. Your leg, right?"

"My knee. I had to get a prosthetic implant."

"Is that doing okay?"

"Doesn't bother me much unless it's cold out."

The waitress walked up with two glasses of tea, straws, and napkins. "Your food is almost ready."

"Rachel gives you much credit for her dad and mom getting right with the Lord."

"I don't deserve credit. God may have used me to accomplish His plan, but it was all God."

"Amen. Well said."

The pastor saw the waitress bringing their meal. She sat the trays down and said, "Enjoy."

"Let's give thanks," the pastor said.

They both bowed their heads.

"Father, we thank You for this opportunity to share a meal. I thank You for Michael, whom You have sent to our little church. Thank You for bringing him through the things he has gone through these last few weeks. We give You thanks and praise in Jesus' name, amen."

"Amen," Michael said.

"So, you switched to the Army Reserve?" the pastor asked between bites.

"Yes sir. It was either that or retire. I chose not to retire just yet."

"I see. How is it going with the new job?"

"I'm adapting. I think it's going well."

After several minutes of small talk, Pastor Hatcher said, "Michael, I had two reasons to meet with you. The first was to get to know you, and the second was to keep you occupied."

"Occupied? I don't think I understand."

"When we leave here, I am going with you to the reserve center. The general has something planned, but he asked me not to divulge the details."

"You have my curiosity piqued."

"We can leave as soon as we finish our meal. I'll follow you, and this is on me. It's not every day I get to eat with a soldier."

"Thank you. I'll get it next time."

They left and soon pulled into the gate at the reserve center. A soldier stood at the gate, and Michael stopped to tell him the pastor's vehicle was with him.

"Hooah, Sergeant."

They parked and noticed all the soldiers standing in formation.

"I didn't know we were having a formation. I'd better get down there,"

Michael said.

"The formation is for you. You need to go up front and find the general. I'll take a seat."

Michael did as the pastor directed. He noticed people in civilian clothes, sitting in rows of chairs in the front of the formation. Someone waved, and he was surprised to see his mother, Missy, and Mark sitting there. He scanned through the crowd and saw more people he knew: Monica, Rachel, Sarah, Heather, and Violet. The pastor sat beside Rachel.

Gen. Davidson motioned to Michael, and Michael stood beside him. A major general walked to the podium. Michael assumed he was Gen. Davidson's boss.

"We are here today to honor two of our own: Brigadier General Thomas Davidson and Sergeant First Class Michael Logan. They have recently returned from a tour of duty in Kuwait. While there, they were wounded in action. It is with great pleasure that I award both of these fine men with the Purple Heart."

The major general pinned the award on them, saluted, and shook their hands. Gen. Davidson then walked to the podium while Michael remained standing. The general cleared his throat as the crowd applauded. He looked out over the crowd and saw his family and Michael's.

"I have not known SFC Logan long, perhaps a month or two. But in that time, I have gotten to know him well. We were wounded in the same firefight and spent time in the same hospital, and now he works here. Some of you have gotten to know him, also. If you haven't, make sure you do. Sergeant Logan is a fine man."

The general's voice cracked as he gripped the podium and he cleared his throat. "I can tell you, I would not be standing here today if not for this man. Sergeant Logan has proven himself to be a man who works well under pressure. We were attacked while in Kuwait. Sergeant Logan eliminated the immediate threat, then ordered his men to open fire on the remaining hostiles. I was hit, and Sergeant Logan left his covered position, putting himself in danger of the bullets raining down on us. He pulled me out of the line of fire and to safety. In the process, he was hit. He began administering first aid to me before he realized he needed first aid, too. SFC Logan, I thank you for your courage, patriotism, and friendship. I am pleased to award you the Bronze Star for Gallantry."

The general walked to Michael and pinned the award beside his purple heart. He saluted and shook his hand. The crowd applauded. The general then invited him to speak.

Michael walked to the podium and waited for the applause to die down.

"Everything you've heard here today is true. But I would be amiss if I did not give the credit to whom it belongs: God. I am convinced of it. The general and I stand before you today because we serve a risen Savior."

Several people wept, including Michael's mother and Rachel.

"I thank you, General, for this award and recognition, but, honestly, it is not me but God who deserves the glory."

Michael left the podium as everyone stood and applauded. The general, CSM Samson, and the major general shook his hand.

As the formation was dismissed and people began shaking hands, Michael approached his mother. He hugged her and spoke to Mark and Missy. He began introducing people to them: Rachel, Monica, Sarah, Heather, Pastor Hatcher, and Violet.

Michael enjoyed getting all the people in his life together. Gen. Davidson walked up and patted him on the back.

"Mrs. Logan, you raised a fine son."

The awards ceremony had been a reminder of the events of a few weeks earlier — and a reminder of God's goodness and mercy.

On Saturday, when Michael drove to the Davidsons, he made a point to seek out Monica and talk to her.

"Monica, would you go to dinner with me tomorrow?" Michael asked.

"You and Rachel not hitting it off?"

"No, nothing like that. I just want to spend some time getting to know you."

"Sure. I'll go to dinner with you on one condition. You take it easy on the God talk."

"Okay, we can set some ground rules. If I hit home and you feel like I need to back off, you point at me."

"Point at you? Sounds good."

"That way, you won't feel you need to leave, which is exactly why we haven't got to know each other."

"Agreed." She walked away, jokingly pointing at him.

On Sunday morning, Michael gathered in church with Rachel. She knew his plan for that evening and wished him well. She wanted to see her sister come to God. Michael might provide the guidance Monica needed.

The general and Sarah sat next to them. When the singing began, Michael was surprised at the pure, deep bass tones the general belted out.

Pastor Hatcher preached from John 4 — the story of Jesus and the Samaritan woman at the well. Michael had heard the story preached several times, but as he listened, he noticed something different.

The pastor explained that Jews avoided Samaria because they disagreed with events in the Samaritan's past. Jews would walk around the region to ensure they didn't even get Samaritan dirt on their sandals. But Jesus didn't avoid the region. He walked the most direct route to Galilee, right through the middle of Samaria.

While Jesus was at the well, a sinful woman approached. Jesus asked for a drink, and even she was surprised that a Jew spoke to her. She asked, "How is it that thou, being a Jew, askest drink of me, which am a woman of Samaria? For the Jews have no dealings with the Samaritans."

The pastor made other references to Jesus eating with publicans and sinners. He did not avoid them but sought them out. Jesus came to save the sinners.

Michael felt convicted, as if the pastor was speaking to him. He had avoided Monica because of her drinking and attitude toward God. Jesus would have walked straight to her, but he had done the opposite. He saw his error. He had acted just as the Pharisees Jesus scolded.

As the service concluded, Michael turned to Rachel. "I think that sermon was meant for me."

"How so?"

"Your sister is just like the woman at the well, and I have avoided her."

Rachel put a hand on his arm and realized he was right. "Speak to her tonight. You may get through to her."

The general overheard the conversation and was curious.

"Is everything okay?"

"Yes. I'm going to have dinner with Monica tonight and try to lead her to the Lord," Michael said.

"I wish you luck. I think she feels alienated now that she is the only one who isn't a Christian."

"I know now I can no longer avoid her as I have done in the past. Pray for me tonight."

"We will," Sarah said.

That evening, Michael waited on Monica outside a local restaurant. In only a few minutes, he noticed her walking toward him.

"Good evening. You look very nice."

"Thank you."

They went in and were seated right away. Monica picked up the beverage menu and began considering a wine but glanced up at Michael and changed her mind.

"Sweet tea, please," she said when the waitress asked what she wanted to drink.

"Same for me. Thanks," Michael said.

"Get whatever you want. It's on me," Michael said.

"I think I'll try the fish."

"Sounds good, but I think I'll go for the steak."

The waitress returned with their drinks and took their order. When she stepped away, Michael said, "So, tell me about yourself. All I know about you is that you are a nurse."

Monica smiled and looked at the ceiling.

"Well, I was raised an army brat." She laughed. "I was born in North Carolina. When I graduated from nursing school, I bought a house here. I'm thirty years old and single, and I work in the recovery wing of the hospital. Not a lot more to tell."

"Have you ever been married?"

"No. I was engaged once, but it didn't work out. How about you? I noticed you are still single. No ex in your life?"

"I was engaged once, but we broke it off."

"May I ask why?"

Michael shifted in his seat. "Can we hold that one until our next dinner?"

Monica joked. "Oh, next time. Feeling pretty confident about a next time?"

"You're right. I shouldn't assume that."

Monica giggled. It was one of the rare times he had heard her do that.

"We will see how the evening goes. I'll let you know if there will be a next time," she said.

"Fair enough."

"Are you and Rachel getting serious?" Monica asked after a moment of silence.

"We have had dinner a few times and go to church together."

"She is my sister, and I don't want anything to come between her and me. I love her, even if she gets on my nerves at times."

"I have a sister, too. I know what you mean."

"Do you have feelings for Rachel?"

"I like her. Does that count as feelings?"

"Just seeing where I stand. I want to make sure you aren't a playboy."

"No, that's not me. I have had less than five dates in the last five years."

"You sound like me. This is the first time I have been out in …" She looked at the ceiling again. "I guess it's been three or four years."

"I'm glad you accepted my invite."

"Dad built you up like a superhero, so I was curious."

"I'm an average man — definitely not a superhero."

The waitress returned with salads and rolls. They thanked her.

"It should only be a few more minutes on your food," the waitress said.

"Do you mind if I ask the blessing?" Michael asked.

"No, go ahead."

"Father, thank You for this opportunity to spend time with Monica and share a meal. We give You thanks and praise in Jesus' name. Amen."

As Michael opened his eyes and looked up, he could tell that Monica was uncomfortable. She had changed her expression back to the scowl he was familiar with. She picked up a fork and began eating her salad.

Michael knew he needed to hold off a moment before he asked anything. He stirred his dressing into his salad and took a bite.

"That's pretty good. I don't eat a lot of salad, but that's a pretty good one."

Monica shifted her mood back to the conversation.

"Yes, mine is good, too."

Michael felt he was struggling with what to say next. He wanted to speak to her about the Lord, but she was already showing signs she did not look forward to that conversation. He thought a prayer, *Help me, Lord. I'm drowning here. Give me the words to speak.*

Just then, Monica laid down her fork and looked Michael straight in the eye.

"I get weird about God because I don't understand much about Him."

Michael was thrilled it was Monica who had brought up the subject. He thought another quick prayer, *Thank you, Lord. Nicely done.*

"I have been a Christian my entire adult life, and sometimes I struggle with understanding. Don't think you are alone in that."

"What I mean is I have gone to church with Rachel, and I'm lost. I have no idea what the pastor is talking about."

"I know what you mean. Some pastors forget the basics because they assume the congregation is more advanced in their spiritual walk."

"So, what are the basics?"

"I would say knowing Jesus is the Son of God and *is* God. Knowing that He came to live among us to save sinners and that we need to spread His news of salvation. Knowing that He died for our sins and rose from the grave. That's the basics."

"I still don't get it."

"Much of understanding comes with a relationship with God. Once you accept Jesus, you get more understanding. It's called faith. We have faith in a God we have never seen. But we know He is there. I talk to Him every day. He doesn't actually talk back, but I hear Him in other ways."

"Like what other ways?"

"In His Word, the Bible."

"I see."

The waitress approached and set their food in front of them.

"Can I get you anything else?"

Michael motioned questionably to Monica, who shook her head. He looked at the waitress and replied, "No ma'am, we are good. Thanks."

Michael began to cut into his steak and continued to speak.

"Monica, do you know that Jesus loves you?"

The sound of Monica dropping her fork onto her plate seemed as if it rang throughout the entire restaurant. She sat there staring right through him with several emotions in her eyes. She lifted her hand and pointed at Michael. He knew to stop for the time being.

After dinner, as Michael was driving home, he decided to stop in at Rachel's. He thought she might be wondering how things went. He walked up to her door and noticed a light on. Hopefully, she was still awake. He knocked, and the porch light came on a few seconds later. Most likely, Rachel was looking out the peephole.

"I didn't expect to see you this evening. Come on in," Rachel said.

"I figured you might be curious about how long your sister sat still."

"Yes, I'm a little curious."

"She stayed all the way through, and you may not believe this, but she brought up the subject of God."

"That's great."

"We talked more than we ever had before. We did reach a point where she had enough. I asked her if she knew Jesus loved her, and it hit her pretty hard."

"Wow, sounds like dinner wasn't a bad idea, even if it was mine," Rachel said, jokingly patting herself on the back.

Michael changed the subject. He had something he wanted to ask her all week.

"Rachel, last Sunday, you said we were just friends. I hope you know that is not my intention. I feel God has brought us together."

Rachel remained silent as a tear fell down her cheek. She wiped it away and sniffed.

"I do, too. You are everything I have wanted in a man."

"I feel the same way. So, why do you feel we are only friends?"

"It was my idea for you to take Monica to dinner, but I couldn't help but feel jealous," she admitted.

He reached over and hugged her, and she began to cry.

"I'm sorry. We can figure another way to reach her."

He held her a few more minutes, glad she had confirmed her feelings for him. Her just-friends statement had gnawed at him all week. He pulled away and looked at her.

"Are you okay?"

"Yes, I'm fine. I'm glad we had this talk."

"Me, too. I had best be getting out of here, though. We both have to work tomorrow."

Rachel walked to the door with him. As she put her hand on the knob, Michael stopped her. They embraced, and he kissed her. She laid her head on his shoulder and cried again. He gently raised her chin to meet his eyes.

"I don't want to lose you, Rachel. I've waited a long time for you."

The next day at work, Michael felt as if a huge weight had been lifted off him. He was glad he and Rachel had confirmed their feelings for each other. He spent most of the morning feeling as if he were on a cloud — the happiest he had been in a long time.

After lunch, the general walked in and shut the door.

"Do you have a minute?"

"Is anything wrong?" Michael asked, knowing this was probably related to his dinner date with Monica.

"That depends on what folks consider wrong."

Michael understood that the general was concerned about both of his daughters.

"Do you think I was wrong to take Monica to dinner?"

"Yes and no. I understand why you did it, and Rachel does as well, but Monica may have questions about your motive."

"I understand, sir. I probably should have chosen another avenue to reach Monica. Rachel and I spoke about it last night, and I discovered I had hurt her. It was her idea, so I thought it was okay."

"Seems you don't know much about women. It's never okay, even if they say it is."

"I learned that lesson the hard way. How would you recommend I try to witness to Monica?"

"Don't assume I know any more about women than you. I have been married a great many years, but I still haven't got Sarah figured out. Maybe you should have included Rachel."

"I believe that would have been the right choice. I could have avoided all this. I just felt the Lord leading me to speak to Monica."

"I'm not overstepping what God is telling you. Just do it in a way that saves both their feelings."

The general got up and placed his hand on the doorknob.

"Michael, you are a good man, and I'd be proud to have you in the family. I've already told you they both admire you. You can love one of them, but don't hurt the other."

"I won't."

Gen. Davidson left and walked down the hall to his office. Michael sat there a moment, thinking how he had messed up. He recalled the dinner with Monica. Had he said anything to lead her on? After a moment, he realized he had. He left Monica thinking he and her sister were just friends. Just friends. There it was again.

That evening, he checked the mail before climbing the stairs to his apartment. He opened the box to find a letter from Dutton. He carried it in, laid it on the counter, grabbed a quick shower, and knocked on Violet's door.

"Come in, Michael. Supper is just about ready."

"Thank you, Mrs. Thompson. I have been looking forward to this all day."

They sat at the table, eating and enjoying each other's company. Michael needed a friendly voice after the day he had.

"I was very impressed with the ceremony they had for you. I haven't asked you about what happened in Kuwait because I respect your privacy.

Walter never talked about Normandy until he got sick at the end."

"Thank you. I was glad you were there. It seems all the people in my life were there."

He thought of Rachel, sitting beside his mother and both crying.

They finished their meal, and Michael helped with the dishes before returning to his apartment. He walked by the counter, picked up the letter from Dutton, and sat on his cot.

He opened it and read the following:

> SFC Logan,
>
> I hope this letter finds you well. I was thankful to receive your letter expressing your concern for us. When the bombing started, they pulled us off the line. Almost immediately, the Iraqis began surrendering. We are now escorting and processing POWs. Hundreds every day are walking south, carrying a white flag. Turns out that only a few have the same motivation as Saddam. We take them down to the reserve units for holding.
>
> I wanted to tell you about the investigation, or witch hunt, as Boone and I call it. We were questioned for several days by several people, and I lost my respect for the battalion commander. It seems he is the only one who wants to slam us. He chewed us out pretty good. He pulled 1st Lt. Samuels out and replaced him with some tanker lieutenant. SPC Thomas is ready to pull his hair out.
>
> I don't know where this is going. Boone has decided to get out when we are done here. He has had enough and looks forward to going into the ministry. He gives you a lot of the credit for that. We both miss our Bible study time.
>
> Well, I have to get back to work. Boone sends his regards. Write again when you get time. You know how getting mail pumps you up. Thanks for helping me along the way. I will never

forget you, and I pray we can meet again someday.

SPC Dutton

Michael smiled as he finished the letter. He was glad to know his men were safe. The investigation did not concern him at all. The letter only confirmed his suspicions of his battalion commander. He just needed Jesus in his life. Maybe then, he wouldn't be so grumpy.

He laid the letter on the counter, picked up his Bible, and spent the next few hours reading until he got sleepy. He placed the Bible under his cot, got up, and picked up the jar of sand. He shook it and looked at the grains falling back into place.

"Miss you guys."

Later in the week, Michael grabbed his clothes basket and headed to the laundry room before he went to work. He had learned that the weekend was not a good time to get a washer in apartment living. He was surprised to find someone already there with the same idea.

"Good morning, Heather."

"Good morning, Sergeant Logan."

"You can call me Michael."

He put his clothes in a vacant washer.

"Chris has never called you anything but Sergeant Logan in his letters. It would take some getting used to."

"Have you heard from Boone? I got a letter yesterday from Dutton."

"Yes, I got one the other day. He was surprised to hear we are neighbors."

"I would say so. It surprised me as well."

"He has decided to get out when his time is up."

"Yes, Dutton mentioned that."

"Did he also tell you Chris and I plan to marry soon after he gets home?"

"No, he didn't. Congratulations."

"Thank you. You have to save the date. We both want you there."

"Okay, sure. When's the date?"

"Not sure yet. We just started talking about it. It should be this year, though. He's due to leave in June, but that depends on the war. They may still have the freeze on ETS (Expiration Term of Service)."

"That's true. Just let me know. I'll be there."

Heather began folding her clothes. "You need to bring Rachel, too. She tells me a lot about you."

Michael laughed. "Okay, I'll ask her."

"You will get a formal invitation, but I wanted to mention it now."

"I hear he is going into the ministry. Will he be attending seminary around here?"

"Yes, I have been looking into that for him. There is one here in Charlotte."

"That's good. Sounds like you guys have it figured out."

"I hope so. I worry about him, especially now that the war has started."

"Just pray for him and write to him every chance you get. Letters mean a lot. It reveals the reality of things in the real world that you forget about while serving."

"That's what he said."

Heather paused to finish cleaning out her dryer. "Mrs. Thompson tells me you two are eating together a few days a week."

"Yes, on Monday, Wednesday, and Friday."

"I have tried to get her to eat with me, but she will never do it. I take her to dinner after church on Sundays, but that is all she allows."

"That helps. I think we have the whole week covered. We are fortunate to have her as a neighbor."

"Yes, she is a good woman."

Heather picked up her basket. "Well, I must get ready for class. It was good speaking to you. Say hello to Rachel for me."

"I will. Tell Boone hello for me."

After Heather left, Michael sat and sorted his thoughts. He wasn't sure if he wanted to go by the Davidsons on Saturday and face Monica. The general had given him a few things to think about. He decided he needed to get away for the weekend. On Friday after work, he would head home and see the family. He called Rachel and arranged for them to get together when he got back on Sunday.

When Michael arrived home, his mother was already in bed. But when she heard his vehicle pull up, she got up to greet him. They talked for a few minutes, and both soon decided to turn in for the night. Michael went into his room and reasoned he would soon have to purchase a bed since he only slept in one when he went home.

He needed the weekend to rest and reflect on the past week's events. Still, he couldn't help but feel he was running from his problems. Monica had proven to be a challenge. It would require much energy to bring her to the Lord. He fell asleep, understanding nothing is promised to be easy.

The following week, Michael sat in his office, reviewing a mountain of paperwork when the general came charging in. He had a very concerned, almost fearful, look on his face.

"Monica just called. She needs you at the hospital right away."

Michael grabbed his hat and rushed out the door.

"She is helping out in ICU this week. Go there," the general called to him.

Michael jumped in his truck and sped off, wondering what kind of emergency he was walking into. In only a few minutes, he arrived and ran to the entrance. He got directions for the ICU from a volunteer working at the front desk and continued his urgent pace until he came to a nurse at the ICU desk.

"Where is Monica Davidson?" he asked.

"She is in that second room on the left. She's expecting you."

Michael walked into the room to see Monica hanging an IV bag. Her eyes were bloodshot and puffy. He knew she had been crying.

"Michael, thank goodness. You have to help."

"How can I help?"

"Pray for this woman."

Michael looked at the woman in the bed. He could tell she was in pain. She had bandages around her head, tubes in both arms, and several monitors attached. One eye was swollen shut and discolored — red, blue, and black. The same side of her face was swollen, and her lips were split.

"Her husband beat her. She may not make it. Pray for her, please," Monica pleaded. "She doesn't deserve this."

Michael took the woman's hand and felt a slight squeeze. She slowly opened one good eye and looked at him with a medicated, far-off stare.

"You are a soldier?" she whispered.

"Yes ma'am. I came to pray for you."

"I knew you were coming. I saw it in a dream."

"Ma'am, do you know Jesus?"

She closed her mouth and eye as tears formed. She shook her head.

"Would you like to know Him?"

"Yes."

She began crying and squeezed his hand tighter through her pain. Michael moved closer to her.

"Jesus is giving you another chance."

The woman nodded her approval as she remained focused on Michael.

"Do you believe in Jesus and that He rose from the grave?"

"Yes, I do," she whispered through her pain.

"Ask Jesus to forgive your sins. Ask Him to save you and come into your life."

The woman took several breaths to calm herself. "Jesus, I need You. Forgive my sins. Save me, Lord."

Michael felt her hand go limp. The monitor began a constant alarm that alerted Monica, and she pushed him out of the way.

"She's flat-lining. Move."

Michael stepped out of the way as doctors and nurses rushed in. They began resuscitating her, and after a few minutes, one doctor checked for a pulse. He looked at the clock on the wall.

"Time of death, 11:47 a.m."

As the medical staff left the room and turned off the monitor, Monica turned toward the window and cried. Michael understood that she had always worked in recovery. She was used to seeing people getting better. ICU was different. Now, she was seeing people come in with pain and trauma — some requiring surgery, and some not surviving.

He laid a hand on her shoulder. She brushed it away and turned to him. He saw anger and resentment.

"God was supposed to save her. Why did she die?"

"Monica, God gave that woman another chance to accept Him. She took that last opportunity. She left all that pain behind and went on to be with the Lord."

"But why didn't God let her live?"

"It was His will that she left this place. We can make our requests, but God makes the decision. And God did save her."

Monica stormed out of the room — confused and frustrated.

Michael watched her leave and then turned to the woman lying in the bed. He held her hand.

"I didn't get to know your name, ma'am. I'm thankful that you are with our Lord. The angels are rejoicing that your soul was saved."

He walked out but never saw Monica.

As he returned to his office, the general came behind him and shut the door.

"What happened?"

"A woman took the wrong end of her husband's anger. He beat her badly. Monica was upset about it and wanted me to pray for her."

"Is the woman okay?"

"She died after accepting Jesus."

"And Monica doesn't understand?"

"No sir. I tried to explain that God gave the woman one last chance, but Monica didn't understand."

The general took a moment to respond. "We've all been there. Understanding takes time. You've given her a lot to think about. Don't be discouraged. God is working on her heart. We need to stay the course."

The general was right. Michael had felt overwhelmed and unsure of how to reach Monica. They prayed together that God would give them the words to speak and the patience to use them.

Monica didn't come to the family dinner that Saturday. Sarah called her, but she said she wasn't feeling well. Michael and the general knew, however, that she was upset. Upset with Michael, upset with God, and upset that a husband could beat his wife and cause her death.

"Maybe we should ask Pastor Hatcher to speak to her," Rachel suggested.

The general called and left the pastor a message. Michael was relieved to accept any help with the situation.

Michael and the general had drill the following weekend, so there was no family dinner. Sarah had gone out with the girls for dinner, and she and Rachel tried to get a read on Monica's situation. She ate with them but didn't speak much about the incident — only to say she didn't plan on working in ICU anymore.

At work the next week, things took a turn for the worse. The general called a formation. He stepped to the front to address everyone but had his head lowered with his hand over his eyes, concealing his tears. Everyone felt moved by his hesitation to give his news.

"I have just received word that at approximately 12:40 EST, an Iraqi scud missile targeted the barracks in Dhahran. Defenseless army reserve soldiers were attacked as they prepared for bed. The first report shows ninety-eight soldiers were wounded, and twenty-seven died. I ask that we observe a moment of silence for our fellow service men and women."

Several in the formation cried. The news had been a shock. No scud missiles had hit their target since the war began, but now the Iraqis were lucky. It was the most significant loss to a single unit in recent history.

The general asked Logan to offer a prayer for those affected.

Logan stepped to the front of the formation and took a moment, not believing the news he had just heard.

"Father, we give You thanks that You are our God. We ask that You would shower Your mercy on everyone who has been involved in this brutal attack. We ask for healing for the wounded and comfort for the family and friends of those who lost their lives. We ask these things and give you praise. In Jesus' name, amen."

Three days later, a cease-fire was called. Saddam was pushed out of Kuwait. The war was over, and US and allied forces declared a victory.

CHAPTER 6

The summer soon arrived, and Michael Logan's old battalion pulled out of Kuwait and returned to Germany. Dutton and Boone made plans for their futures as the time drew near for their ETSs. Boone chose to get out and return to North Carolina and pursue the ministry. He had moved back in with his mother until he and Heather could marry.

Heather was planning as quickly and efficiently as possible. Her every spare minute was involved in the details, and Boone was supportive, even though she changed her mind several times about the venue, dress color for the bridesmaids, tux color, and choice of meat for the reception.

She had enlisted Rachel's help, and Rachel threw herself deeply into the task. Michael noticed Rachel used this opportunity to prepare for her future wedding. Mental notes were taken about what she should avoid and whom she could use for catering, flowers, and pictures.

Boone had begun seminary and took a part-time job as well. Michael saw him every Sunday at church and at least once or twice a week when he stopped by Logan's apartment on his way to visit Heather.

Dutton had chosen to stay in the army. He reenlisted and was sent to Fort Bragg. Soon after arriving there, he was sent to airborne or "jump school," as most soldiers call it. The move had pleased Michael since now both his soldiers were nearby. Fort Bragg was only a two- to three-hour drive from Charlotte.

The three planned to get together after Dutton returned from jump school and knew his schedule. If this weren't possible, they would all be at Boone's wedding since Dutton was the best man.

The general had traded his golf clubs for a fishing pole. He and Michael spent many hours on the lake, with the remainder of the family tagging along on the pontoon boat. The general had even considered buying a bass boat. He had joked that fishing was almost as expensive as golf with the numerous lures he lost as he learned to cast.

Monica had slowly worked her way back into the family get-togethers but did not speak much about the incident in ICU. Michael and Rachel had spoken with her many times, trying to give her understanding, but it seemed she had a barrier that would not allow it.

Violet continued to cook for herself and Michael. Every Sunday at church, she would give him a shopping list and smile. Michael realized that Violet enjoyed feeling productive as much as she liked to cook. The arrangement had given her something to live for.

Rachel and Michael continued to strengthen their relationship. Everyone now knew they were meant for each other. The general and Sarah were well pleased. When Michael was at the Davidsons, Rachel had an arm around him, or they held hands when they walked. The parents knew they would soon have a son-in-law and were happy with her choice.

Master Sgt. Hill retired, and Michael's leadership style was effective. CSM Samson commented on improving production and morale, even though MSG Hill hadn't done much differently from Michael. The only real difference was that Michael refused to micromanage. His soldiers knew more about their job than he did. He assigned the task and left them alone to work on it.

Michael was surprised to find many of his soldiers coming to him for professional and personal advice. He listened and offered a few suggestions. By the end of the conversations, the soldiers had found the answer they needed on their own. Michael didn't want to make decisions for them. He wasn't a parent.

The soldiers enjoyed working for him, and he didn't have any that he had to stay on. Most days at work, he realized it was time to go home not long after getting there. Everything went smoothly.

He had also furnished his apartment. He had not delayed because he was lazy or cheap but because he didn't need the added comfort. After sleeping on the ground as a soldier, he felt a cot was a luxury.

Pastor Hatcher and Michael had gotten to know and respect each other more and more. It did not surprise Michael when one Sunday after church dismissed Pastor Hatcher asked to speak to him in his office.

"Michael, the church will hire an associate pastor, and I wanted to get your thoughts on the subject. We have a few applications, but I have one at the top of the list, and it has you listed as a reference."

Michael smiled, knowing he was talking about Chris Boone.

"Yes sir. What would you like to know?"

"We are looking for someone to strengthen the youth program and occasionally fill the pulpit. Do you think Chris is up to the task?"

"Boone is a man of God. I have watched him grow in his faith over the years, and I feel certain he will be God's man when he's old and gray."

"I know he hasn't been in seminary long, but that doesn't even concern me. Can he stand the trials he will face?"

"I believe he will give his heart and soul for God. The trials are meant to make us stronger. He will continue to get stronger."

Pastor Hatcher laughed. "So, you are giving a thumbs up to Chris?"

"I am. I've known him long enough to say that without reservation."

"Good. Chris it is. Would you like to sit in next Sunday after church when I tell him?"

"I would like that."

"Heather and he have asked me to marry them, and I plan to talk to them then."

"If you want to mention the associate pastor position first, I can leave for the second part. They may want privacy."

Michael drove home, feeling as if his son had taken his first steps. He remembered the years when Boone's feet were right there between himself and Dutton as he stood in the turret of the Humvee. His eyes always searched out the dangers that lay ahead. He remembered the countless Bible studies and conversations about God. God had called Boone to preach. Michael was glad that Chris had obeyed the call.

As Michael climbed the steps to his apartment, Boone called over the banister. "Sergeant Logan, can you come up for a minute?"

Michael walked into Heather's apartment to find Rachel and Heather seated on the couch. Boone shook Michael's hand as he came in.

"Sergeant Logan, Heather has something she wants to ask you."

"Fire away."

Michael took a seat and waited for Heather to speak. She cupped her hands over her mouth nervously. Rachel looked at him, smiling.

"Would you give me away?"

Michael's eyes opened widely. He did not know that Heather's father was out of the picture.

"I would be honored."

Heather hugged him and squealed with excitement.

"Thank you, thank you, thank you."

"We are meeting with the pastor next Sunday to discuss the wedding. He will be marrying us in the church," Boone said.

Michael smiled. "Sounds good. Do you know the date yet?"

"We have it narrowed down to August. And Rachel is the bridesmaid," Heather said.

Rachel seemed to glow when Michael looked at her. Just saying wedding stirred her attention. They had both mentioned what they wanted out of life, but Michael hadn't asked her yet. He didn't want to rush anything. If it were God's will, it would happen.

On Saturday, Michael arrived at the Davidsons, and the general was busy preparing the grill.

"Michael, I have something I wanted to run by you."

Michael sat in a chair beside the grill.

"What's on your mind?"

"I was thinking of putting together a family trip to Israel. You included. The five of us. What do you think?"

"I have always wanted to go. The closest I have ever been was when we were in Kuwait."

"Me, too. I found they have guided tours of all the points of interest. It lasts a week to ten days. The tour goes through the Sea of Galilee, Nazareth, Caesarea, Jerusalem, Mount of Olives, Bethlehem, and the Western Wall."

"Rachel and I have the wedding for Heather and Boone sometime in August. When were you thinking?"

"Sometime in September. The temperature is in the 80s for the high."

"Sounds good."

"Sarah is fine with it, but I must ask the girls when they arrive. You may need to help me convince Monica."

"I can try."

The general placed the meat on the grill as Michael reflected. He had noticed an "all in" attitude with the general since he had returned to the Lord. Michael was thankful that he and Sarah had committed. Before, the general would exit when there was God talk, but now he initiated it.

Soon, Rachel and Monica walked out the back door and approached them.

"There are my babies," the general said. "Come on over, girls. We have something to ask you."

After they sat, the general asked if they would like to go. To his surprise, both agreed. Monica liked to travel. It did not matter to her where they went. Michael prayed she would get more out of it than just a family vacation.

"What is there to see in Israel?" Monica asked.

The general looked at Michael to take the lead in the conversation.

"Well, one of the places we will visit is Bethlehem," Michael said.

"That's where Jesus was born, right?"

"Yes, that's right. And we will stop at Caesarea."

"I'm not familiar with that one," Monica said.

"Caesarea is a town on the Mediterranean Sea. Herod dedicated it to Caesar since Rome occupied Israel during the days of Jesus. Much of the architectural design has Roman influence. It's the town where Peter, a disciple of Jesus, converted Cornelius, a Roman centurion. This is the first evidence of a non-Jew following Christ. It's also where the Apostle Paul was imprisoned for nearly two years."

"Sounds interesting. You seem to know a lot about Israel."

"Well, it's all in the Bible. Every place we will go has a significant meaning to Christians."

"It sounds like a very educational trip. I'm looking forward to it. I need to get back in and help mom, though. Please excuse me," Monica said.

"That went better than I expected," the general said.

"I agree. I didn't expect her to engage with Michael," Rachel said.

"She does seem to be over her ICU experience," Michael said.

After the Sunday service, Michael went to the pastor's office. In a few minutes, the pastor came in with Heather and Boone. They were surprised to see him sitting there.

"I asked Michael here to witness the first part of our discussion. We can talk privately about the wedding afterward," the pastor said.

Heather and Chris nodded and glanced at each other curiously.

"Chris, I received your application and noticed you put Michael down as a reference. We have had a conversation, and we both agree you would make a welcome addition to our church staff."

Heather covered her face to conceal her emotion as Chris stood and shook the pastor's hand.

"Thank you, sir. I appreciate this opportunity." Then, he turned to Michael. "Thanks, Sergeant Logan."

Michael stood and shook his hand. "I knew God had a plan for you, and the thanks go to God."

Michael left the office, relieved Boone had taken a huge step in his Christian walk. He was maturing right before his eyes.

A few weeks later, Dutton finished jump school and drove out to Charlotte to visit with his old crew. Boone and Michael took time off to make the trip worthwhile. They all met at Michael's apartment to catch up on recent events.

"So, how did jump school go?" Michael asked.

"It went well. I never planned on going airborne, but I was good with it by the fifth jump."

"How often do you have to jump with your unit?" Boone asked.

"I think once a month to keep your pay status, but I haven't jumped with the unit yet. How is seminary going, Boone?"

"So far, it's easy. We have been covering the Bible's different books and authors. We are getting into the books of Moses and Jewish history right now."

"You'll get it. I have no doubt," Michael said.

"Thanks for your vote of confidence, Sergeant Logan. I hope I don't let you down."

Michael had been able to spend more time with Boone since Boone and Dutton got back from overseas, but this was the first time Michael had seen Dutton since the day he got shot. Dutton seemed to have something to say but chose to keep it hidden.

"Something you want to talk about, Dutton? You seem like you're carrying a heavy load," Michael finally asked.

"I figured if anyone would notice, it would be you, Sergeant."

"What's on your mind?"

Dutton hesitated but thought it better to bring his issue out.

"I've had a few sleepless nights since that morning in Kuwait. I keep playing it over and over in my head. Sometimes, it feels like the whole thing was a dream and didn't happen. Do you guys know what I'm talking about?"

Boone answered first. He had not spoken about that day since it happened.

"I was with you, remember? Even though you didn't speak about it, I knew what you were going through because I was, too."

"I have tried to push it out of my mind. I don't think about it much," Michael said.

"Sergeant Logan, you do realize that all three of us have taken another's life?" Dutton said.

Michael thought for a second before he spoke. "Yes, we did that, but it was us or them. We didn't go looking for trouble; it found us. We were soldiers, sworn to defend the Constitution of the United States against all enemies, foreign and domestic. Don't feel guilty. We did what was asked of us."

"I don't think I feel guilty, just different. I remember the empty feeling I had when the chopper took off with you on it," Dutton said.

"Not to mention, we had a battalion commander who wanted a pound of flesh," Boone added.

"The general has assured me we need not worry about the investigation. He stands with my decision and our actions," Michael said.

"How is the general?" Dutton asked.

"He is well. He lives not far from here. I told him you were coming by, and he made me promise I would bring both of you over to his place."

After a quick call to the Davidson residence, the trio visited with the general. As they got out of the vehicle and followed Michael to the back yard, both young men commented on the beauty around them.

Gen. Davidson was standing at the grill and already had a few burgers heating up.

"Evening, General. I brought the old crew. You remember Dutton, don't you?"

The general held out his hand. "I sure do. We had breakfast together not long ago. How is the 82nd treating you?"

"So far, so good, sir."

The general motioned for everyone to take a seat. He turned the heat down on the grill and joined them.

"Michael and Chris, tell me you guys had to pull POW duty after the war started. How did that go?" the general asked.

"It was an easy detail. No one resisted. Everyone we encountered wanted food and sleep. Saddam was not taking care of them very well."

"That's what I hear. I also heard you had a little shake-up with the chain of command."

"Yes sir. Our platoon leader was relieved, and we got a replacement that tried his best but struggled with the change. He wasn't a scout, nor did he want to be."

"I have wished many times that I could have met your battalion commander. We could have had an interesting conversation."

Michael laughed at the general's attempt at humor.

"General, I wish I were a fly on the wall to hear that one."

The general looked at Michael and nodded, grinning with an executioner-type expression. The young men understood that the general didn't think favorably of the battalion commander either.

"General, the three of us discussed the investigation just before coming here. I told them they have nothing to worry about," Michael said.

"Don't worry about it, men. You were in the right, and I will stand with my hand on the Bible and say that in court if it ever comes to it. I have considered calling your old division commander and seeing where he stands on it, but I think it's over."

Michael looked at both Dutton and Boone. "The general and I were investigated while in the hospital but haven't heard any more about it."

Dutton and Boone both breathed a little easier after hearing the news. They had been carrying worry around for several months like a chicken waiting to have his head chopped off.

"I think me getting sent to Fort Bragg was a blessing. I was glad to get out of there," Dutton said.

"Move on with your life and put it behind you. In my opinion, it's over," the general said.

The general changed the subject and teased Boone. "Chris, have you and Heather got a date for the wedding yet?"

"I think she is close to finalizing it. All I can tell you is sometime in August."

The four continued to talk and enjoy a burger. Afterward, the general loaded everyone on the boat and took them out on the lake. Michael listened to the general tell some of his fishing stories. He wasn't sure if he would have ever seen them again. But God brought them back into his life, and he was grateful.

After several days of visiting, Dutton went back to his unit. He had stayed with Sgt. Logan and slept on the cot. Their time together brought back a lot of memories. They were looking forward to the wedding so they could get together again.

The following Saturday at the Davidsons, Michael was seated with the general in the back yard when Monica approached, wine glass in hand. She hugged her father and greeted Michael.

"Hey, Michael. How have you been?"

"I'm doing well. Hope you are, too."

"I am. But I have been thinking about our upcoming trip. I can't wait. Tell me some more about it."

Michael hoped she was excited to learn more about the Lord, but he doubted it. She was most likely only concerned with the names of the towns they would visit and a brief history.

"I think the general mentioned we will visit the Sea of Galilee. In that region, Jesus called his first disciples: Simon Peter, Andrew, James, and John. They were all fishermen in that area. It's also where Jesus performed several miracles."

"What kind of miracles?"

"Jesus walked on the water and fed thousands with just a few fish and loaves of bread. It's also where the Jordan River flows from. Jesus was baptized there."

"Where else?"

"Nazareth is a town in the region of Galilee, where Jesus grew up. He was born in Bethlehem but was known as a Nazarene."

"Why wasn't He raised in Bethlehem?"

The general looked on and smiled at his daughter's questions.

"Well, when Jesus was born, it threatened a ruler named Herod. He was told that a king of the Jews was to be born in Bethlehem, as told in prophecy. Herod didn't want to give up his throne, so he had all the male children under two killed," Michael answered.

"That's awful."

"I agree, but an angel told Joseph — Jesus' earthly father — to take the child and flee to Egypt. They stayed there until Herod died. When they headed back, they stopped at Nazareth."

"Well, that's good."

"The Bible doesn't paint a pleasant picture of Nazareth. It seems it was not high on the 'must-see' locations in the area."

"But Jesus was there. Wouldn't that be reason enough?" Monica asked.

"You would think so, but the townspeople rejected Jesus as the Messiah. When He began His ministry, He didn't stay in His hometown long because the people didn't believe."

Monica seemed as if she was thinking about what was being discussed. You could almost see her displeasure with the people of Nazareth. However, she quickly made her familiar escape. Everyone commented that she seemed to be taking a few more spoonfuls of "God" talk each time he and she got together. Still, Michael could tell she wasn't entirely comfortable. If God was working in her heart, Monica was resisting a lot.

On Sunday morning, Pastor Hatcher made a few announcements after the service.

"I wanted to introduce everyone to our new associate pastor. Many of you have met him since he left the army and returned home. I feel very encouraged that Chris will be a strong voice for God."

Pastor Hatcher motioned for Chris to come up as everyone applauded. He laid a hand on Chris' shoulder as he continued.

"Also, I have been asked to announce the wedding of Chris and Miss Heather in just a few weeks. The wedding will be here, and you are all invited." He looked at Heather and asked, "Do we know the date yet?"

Heather shook her head and said, "We are getting closer, though."

Pastor Hatcher laughed. "Yes, just remember that Jesus is coming back, too."

Everyone chuckled as Heather blushed and gave a thumbs up. She knew she needed to nail down a date.

The pastor motioned to Chris to take the podium. "Chris, would you like to say anything?"

Chris stepped up and looked over the congregation.

"I look forward to getting to know you all. I have been gone a few years while in the service, but it's good to be home. I see many old friends out there. Heather and I grew up in this church, and it seems fitting that we should be married here. Also, I thank you for choosing me to serve as your associate pastor. Thank you."

Everyone applauded again as he stepped down and returned to his seat. Michael was proud of him. Boone had come a long way in his spiritual walk, and Michael had been there to witness it. The memory of a scared young private entering his office in Germany came to mind. Neither Boone nor Dutton had known what to expect as they walked in and shut the door. Now, Boone was taking another step — a step that would cement his devotion to the Lord. Boone was no longer talking about it; he was doing it.

Supper with Violet became something Michael looked forward to. Their conversations grew longer and more personal. The approaching wedding gave Mrs. Thompson a special feeling.

"Michael, I certainly am happy for Heather. She seems to have found her a good man."

"Yes, Boone is that."

"And he's a pastor now. I look forward to hearing him preach."

"I am, too. We will both be there for his first time, Lord willing."

"You both served together, right?"

"Yes ma'am. We were in the same platoon — same crew, actually. He was my gunner."

"I can't imagine him behind a gun."

"Oh yes, he was one of the best."

"Well, I couldn't imagine my Walter in the infantry either. He was such a gentle man."

"I guess war brings out a different side of us."

"I suppose you are right."

"Mrs. Thompson, is that a picture of Mr. Thompson?" Michael asked, pointing at a framed picture of Mrs. Thompson's husband on the wall — most likely his basic training picture.

She turned, smiled, and got up to take it down. She sat back down and turned it to Michael.

"Yes, that's my Walter. He was so handsome, don't you think?"

"Yes ma'am."

She continued looking at the picture and running her fingers over it, as though touching his face.

"We had two children, a boy and a girl. Of course, you have never met them, though."

She got up, placed the picture back on the wall, and sat back down.

"No ma'am, I haven't."

"That's because they never come around. They grew up and moved away. I hear from them occasionally, but only when I call."

"Do they live around here?"

"No. David is in Arizona, and Ruth lives in Texas."

"That's a good way off. Do you ever get to go out and see them?"

"I have been out there, but I just don't get around like I used to. Those plane rides wear me out."

"Well, hopefully they will head back this way for a visit. I'll pray for you and them."

"I appreciate that, Michael. You have been a blessing to me since you moved in. I feel safe with you living next door."

Michael thought about her statement as they continued to talk and eat. He felt a genuine concern for Violet. She had lost her only true love, and her children refused to be part of her life. She was getting by the best she could. The evenings they shared a meal and conversation had blessed them both.

After much planning and re-planning, the wedding day was set for Chris and Heather. The church was decorated with wall-to-wall flowers. The men wore simple black tuxes, and the ladies wore long, flowing pale-blue gowns.

As Michael stood in the back, speaking with the pastor, Rachel walked by and said, "Gentlemen, you both look nice."

Michael felt embarrassed. He had barely recognized Rachel. Her hair was different, and her dress made the beautiful woman he knew seem even more so.

He leaned in and kissed her on the cheek. "I almost didn't recognize you. You look lovely."

"Just lovely?" she joked.

"Beautiful. I was going for beautiful."

"Well, thank you."

Pastor Hatcher stepped into the conversation with a question that caught Rachel's attention.

"It won't be long before the two of you are doing this again, I suppose."

Rachel looked at Michael, waiting for his response.

"Perhaps, you're right. I may have to ask her first, though."

Pastor Hatcher changed the subject, realizing he had stepped over the line.

"Well, we should get to our places. It's time to get this show started."

Michael walked to the back of the church and met with Heather, who was very emotional.

"Thank you for doing this, Sergeant Logan."

"I'm giving you away. I think you can call me Michael."

The music began, and Michael held out his arm for Heather. They started walking down the aisle as everyone stood and looked on. Boone and Dutton were turned to watch them approach. Pastor Hatcher smiled.

"Who gives this woman to be married?"

"I do," Michael said, then stepped back so Chris could take Heather's arm.

Heather took Chris's arm, placed her head against his shoulder, and cried.

Michael sat as Rachel and Dutton positioned themselves beside the bride and groom. As the pastor read the vows, Michael thought of the goodness of God. God had brought his soldiers back into his life, and he was getting to be a part of Boone's wedding. God's plan was far greater than anything he could have imagined.

After the ceremony, Boone's mother approached Michael in the fellowship hall while everyone was seated.

"Sergeant Logan, I certainly appreciate your guidance with Chris. He speaks highly of you."

Rachel walked up and nestled her arm in his.

"All I did was point him to God, ma'am. He walked where he was led."

"Well, I thank you for keeping him on the right path. Chris has given you much credit for being the male role model he needed."

"Thank you ma'am. He's made both of us proud."

Boone's mother wiped a tear and took her seat. Michael and Rachel sat as Dutton walked to the microphone for the best-man toast.

"I met Chris a few years ago. It was our first day of basic training. We became friends almost immediately. We shared a love for the Lord, and after finishing basic and advanced training, we were shipped to Germany for our first duty station. We both grew up, in a way, under the leadership of a strong Christian sergeant. Chris talked about his desire to marry Heather someday, but neither of us thought SFC Logan would give his bride away."

Everyone laughed.

Dutton turned to Boone. "Chris, you are my best friend. I can't imagine going through what we have been through with anyone else. Heather, I felt like I knew you before I ever met you. He talked about you all the time." Dutton raised a glass. "To the bride and groom. May you both continue to grow in your love for each other and God."

Everyone stood and applauded. Boone grabbed Dutton's hand and pulled him in to hug him. Heather and even Rachel were both crying. The general nodded to Michael from a few tables away. Michael realized he would soon have to ask for his daughter's hand. The general seemed anxious for the conversation.

After a brief honeymoon, Chris moved in with Heather. Michael saw him nearly every day. They would discuss the classes Chris was taking in seminary, and occasionally, Chris would ask questions for better understanding.

"Sergeant Logan, we are studying the kings of Israel and Judah. I could use some help."

"They get tougher to understand as time progresses. After David and Solomon, it seems to move faster," Michael said.

"Exactly. And some were good, and some were evil. I have to write a paper on one of them. We can't use Saul, David, or Solomon, though. Who do you recommend?"

"I have always liked Josiah," Michael said. "His father and grandfather were wicked, but he chose a different path."

"Yes, that's right. He was the one who began to reign at eight years old and later found the Book of the Law."

"That's the one. He tore down all the idols of the false gods and sprinkled their ashes on the graves of the priests who served under his father and grandfather."

"That's making a statement," Chris said.

"Right. He brought the one true God back to the people and condemned any false worship."

"I think you inspired my choice. Josiah was a king for God."

"You may remember God had promised wrath on Judah because of the wicked ways of his predecessors, but God spared Josiah from witnessing it. He promised that he would go to his grave in peace before God brought judgment on them."

Chris began to make feverish notes as he received the message.

"Thank you. I wasn't sure who to choose, but I could probably write the whole paper in an hour now."

"I'd like to read it when you finish it," Michael said.

"You bet. Let me get out of here and get started. The Spirit is moving me."

Michael smiled as Chris hurried off. God was undoubtedly leading him, and Chris was following.

"Do you think it's too soon to put Chris in the pulpit?" the pastor asked Michael one Sunday after the service.

"Not at all. He's going to have to do it eventually. Might as well be sooner than later."

"I don't want to overwhelm him. Maybe I'll give him a two weeks' notice."

"I overheard your conversation about Chris preaching. I wonder what he thinks about that," the general said, walking up after the pastor left.

"I believe we can tell by his expression that he is up to the task," Michael said, pointing at Boone's face as he talked to the pastor.

"I believe you're right. I look forward to hearing his message."

Chris never asked Michael what to preach for his first message. Michael would have told him to preach whatever God put on his heart.

After the pastor opened the service, he made a brief introduction and then sat on the front row as Chris walked to the podium. Heather was already crying. Dutton was seated next to Michael and Rachel. He wasn't about to miss Chris's first sermon.

Chris grasped the sides of the podium and looked down with a moment of silence that seemed to grab everyone's attention.

"As many of you may know, I was raised without a father, so my mother did double duty." He pointed toward his mother, who nodded and wiped a tear.

"God's plan is for children to be raised with both parents. Some of the problems in society today are blamed on the absence of a strong male role model. I can remember as a teen being tempted to make bad choices. My mother would reel me back in, but something was missing. Something I had never experienced. It led me to seek the path most men take — the path to prove yourself worthy to be a man.

"I decided to join the army and put myself to that test. I had no advice from my dad or uncles. It was something I felt the Lord led me to do. During those first few weeks of basic training, I was like a scared rabbit running from the hounds. It was tough sometimes, but I got through it with help from the Lord and a good friend.

"It was during this time that my faith began to grow. I understood that the army and God were testing me. I believe the shining moment of my time in the service came when Dutton and I were sent to Germany. There, we met a man who would fill the void I had always felt as a child. It was almost as though God brought this strong Christian man into my life to help guide me."

Rachel squeezed Michael's hand and glanced up to see his reaction. Michael smiled at her, then turned back to Boone.

"It's no secret that I'm talking about SFC Michael Logan. You may recall, he gave my wife in marriage just a few weeks ago. Sergeant Logan was the role model I needed as a youth. I tried to imitate and learn from him and grew to think highly of him. I have never told him, but I grew to love him. He was a man that was concerned with the spiritual growth of two young men as much as our physical growth. We became a crew and spent many hours together, studying God's Word and sharing our love for the Lord.

"Sometime later, we were sent to Kuwait. Sergeant Logan had a habit, a good habit, of reading from God's Word and praying every morning before the day began. I can remember many times lying there awake and listening to his worship.

"Sergeant Logan had many portions of Scripture he used in his devotions, but while in the desert, he chose Isaiah. Please turn with me to Isaiah 41, verses ten to thirteen.

"I spent many hours waiting for God to put something on my heart. What would be my first message? I think all pastors have struggled with that. However, I realized God gave me this message long ago while in Kuwait.

"The tenth verse is God speaking, and He deals immediately with what is common in people's fear. He says, 'Fear thou not; for I am with thee: be not dismayed; for I am thy God: I will strengthen thee; yea, I will help thee; yea, I will uphold thee with the right hand of my righteousness.'

"To give it to you in plain English, God says not to be afraid because He is with us. He is our God, so don't worry. He will strengthen us, help us, and bless us. God reminds us 365 times in the Bible that we should not fear. That's a daily reminder for the whole year.

"Many of us read God's Word and feel Him speak to us, but on a morning in Kuwait, I saw Him speak. We were attacked by a group of Iraqis one morning. Sergeant Logan, Dutton, and the general were all there. I saw God's Word in the events that took place.

"Sergeant Logan had studied these verses every morning, and now I heard God speaking and understood. Sergeant Logan bears a constant reminder, as well as the general. They were both hit by enemy fire. Sergeant Logan was hit in the knee. Basically, his kneecap was blown out. General Davidson was shot in his shoulder. Both men have an implant to replace what was damaged.

"I saw God strengthen and help Sergeant Logan. And yes, God held him up with His righteous right hand. You see, Sergeant Logan stood up and ran to the aid of a fallen comrade. He pulled the man to safety, all on a leg that should have collapsed. On a leg that should not have supported his weight.

"If you are curious about the enemy soldiers, let's continue with verses eleven and twelve: 'Behold, all they that were incensed against thee shall be ashamed and confounded: they shall be as nothing; and they that strive with thee shall perish.'"

Boone paused to wipe a tear, remembering the barking of his .50 cal. "'Thou shalt seek them, and shalt not find them, even them that contended with thee: they that war against thee shall be as nothing, and as a thing of nought.'

"That's pretty easy to understand. Here are the four of us. The others are not." Boone closed his Bible and continued. "Since Sergeant Logan and the general left that morning on the medivac chopper, I have studied these verses. God's Word is truth. He is speaking to Isaiah but said the same words to Sergeant Logan on that morning in the desert.

"I thank God that I was there to witness it. It has confirmed any pause I may have had. I can tell you without a doubt God's Word is truth. If you want God to speak to you, pick up your Bible and read. Jesus wants to have a conversation with us. He looks forward to spending time with us.

"When we pray, we are speaking to God, but if we never study His Word, we miss hearing His response. It's a one-sided conversation. As Christians, we better be seeking His guidance.

"If a person hires you to do a job, and you give your references and experience but never find out exactly what the boss wants you to do, the job will suffer. If you wait until the boss says you didn't do that right, you miss an opportunity to get it right the first time.

"I have been in churches where people leave their Bibles in their assigned seats to hold their spot until next Sunday. Are we more concerned about where we sit than taking the Bible home and using it? Worship is more than just Sunday. Open God's Word. He will speak to you."

Chris nodded to Pastor Hatcher, then stepped away from the podium. As Chris began to walk to a seat, Pastor Hatcher took him by the shoulder.

"Hold on there, Chris. Let's close this service together."

Pastor Hatcher stood behind the podium with Chris standing beside him.

"That was a fine message. Chris, would you close in prayer?"

Chris bowed his head and began. "Father, we thank You for Your Word. We thank You for everyone gathered here today to receive Your message. As we go our separate ways, fill each of us with the desire and thirst to study Your Word. In Jesus' name we pray, amen."

Several people made their way to Boone to thank him. Michael approached him, shook his hand, and then hugged him.

"Seems God was speaking to us about the same message."

"Well, you got it first. He spoke to me after you left Kuwait," Chris said.

Gen. Davidson squeezed in beside Michael.

"Fine message, son. I knew God had a hand in the things that happened that day. I have no doubt."

"Yes sir, General. He did."

"I believe your boy is grown up," Pastor Hatcher told Michael.

"Yes sir, and I couldn't be prouder."

Michael had made most of his preparations the last week before the trip to Israel. The only thing he hadn't figured out was Mrs. Thompson. He was concerned that she wouldn't eat well while he was gone. Heather suggested that Violet eat with her and Chris, but Michael doubted she would do it. She was independent and would not accept charity. On Wednesday evening after work, he would get Violet's thoughts.

Michael hurried home, showered, and met with his neighbor for dinner. He could smell the mouthwatering aroma of her labors. He knocked, but the door didn't open. He listened to hear if Violet was busy cooking and hadn't heard him. Perhaps, she had stepped into the bathroom. He knocked again.

From over the balcony, Heather looked down to investigate the knocking. Michael looked up at her.

"Have you seen Mrs. Thompson today? I can't get her to the door."

"She might be in the bathroom. Hang on, and I'll call her."

Heather called. Michael could hear the phone ringing. Heather came back out with a concerned look on her face.

"I hope she hasn't fallen."

Michael knocked again.

"Mrs. Thompson. It's Michael."

He turned the doorknob, but the door was locked.

"What's wrong?" Chris asked as he walked up the stairs.

"We can't get Violet to the door."

"Wait a minute," Heather said, remembering Violet had given her an emergency key to her apartment.

"I hope this isn't an emergency," Michael said.

Heather hurried down the steps. "Hold on. If we go busting in there and she's in the bathroom, we will scare her to death."

"I will apologize for all of us, honey. You'd better open the door," Chris said.

Heather sobbed as she fumbled with the key. The fear of what she might find wore heavily on her.

Heather slowly pushed open the door. "Mrs. Thompson, it's Heather."

The three had only taken a few steps when their fears were confirmed. Violet sat at the table, her Bible opened in front of her. The table was set, and several prepared dishes were awaiting her guest. Something on the stove bubbled over. Chris removed the pot from the heat and turned it off. Michael placed a hand on Violet's shoulder and felt her neck with his other hand.

"She's gone."

Heather turned to Chris and hugged him. Michael dialed 911. In a few minutes, a police officer arrived. By now, a small group of neighbors and passers-by had gathered outside to investigate. The officer moved everyone back to make room for the ambulance and asked Chris and Heather to sit on the couch. Heather was still weeping. The death of her friend had come as a surprise.

"Are you a relative of the deceased?" the EMTs asked Michael.

"No, I'm her neighbor. Her name is Violet. We were meeting for dinner this evening."

"Do you know any next of kin?"

"I know who they are, but I've never met them. She has a son and daughter out west." Michael picked up an address book next to the phone and thumbed through it until he came to the name David. "This looks like it could be her son. David lives in Arizona, and I don't recognize the area code."

"Do you mind if I keep that?" the officer asked.

"The daughter's name is Ruth, but I'm unsure if she is married."

"Heather, do you know Ruth's last name?" Michael asked.

"No, I'm afraid not. I remember she lives in Texas, but that's all."

The EMTs lifted Violet onto the stretcher and secured the straps. Michael moved out of their way as the officer continued.

"Well, we will see what we come up with. You are most likely correct about the son."

"I wish we could be of more help. She was a good woman."

During the remainder of the week, Michael and the Boones kept a close eye on the obituaries in the paper but never found any mention of Mrs. Thompson. They called several funeral homes in the area, but no one had any information to help with their search.

Michael called the police station, hoping to retrieve David's phone number, but the police declined to release the information. It all seemed mysterious. Violet had lived a private life alone, and now it seemed she would go out privately.

She had touched many lives and had several friends at church. Most of all, Heather was close to her. They had made fast friends when they met. Both women lived by themselves, and they shared many memories. Heather thought more of her than just a neighbor who rode to church with her.

Michael sat in his apartment on Saturday before going to the Davidsons. He remembered the spunky little lady he had come to admire. He had walked by her door several times and still expected her to open it, smile, and say, "Come on in, Michael. Supper's ready."

He prayed for Violet and her family. The loss was regretful, but not knowing where she would be laid to rest or when caused him more concern. He would be in Israel, most likely, before anything would be discovered. He wouldn't be able to attend her funeral.

Chapter 7

The Davidsons were packing suitcases in their vehicle as Michael pulled into the driveway.

"We may need to take two vehicles with everything these ladies packed. They may come out here with the kitchen sink next," the general said as Michael walked up.

"No problem, sir. Rachel and I can go in my truck."

"That may be best. We can load your bags in here in case it rains."

The general was sweating as he struggled to move stuff around repeatedly, trying to fit the last piece of the puzzle.

"General, why don't I take Rachel and Monica, and then you can fill the back seat up."

"Fine with me. I've never rode in a pickup truck," Monica said.

"You don't know what you're missing," Rachel said. "The seats are uncomfortable, and the air conditioning blows right in your face. Not to mention, it takes a step ladder to get in. You can ride shotgun."

"Shotgun. What's shotgun?" Monica asked.

"She means you can ride by the door," Michael explained.

After a lengthy workout of loading bags, the group pulled away in two vehicles. Rachel snuggled beside Michael as Monica took her first ride in a truck.

"What do you think?" Rachel asked Monica.

"Loud."

When they arrived, Michael found a parking spot close to the general. They got out and went to help disassemble the puzzle of bags.

"I'm glad we aren't going for any longer. We would have filled Michael's truck bed up," the general said.

They lugged their bags into the airport, got in line, checked in after a brief wait, and then walked to their gate. The general led the way. At one point, they had to pass through a metal detector.

As soon as Gen. Davidson entered, an alarm alerted the security men, who quickly held up their hands for him to stop. One man waved a wand over the general.

"I have an implant," the general explained.

The explanation was ignored, and the repeated waving of the wand continued.

"Sir, did you remove all your items from your pockets?"

The general huffed. "Yes, I did. I have an implant."

Again, the explanation was ignored.

"Sir, I'm going to ask you to step into this room so that we can search you."

"Search me? I told you I have an implant."

The general was ignored for a third time but complied with the request. The line began to move again, and all three Davidson ladies jumped in front of Michael.

"Good thinking," Michael said.

As Michael passed through security, he was met with the same alarm and alert attention. Rachel stood on the other side, waiting with a light-hearted grin. She knew it was coming. The same interrogation ensued, but Michael didn't explain anything. He had already seen that it was useless. He was motioned into the same room where the general had his shirt off as an officer waved a wand back and forth over his shoulder.

Gen. Davidson looked at a second officer who made eye contact with him. "I already told this man I have a metal implant."

"Yes sir. We can see that now. You can dress and be on your way. Enjoy your flight."

The general's face was flushed. Michael could tell he was upset. He had served in the military his entire life, been wounded in combat, and was made to feel like a criminal. He looked at Michael as the wand was being passed over his knee.

"Good luck, Michael. You are guilty until proven innocent in here."

As the general left, the officer asked, "Sir, can you pull up your pants leg?"

Michael obeyed but could not reach a point that satisfied the security man.

"Sir, can you please drop your trousers to your ankles?"

Michael said nothing and did as directed. The wand was passed over his knee several times until he finally looked at the second officer as if to say, "Enough is enough."

"You can dress and rejoin your party. Enjoy your flight."

Michael left the room to find the Davidsons waiting at a nearby wall. Sarah tried to calm the general, fearing his frustration might affect his blood pressure.

"I didn't know we were traveling with two criminals," Rachel said.

The general gave her a stern look and then smiled, joking with his best Scooby Doo line: "And we would have gotten away with it if it wasn't for you meddling kids."

They all laughed, and the general seemed to regain his composure slowly. After a brief wait, they entered the plane and searched for their seats. Gen. Davidson and Sarah sat in front of Rachel, Michael, and Monica.

"You girls behave yourselves, or I'll stop this plane and spank your rumps."

"Yes sir," Monica said, saluting her father.

After being in the air briefly, Monica asked, "Dad, when we arrive in Tel Aviv, we are getting picked up in a bus, right?"

"Yes, we will catch a bus to Jerusalem, where we will stay."

"Jerusalem? You haven't told me about that one," Monica said to Michael.

"Jerusalem is probably the most holy city to believers. It was the capital in Jesus' day and where a kangaroo court tried Him. He was crucified just outside the city gates."

"I knew that," Monica said. "Just wanted to hear it."

Monica sat back, put her headphones on, and shut her eyes.

Everyone tried to nap, but Michael couldn't accomplish that task. He was excited, like a kid waiting for Christmas morning. Going to Israel was a dream come true. Many Christians make the trip in their lifetime, and now it was his time.

He was thankful that the general had invited him to accompany the family. It also allowed Rachel and him to spend more time together. He glanced at her as she napped.

After several hours, the plane began its taxi into Munich, where they would change planes.

"Are we there already?" Rachel asked after Michael woke her up.

"Not hardly. We are changing planes in Germany and have about three hours before we take off again. You know what that means?"

Rachel looked at him with a half-alert expression and a matching response. "What does it mean?"

"*Jagerschnitzel.*"

The general overheard the conversation and spoke the best broken German he could. "*Jagerschnitzel mit pommes frites bitte.*"

"What did he just say?" Rachel asked.

"He said he will have French fries with his, please," Michael interpreted.

Monica yawned and stretched as the plane touched down. "I understood French fries, so I'm having what Dad said," Monica said.

"Do you want to share mine, or do you want your own?" Michael asked Rachel.

"I want my own, but what exactly is *Jagerschnitzel*?"

"It's a breaded veal or pork cutlet smothered in mushroom sauce and noodles. Germans are considerate with portions is why I asked."

As they stepped off the plane and started down the hall, Michael saw what he was looking for: a sandwich board advertising schnitzel. Sarah quickly stopped him, knowing what the girls would soon find out.

"Michael, I will share Tom's. You can get me a water, please."

Michael stepped to the counter with Rachel close beside him.

"Guten tag. Ich haben nicht duetche marks. Ist dollars, okay?" (Good day. I have no German money. Are dollars okay?)

"Ja, das ist sehr gut" (Yes, that is very good), the woman behind the counter replied.

"Wunderbar. Vier Jagerschnitzel mit pommes frites und funf wasser bitte." (Wonderful. Four Jagerschnitzel with French fries and five waters, please.)

"Zwanzig dollar bitte." (Twenty dollars please.)

Michael paid, and Rachel looked at him in amazement.

"I didn't know you spoke German."

"I don't, but I can order food. I lived here for several years. At some point, you've got to eat."

The woman laughed. "That's true. And your German is not bad either. Here are your waters, and I'll get your food."

"How do I say thank you?" Rachel asked.

"*Danke* for thanks, or *danke schon* for much thanks."

The woman returned with two platters, and another person brought the remaining two. Each had two cutlets piled high with noodles and fries on the side.

"Danke schon," Rachel said.

"You're welcome. Enjoy," the woman replied.

Michael thanked the woman and carried the platters to a nearby table without chairs, where the remainder of the family waited. He placed each meal on the table. Each person had just enough room. He said the blessing and then looked at Monica and Rachel, who both gazed at their plates in disbelief.

"You'll both manage," Sarah said.

Rachel began tasting cautiously. "I should have listened to Michael. I will never eat all of this."

Monica tried her meal and chose to stick with the fries.

"If you girls have a problem with this, you will starve in Israel. You can't be finicky when you go to different countries," the general said.

"What do you think was in the suitcases you loaded? Rachel and I brought enough snacks to get by," Monica said.

After a two-hour layover and four more flying hours, they finally arrived in Tel Aviv. They retrieved their luggage and met on their tour bus to take them to Jerusalem. Many of the passengers on the plane from Munich were on the same tour.

"I am worn out. Flying all day takes a lot out of you," Rachel said.

"Me, too. I will sleep well tonight," Michael said.

As the bus pulled up to their hotel, the tour guide stood and spoke in nearly perfect English.

"Ladies and gentlemen, may I have your attention? Thank you for choosing Israel for your vacation. We welcome you. You may retrieve your bags and check in when we unload at the hotel. It is now 10:00 a.m. Israel time, so you can rest and relax until 4:00 p.m. We will meet in the hotel's conference room to discuss the itinerary for this week, and afterward, we will move to the buffet for the evening meal. Once again, Israel thanks you."

As the general stood in line to check in, the ladies and Michael sat in chairs in the lobby. They were all exhausted. In a few minutes, the general rejoined the group with interesting news.

"Well, somehow, our reservation got messed up."

"How?" Sarah asked.

"Our three rooms with two beds are now two rooms with two beds and an adjoining bathroom."

The general looked at Michael. "I believe the only solution is for Michael and I to take one and you ladies to take the other."

"Fine with me," Michael said.

"Sure, that's fine. The girls can take one bed, and I'll take the other."

They loaded on the elevator and located their rooms. After entering, the girls and Sarah opened the door that separated each room and surveyed them both. They discovered they were the same.

"Which bunk do you want, Michael?" the general asked.

"It doesn't matter, sir. You choose."

"Since I'm right here, this one is perfect. Wake me in a week."

"Michael, I wanted to warn you Tom snores a little," Sarah said.

"Everybody snores, darling."

"Not like you."

"You are right, but we will manage. You ladies must get unpacked and rest before we go down this evening."

Everyone understood that the general wanted an undisturbed nap. Michael stretched out on his bed after the ladies left, and in only five minutes, the snoring was confirmed. Michael lay there looking at the ceiling. It was going to be a long week.

A few hours later, the general awoke and seemed to be recharged. He sat up and looked at Michael to confirm he was awake also.

"I feel much better. That nap was just what the doctor ordered."

Michael sat up, glad that the torture had ceased for the moment. He grabbed his suitcase.

"I am going to get unpacked. I was trying to keep quiet while you slept."

"You didn't take a nap?"

"No sir."

"Well, you will sleep well tonight."

"I hope so."

After a brief presentation from the tour guide, the family was led to the buffet. Michael and the general went through the line, smiling at the unknown dishes. The ladies took a more cautious, selective approach.

Michael and the general sampled a little of everything. There was fish, chicken, vegetables, soups, and bread. The typical American greasy, fried choices were not present. They noticed eggplant and chickpeas in several of the dishes.

"Someone told me I have to try the falafel," Michael told the general.

"Think I'll try it, too. The two men sat down as the ladies continued to make laps around the buffet, trying to decide. They each came back to the table with baked chicken and salad.

"You girls don't have much on your plates. You're missing out," the general said between bites. "This falafel is delicious, isn't it, Michael?"

"Sure is."

Michael looked at Rachel as she nibbled at her food.

"You aren't adventurous?"

"Not when it comes to food. I like to know what I'm eating."

Michael offered her a bite of his falafel.

"Here, try this."

She took a bite, smiled, and asked, "What is in that? It's pretty good."

"Mostly chickpeas, flour, and garlic, I think. It's kind of like a hushpuppy without the grease."

"I like the crunchy coating."

"Do you want to try any of these other dishes?" he asked, pointing to his plate.

"No thanks. I'll eat what I have. Maybe tomorrow."

"I don't know what half of what I ate was called, but it was all delicious," the general said.

"I may gain a little weight while here," Michael said.

The ladies smiled politely as they took their time eating. Both men could tell they did not enjoy middle eastern cuisine.

After dinner, as Michael sat on his bed and thumbed through his Bible, the general said, "Michael, I was giving a little thought to the situation with Mrs. Thompson."

"Yes sir. I haven't been able to find anything on her. It's got me puzzled."

"Well, I was thinking. Her husband served in WW II, right?"

"Yes. He fought at Normandy."

"Chances are he had a military funeral. If that's true, Veterans Affairs would have a record of his resting place," the general reasoned. "You need to contact Graves Registration with the V.A. I am sure Violet was buried with her husband."

"You are right. I don't know why I didn't think of that," Michael replied.

"That's understandable. You got hit with her loss and trying to prepare for this trip all at once."

Rachel walked in through the open door that separated their rooms and sat on the bed next to Michael.

"Your dad may have just figured out how we can find Violet."

"That's great."

The general got up to use the bathroom.

"Michael, with three women, you better use the bathroom even if you don't need to. Chances are good someone will be in there otherwise."

"Here, Mom wants you to have these," Rachel whispered to Michael after the general left.

He looked down to discover several packs of foam earplugs.

"Tell her thanks."

Sarah had endured his snoring for years and had made the necessary adjustments but never complained. He admired her tenacity.

The following morning after breakfast, the tour group loaded on the bus and set out for the Sea of Galilee. Michael noticed Monica being quiet and attentive to the passing scenery.

"I hope your sister enjoys this trip and gets something out of it," Michael told Rachel.

"Me, too. She asked a few questions last night before we went to sleep. She actually brought up Jesus."

"That's great." He looked out the window as the bus moved down the road. "It humbles you to see the things that Jesus saw and walk where He walked."

"Yes, it does."

The bus stopped at the southern portion of the water near the Jordan River.

"This is the Sea of Galilee," the tour guide explained. "It's also referred to as the Lake of Gennesaret. Jesus was walking along the edge of the water one day and saw his first disciples: Peter, Andrew, James, and John. They were returning from an unsuccessful fishing trip. They were washing their nets but had caught no fish. Jesus got into Peter's boat and asked him to push off. Jesus told him to head for the deep and cast his net. Peter explained that they had already tried that all night, but it didn't produce anything. Still, Peter did as commanded, and his net filled with fish. So much so that he called to the others to come and help. Peter was humbled and asked Jesus to depart from him, for he was sinful. Jesus then said, 'Fear not, from now on, you shall catch men.'"

Michael glanced at Monica, who alertly listened and looked on. It seemed she was trying to imagine what the tour guide described.

"I think God has her attention," Michael said to Rachel.

"I believe you're right."

The tour guide further explained the Jordan River. "The river that flows out of Galilee is the same river that Joshua and the people crossed to go into Jericho. John the Baptist preached along this valley, baptizing believers and even baptized Jesus in these very waters."

As they walked away, several people, including Monica, bent down to dip their hands into the water. Michael smiled as he knelt beside her, letting the water run through his fingers. He could tell she was being ministered to.

The tour continued with a boat ride that slowly moved along, powered only by the wind pushing the large sails. Michael remembered Jesus preaching to the multitudes who gathered on the shore and His walking on the water.

The tour guide spoke as everyone looked on in amazement and wonder.

"Jesus performed most of His miracles in this region. He turned water to wine, healed a nobleman's son, drove out an evil spirit from a man, healed Peter's mother-in-law, cleansed a man of leprosy, healed a Roman centurion's servant, healed a man with a withered hand, calmed the sea, healed the woman with the issue of blood, raised Jairus' daughter back to life, healed blind men and the mute, fed thousands with only a few loaves and fishes, and paid the tax with a coin from a fish. All of that was done in this region."

Monica looked across the water, staring into the endless blue. Jesus had been where she now was. Michael was thankful she was getting this opportunity and that God was speaking to her.

That evening after their meal, Michael asked the general, "Sir, did you notice Monica today?"

"Yes, I did. Seems our coming here may be a blessing."

"I agree. I wonder if she would like to talk about our day?"

"I don't know. Let's ask her." The general called through the open door to the ladies in the other room. "Monica, do you have a moment?"

She walked into the room, followed by Sarah and Rachel.

"What do you think of the trip so far?" the general asked.

Monica sat on the bed beside the general. "I am enjoying it. It's like the Bible coming to life. There's so much history here."

"Glad you are enjoying it. Is there anything you have questions about?" Michael asked.

"No, not really. The tour guides did a good job with their presentations. I'm looking forward to Caesarea tomorrow."

"We all are," the general said.

That night, Michael lay awake as the general began his assault on anyone in the next room or rooms. How did the paint not peel from the walls with his loud and labored breathing? Sarah deserved a medal for distinguished service.

Michael had found that if he put the earplugs in and wrapped his pillow tightly around his head, he could drown out enough of the noise to sleep. He knew that eventually his sleep deprivation would take care of itself.

The next day, the tour set out for the waterfront town of Caesarea. The Roman influence could still be seen in some of the older ruins. Monica took it all in again and paid considerable attention to what was being said — almost like a student cramming for a test.

The next day, they arrived at Nazareth — the final time they would have to endure a long bus ride. The remainder of the locations were all less than ten miles from Jerusalem. The tour guide showed a house that would have been present in Jesus' day. It was only four walls and a stick roof with grasses laced into it. The dirt floor reminded everyone how comfortable they had it now. The room was dark, except for the light that shined through cracks in the roof. There was no bathroom, no running water, and no air conditioning. Jesus lived with an average family in an average house. The house He lived in was most likely similar to everyone else's in Nazareth.

On the fourth day, the group set out for Bethlehem and were taken to a hollowed-out, cave-like enclosure.

"This is probably what Joseph and Mary had to settle with when they came here," the tour guide said. "This is where people would keep their livestock while visiting. When Jesus was born, He was wrapped and laid in a manger, much like the ones you see here."

Several people in the group were moved to tears as they imagined Jesus, the King of kings, being born in a cave. Monica seemed moved as well. Seeing it for the first time was a profound experience. Jesus didn't come as royalty but had humbled himself.

The tour guide reminded the group what God had promised through the prophet Micah: "But thou, Bethlehem Ephratah, though thou be little among the thousands of Judah, yet out of thee shall he come forth unto me that is to be ruler in Israel; whose goings forth have been from of old, from everlasting" (Micah 5:2).

"Jesus had come to be born as a child and grew up as we all have. God the Son lived among the people," the guide concluded.

Michael tried to imagine how wonderful it would have been to be there where Jesus stood.

On the next to the last day of the trip, the tour made its way up the Mount of Olives. Hundreds of graves lined the slopes. People had been buried there for thousands of years.

"At the bottom is the Garden of Gethsemane. It was here that Jesus prayed with His disciples before being arrested. He was led away to Jerusalem and questioned before the Sanhedrin," the guide stated. Then, he commented on the cemetery. "This hill is sacred to most believers. Jesus was taken from here, and after He was crucified, He ascended to heaven from here. Many people have been buried here to be closer to God. It is believed when Jesus returns, He will return to this mount."

The group soon reached a point high enough to see over Jerusalem.

"You may have read that when Jesus went away to pray, He usually climbed a mountain. This is one He prayed on many times. It's almost like Jesus wanted to be closer to the Father," the guide said.

"Beautiful here, isn't it?" Michael asked Monica.

"Yes, it is. I'm glad we came here."

"Me, too. Seeing the things Jesus saw hits you in the heart."

"Yes, I suppose it does," Monica said.

Monica walked away from Michael and continued to survey the scenery. He stepped back to Rachel, who had heard the conversation.

"Give her time, Michael. She's got a thick shell around her," Rachel said to Michael.

The general and Sarah glanced in their direction. Everyone hoped and prayed for Monica to accept Jesus. The trip seemed to motivate her spiritually, but Michael wasn't sure if it was only understanding she was seeking.

That evening at the buffet, Michael had his favorite meal. He had concocted it himself. He stuffed a piece of pita bread with salad, falafel, and baked fish. He then spooned a little lentil soup on top. The general had even tried the strange combination and agreed it was delicious.

The ladies had exhausted their snacks and would now have to eat from the many selections on the buffet. Monica went with the familiar. She sat down with a falafel burger but soon found familiarity only in the looks. The taste was not the same.

"When you expect something to taste like a burger, it catches you off guard when it doesn't. However, it's not bad," she said.

Rachel and Sarah let down their guarded curiosity and sampled several dishes.

"There you go. You will like it; trust me. I haven't found anything I didn't like," the general said.

"Tom, you would eat the phone book if it had gravy on it," Sarah said.

"I didn't get to be this big by being picky," he chuckled.

Everyone laughed. Sarah was right. The general wasn't hard to please when it came to food. He liked it all.

The final day of the tour entailed walking through Jerusalem and visiting the Western Wall. Once again, the tour guide offered a brief education.

"Archeologists have found iron gates in some of the construction of the former city. Jerusalem has been torn down and built back so often that they're still unsure how old the gates are. David captured the city during his reign as king and moved the capital from Hebron to Jerusalem. His son, Solomon, built the first temple here. Since then, the city has been destroyed twice, besieged twenty-three times, captured and recaptured forty-four times, and attacked fifty-two times.

"God warned Israel through many prophets of the Old Testament. False idols and worship of false gods caused the destruction and captivity of the people. But God promised He would not completely remove His people, Israel.

"In Jerusalem, during Jesus' days, the Sanhedrin was the ruling council. The priests or judges were appointed to sit as tribunal. Most people looked at them as the most educated in the sacred writings. When Jesus came along and claimed to be the Son of God, the Sanhedrin believed He was speaking blasphemy. They knew they had to deal with Jesus soon.

"The Passover celebration was approaching, and many people were coming into the city to be part of it. You see, Jesus was crucified mainly because He got in the way of traditions and profits. The Sanhedrin could not allow this, so they hired Judas, a disciple of Jesus, to tell them where Jesus was so they could take Him into custody.

"As you remember, Jesus prayed in the Garden of Gethsemane when Judas betrayed Him. He was brought to the city under the cover of darkness and presented before the authorities without all the members present. Both of these acts broke tradition.

"He was then sent to the Roman governor, Pilate, who found no fault in Him. Pilate sent Jesus to Herod, the Roman puppet leader of the Jews, but Herod sent Him back to Pilate, and Pilate then called the chief priests.

"Pilate again told the authorities he found no fault in Jesus and nothing worthy of death, but they persuaded him to do as they requested. They shouted, 'Crucify Him, Crucify Him.' Jesus was led out the city gates to Golgotha, or the place of the skull. Luke is the only one who calls the place Calvary. Jesus was ridiculed and spit upon. He was beaten, bruised, and finally hung on a cross by Roman soldiers, where He died."

Next, the guide took the group to an open tomb for an understanding of the resurrection of Christ.

"This is a burial tomb much like Joseph of Arimathea had. He brought the body of Jesus to his own intended resting place. He wrapped Jesus in linens and laid Him inside. The day following the Sabbath, women brought spices to anoint Jesus but found the stone had been rolled away. He was not there. He had risen. Many witnessed Jesus alive after this, and sometime later, He ascended back to heaven."

Michael and Rachel stood there listening, waiting their turn to look inside the empty tomb. Monica stepped inside and returned with tears in her eyes a few moments later. She walked over to Michael and her sister as they stepped in. Rachel was moved to tears as well.

"Jesus was the perfect sacrifice. He paid our sin debt so we can come into God's presence," the guide added.

That afternoon in the hotel, everyone was packing for the trip home the following day. All three of the ladies walked into the men's room. Rachel got Michael's attention as he bent over his suitcase.

"Michael, Monica wants to ask you something."

Monica stepped closer to him and took a deep breath. She tried to speak, but her emotions overwhelmed her.

"Come sit here, please," Michael said.

She quietly sat and sniffed. "Michael, I want Jesus to come into my life."

Sarah walked to the general, who wrapped an arm around her and looked on. It was finally happening. Monica was tired of running. God had not given up on her, and now she was listening.

"This week, you saw with your own eyes the history of Jesus. You saw where He was born, raised, crucified, and rose from the grave. Do you believe that to be true? Do you believe in Jesus?" Michael asked.

Michael looked into her eyes and saw a woman who had never been where she was before. It was as if he saw into her heart. The thick shell she had kept around herself seemed to melt away.

"I do. I believe. I want Jesus to save me. Will you show me how?" Monica asked.

Michael felt his heart throbbing in his chest. The prayers made by many were about to be answered. He laid a hand on her shoulder.

"Close your eyes and ask God to forgive your sins. Ask Him to come into your life and save you."

Monica thought a moment. She had never prayed before. She wasn't sure how she should begin or in what order.

"When we pray, it's whatever comes to your heart. Say it in your own words. You can do that, right?" Michael coached.

Michael was surprised at her words.

"Father, I ask that You would forgive my many sins. Come into my life and fill me with Your mercy and grace. I thank You for loving me. I thank You for being my God, and I give you praise. In Jesus' name, amen."

Monica wept as the whole family wrapped their arms around her.

"I believe this trip was a blessing, and I'm glad we were all here to witness it," the general said.

Michael grabbed Monica by the wrist. "Congratulations. Welcome to the family of God."

Michael had planned to catch up on his lost sleep when they boarded the plane the next day, but Monica was supercharged in Christ. She wanted to talk about the trip and how she had felt the Spirit move in her at different times. She mentioned the tour guide speaking and seeing things so clearly. Michael listened with a smile on his face. He could sleep when he got home.

Michael remembered how much of his time had been spent avoiding Monica. He knew God had sent him on a journey to save the lost, but he didn't think Monica was included in that task. He knew Jesus offers forgiveness for all who had sinned, but he needed to be reminded of that. God had to show him Monica was to be counted as a child of God.

Most of the day was spent flying, and the whole family seemed excited and alert when the plane approached Charlotte. Israel had been a dream come true for everyone involved, but it was good to be home.

Michael carried his suitcase up the stairs to his apartment. He looked at Violet's door as he set his bag down and retrieved his key. She would have enjoyed hearing about his trip but had taken a far greater one. She didn't get to see where he had been, but she was with the Lord.

As Michael opened the door and turned on a light, he noticed a folded piece of paper lying on the floor that had been pushed under the door. He shut the door and set his bag down. He sat in a chair and opened the note.

Mr. Logan,

My name is Ruth. I am Violet's daughter. She told me about you and the kindness you showed her. We just finished cleaning out her apartment, and I wanted to take a moment to thank you. I would have liked to meet you. We had a small family service at the graveside. She would have wanted you to know where. Mom is with Dad now. Her body was laid to rest in the National

Cemetery in Salisbury, but her soul is with Dad and our Lord in heaven. Thank you for being a friend and good neighbor.

Ruth

Michael closed the note and wept for Violet for the first time. He was glad to know where she was, and he would plan to visit her grave as soon as he got a little rest. He thanked God for putting Violet in his life. She was almost like a grandmother to him — more than a neighbor. She was a good woman, and he would miss her.

After an extended nap, Michael was awakened by the phone ringing. He lay there half asleep, waiting for the answering machine to pick up. Chris was on the other end.

"Sergeant Logan, just checking to see if you made it back yet. Call me when you get home."

Michael sat up and rubbed his face, trying to wake himself. He glanced at his watch and focused on the green-lit number: 1742. Chris had just gotten home. He got up, stretched, and walked to the bathroom. The answering machine blinked four messages.

A few minutes later, Michael knocked on the Boones' door. Heather opened the door.

"Sergeant Logan, glad to see you made it back. Come on in."

"It's good to be back. Is Chris around?"

Chris walked out of the bathroom. "Welcome home. How was your trip?"

"It was great. I'll tell you about it after I get over this jet lag. I got a note from Violet's daughter. I know where Violet is buried."

"That's great. We saw a moving truck leaving the other day and assumed it was her family. We didn't get to ask them anything, though."

"She's buried in Salisbury at the National Cemetery with Walter."

"Thank heavens. We had gotten nowhere since you left," Heather said.

"So, do you guys want to go to the cemetery with Rachel and me after church?" Michael asked.

"Yes, we do," Heather said.

"Sounds good to me," Chris said.

Michael returned to his apartment and noticed the messages still blinking on his phone. Rachel had called him just before he had gotten home. He dialed her number. She answered on the first ring.

"Hey, Michael. I just wanted to see if you want to have dinner here tomorrow evening."

"Sure. That would be great. I also wanted to ask if you wanted to go to the cemetery tomorrow after church. I know where Violet is."

"That's fine with me. That will make us have a late dinner, though."

"How about I buy you dinner so we aren't rushed?" Michael offered.

"Okay, I'll fix dinner next Sunday."

"Chris and Heather are going, too."

"Can we do a movie over here after dinner?"

"That sounds good."

"I'll see you in the morning. I may take a nap."

Michael was up at 0400 the following day and spent time with God. He had a lot to be thankful for. The mystery with Violet had been solved, Monica had accepted Jesus, and the trip to Israel had been a blessing.

As he walked into the church, Pastor Hatcher approached him and shook his hand. "Welcome back, Michael. How did the trip go?"

"We had a good time. It was humbling to see all the places Jesus had been."

"I would say so. I hope to go someday."

"It's well worth it. Rachel's sister, Monica, got saved while we were there."

"That's a bonus."

"She is coming to church this morning."

"I'll make sure I speak to her and welcome her," Pastor Hatcher said.

A few moments later, Rachel walked in and sat beside him.

"You look very nice," Michael said.

"Thank you. You do, too."

Sarah and the general sat next to them. As Monica approached them, Pastor Hatcher stopped her to shake her hand and greet her.

Monica wiped a tear as she concluded her conversation with the pastor and sat beside Sarah. Michael and the family greeted her. She smiled, and Michael saw a different woman. She no longer had the rough exterior with the scowled expression. He could see her joy.

Boone and Heather sat in front of them. The pastor addressed the congregation after the opening prayer and a few hymns.

"It's good to see everyone this morning, and we are glad to have Michael and the Davidsons back with us. We're glad their trip was safe and fruitful. Seeing the places Jesus was during His ministry is something all of us would enjoy. But an even greater joy is when a family member comes to Christ." Pastor Hatcher motioned toward the Davidsons. "Monica accepted the Lord this past week and asked me to thank all of you for your prayers."

Michael and Rachel glanced at Monica to see tears streaming down her cheeks.

"She has asked to be baptized." Several people applauded. "Today, she and her mother and father will do that."

The decision had been kept a surprise. Both, Rachel and Michael didn't know, there would be a baptism that morning. They were overjoyed.

The pastor preached the message, and before the conclusion, Sarah, the general, and Monica got up and walked forward to prepare themselves. Heather and Chris would assist them.

Michael and Rachel remembered the times they had prayed for the family. God had answered their prayers. Michael thought of the journey

God had set him on. He felt sure God had sent him to return the general to the Lord, but he was also surprised when Sarah was saved. His attitude toward Monica had gotten in the way of seeing what God wanted in her life.

Michael put his arm around Rachel as her family members were baptized. "Thank you, Lord," she said.

"Guess you two are wondering how they snuck this past you?" Chris said to Michael and Rachel as they waited for the family to change into dry clothes.

"Yes, I am. We had no idea," Rachel said.

"They called the pastor yesterday when you all got back. I knew about it when you came by the apartment," Chris said.

"I have been a part of the general's surprises before. He got me again."

"Do you all still want to head up to the cemetery?" Chris asked.

"What do you think, Michael?" Rachel asked.

"I guess we need to reschedule that. We can take the family out if you want."

"Well, let's see what they have in mind."

"I'm not putting pressure on you. I think Heather and I are still going," Chris said.

"We can go next weekend, I suppose," Michael said.

A few minutes later, the Davidsons returned to the sanctuary, where many people congratulated them. Their smiles seemed infectious. Monica made her way to Rachel and hugged her.

"Thanks, sis, for not giving up on me."

The tears and sobbing began again. Michael held out his hand, but Monica declined it and hugged him as well.

"I owe you thanks as well, Michael."

"You don't owe me anything, Monica. We've both seen God speaking to you. Give Him the thanks."

Later after lunch, Michael sat beside Rachel on her couch. She started to play a movie but stopped.

"Michael, do you mind if we talk for a while?"

"Sure. What's on your mind?"

"I just wanted to know about us. Where do you see us in a year or two?" Rachel asked.

Michael knew Rachel was anxious to start a life together. His delay in asking her to marry him had concerned her.

"I enjoy being with you, Rachel, and I see us together in the future. I haven't asked you to marry me because we haven't known each other that long."

"So, you do intend to ask me?"

Michael put an arm around her and pulled her into him.

"Yes, you're what I've always wanted. I want to spend the rest of my life with you."

"I feel the same way. It's just that neither of us is getting any younger."

He knew she was referring to children.

"Age is not an issue with getting married. People in their nineties get married all the time."

She lightly slapped him on his arm. "You know what I'm talking about. I was referring to kids."

He laughed, but she didn't find the humor in his joke.

"I know. Sorry, but I'm not worried about us not having children. If God wants us to, we will. Abraham and Sarah were well up in years when they had Isaac."

Rachel exhaled deeply and looked at Michael sternly but didn't say anything. He had hit a sensitive nerve, an area of importance with Rachel.

"Which is more important to you? Marriage or children?"

"I want both."

"So, it's safe to say we will work on the children part immediately."

"Is that okay with you?" Rachel asked.

"I would like to spend time with my wife before a baby comes. But if we are to have ten kids, that's okay, too."

"You just don't see the urgency. Many women in their twenties have two or three children, and I'm knocking on my mid-thirties."

"I understand what you're saying. I guess marriage is at the top of my list. Children will happen if God wills it."

She began crying again, and Michael knew he had upset her. He rubbed her back.

"I'm sorry. I didn't mean to make you cry. "

"Don't worry. I know I'm impatient."

She wiped her tears and went to the kitchen. Michael sat there, unsure if he should console her or avoid the possibly thrown objects. He reasoned with himself, That's precisely why you shouldn't rush into marriage. It takes time to see the crazy come out.

Rachel walked back into the living room. "I'm sorry, Michael. Forgive me. I think I've still got some jetlag. Maybe I should lie down."

"That's fine. I'll call you later this week. I'm going back to work tomorrow."

"Me, too," Rachel said.

Rachel walked to the door and gave him a halfhearted kiss.

Michael walked out, and the door quickly shut behind him. He pulled his keys from his pocket and shook his head. "I guess that was our first fight. Not sure how I came out on that one."

When Michael walked into his apartment, he noticed a message flashing on the answering machine. He thought perhaps Rachel had gotten over her tiff. He pushed the play button but was surprised to hear Monica's voice.

"Michael, I didn't get to thank you for lunch. Also, thanks for being patient and not giving up on me. I appreciate all the times you tried to lead me to the Lord. My life has changed so much."

Michael played the message again and smiled as he heard Monica speak from the heart. He could tell God had changed her.

The following Saturday at the Davidsons' home, Michael carried five steaks he had marinated the night before. The general rose quickly from his chair.

"Let's get them on the grill. I can't wait to taste them."

"My mouth was watering on the ride over here," Michael said.

Monica left the kitchen with a glass of iced tea for Michael and her father.

"The potato salad and coleslaw are ready. Mom is working on the baked beans. I will fix the salad, but let me know when the steaks get close. We don't want the dinner rolls to get cold."

"Sounds great," Michael said.

The general walked out the back door toward the grill with Michael close behind.

"General, is Rachel running late?"

"Yes, she has been way behind at work since our trip. She will be here soon."

The general laid the steaks on the preheated grill and heard the searing sound as he lay each one down.

"Smell that, Michael. I think that's the pleasing aroma they talk about in the Bible when it says sacrifices had a pleasing smell to God."

"I believe you're right."

The general shut the lid and sat down. He sipped his tea and then looked at Michael.

"How long have you been working with us, Michael? Five or six months now?"

"Sounds right."

"I was talking to CSM Samson this week. Seems he is concerned with you being an E-7 and working in an E-8 position."

Michael wasn't sure where the conversation was heading. He thought he was doing a satisfactory job and that CSM Samson was pleased.

"Truth is, I'm concerned, too. The position you hold is for an E-8," the general continued.

"Yes sir. I understand."

"We checked your file, and according to our findings, you are eligible for promotion. Samson mentioned a promotion board coming up but hadn't seen a packet on you."

"I'm only in the secondary zone. That's why I didn't get in a hurry."

"Get in a hurry. You have a 99 percent chance of making it. The unit is short on E-8s. You should let CSM Samson know if the orders were for a Master Sergeant or a First Sergeant."

"Yes sir. I will. I would prefer First Sergeant if there are any companies open."

"There are. I thought you would go that route." He leaned closer to Michael. "Of course, that doesn't mean a thing if you don't get your packet in."

"I'll do that this week."

"Good. You deserve it." The general got up to turn the steaks. "Now, tell me what's happening with you and Rachel."

Michael was hesitant to talk about his personal life. But the general was her father.

"I think Rachel would like to see things moving faster than they are."

"I thought I was the only one. I've been preparing my 'be good to my daughter' speech for some time."

"I just feel we haven't known each other long enough," Michael said.

"Take your time, Michael. Marriage is forever, and it shouldn't be rushed. I support your decision."

They looked up to see Rachel and Monica walking out the back door.

As they got closer, Michael noticed a glass in Monica's hand. She saw him looking and raised it.

"It's sweet tea."

He smiled at Monica as Rachel walked up and hugged him.

"How was your week, Michael?"

"Pretty good and yours?"

"Busy. I am still behind."

Michael noticed she preferred to act as if nothing had happened. He assumed she had talked to her father, which brought on the talk he and the general had just had.

"Those steaks smell good," Rachel said, sitting beside Michael.

"They do, don't they?" the general said. "Monica, they are getting close if you want to start the rolls."

"Are we still planning to go to the cemetery after church?" Michael asked Rachel.

"Sure. We can leave from church if you like. I'm going to fix you dinner when we get back."

"Heather and Chris went last week, and she told me the cemetery is beautiful."

"Rachel, I owe you an apology. I know I hurt you last weekend."

"Thanks, but it's me who needs to apologize. I was showing my impatience. Will you forgive me?"

"You are forgiven," Michael said, leaning down to kiss her.

After church on Sunday, Rachel left her car in the church parking lot and climbed into Michael's truck. She slid over beside him as they pulled away. Michael thought their argument had revealed their true feelings about marriage and children. They would have to compromise. Rachel would have to wait a little longer, and Michael would have to consider asking her to marry him sooner than anticipated.

They pulled into the cemetery and parked on the side of the narrow road. Headstones lined each side — all of them in the same format. True to military standards, they were perfectly aligned and spaced, just like a formation.

Michael pointed down a line of headstones that ended about fifty yards away.

"Boone said she is just past this monument at the end."

As they walked down the row, Michael read the headstones and noticed the dates. They were buried in order of death.

They came to the end and read the stone: Walter Thompson, Pvt, WW II. Violet's name, birth, and death dates were on the back.

Michael stared at the stone, a tear forming in his eye. Rachel took his hand, but both remained quiet, remembering the times spent with Violet.

"That was a wonderful thing you did, eating with her," Rachel finally said.

"I enjoyed her company. She loved her husband and spoke about him many times. Now she's back with him."

"She talked about you all the time at church. Before you came along, she didn't say much."

"I still haven't got used to walking by her door and not seeing her pop out. She reminded me of my maternal grandmother — short, stocky, and spirited."

"I miss her," Michael said.

"We both will."

They stood there deep in thought, until Michael spoke again.

"Mrs. Thompson, I'm glad you are with Walter again and thankful you are with our Lord. I enjoyed knowing you. Say hey to my dad," Michael said.

CHAPTER 8

Michael and Rachel spent the rest of the day together and prepared dinner that evening. She decided to fix a pork roast with potatoes and carrots. Michael was deep frying breaded okra as Rachel scurried about the kitchen.

"Michael, you are supposed to fry the okra, not eat it."

"I'm only eating one or two. It's hard to do this and not eat them."

"Well, just save us enough for dinner."

He walked over and offered her one. She opened her mouth as he popped it in.

"Now you're guilty, too."

When the meal was ready, Michael got out the plates and silverware. Rachel set the prepared dishes on the table, and Michael gave thanks for the food.

"I sure am glad I've got me a woman who can cook," Michael said.

"You sound like Dad. Mom said that's how she won him over."

"Well, I like to eat, so it works out."

"Would you still love me if I couldn't cook?"

"Sure, I would. But eventually, I'd starve to death."

"I know a single man in his thirties can probably cook a little."

"I have survived, but I'm not much of a cook," Michael said.

"Well, I don't mind cooking, but my job won't let me do it every night."

"Not a problem. I don't mind leftovers, and I make a pretty good hamburger helper."

"I like hamburger helper," Rachel said. "You'll have to fix me some sometime."

After dinner, they sat on the couch and talked for a few hours. They had enjoyed spending the day together. Michael didn't see any remains of their disagreement a week earlier. Rachel joked and seemed to be her old self.

As the evening grew to a close, Rachel walked Michael to the door. She put her arms around his neck, kissed him, and held him tightly.

"Why don't you stay the night?" Rachel asked.

Michael was shocked. "I can't," he said.

"Okay, I'll talk to you later. Good night. I'll call you this week," Michael said.

Back at his apartment, Michael reflected on the time when he had been engaged and how that relationship had gone up in flames. He had dated a woman from church. They were perfect for each other. Every spare moment was spent together as the months passed, and they began to plan a wedding. He had made the mistake of moving in with her.

After that, they talked about the wedding less and less. One day Michael woke up riddled with guilt and shame. He told her he couldn't live like that any longer. She broke up with him immediately. He had vowed never to compromise his beliefs again. He asked God for forgiveness, and the relationship was put behind him.

Now, Rachel had put him in a similar situation. He couldn't condemn her, or he would be a hypocrite. They hadn't sinned, but Michael couldn't forget about her suggestion. It surprised him that such a godly woman would suggest a sinful act.

On Friday after work, Michael made the trip home. He needed to clear his head, and the mountain air of home always seemed to cure most of his problems. The porch light was on, but his mother was asleep. He quietly entered the house and made his way to his room. He lay in bed, staring at the ceiling. Sometime late in the morning, he drifted off to sleep.

Michael awoke at 0400 and heard his mother in the kitchen making coffee.

"Good morning, Mom," Michael said, then hugged her.

"Good morning, son. Coffee will be ready in a bit."

He sat at the table, and his mother sensed something may be bothering him. She poured them a cup of coffee and sat beside him.

"What's bothering you, son?"

"Forgiveness."

"Are we talking about you forgiving someone or them forgiving you?"

"I need to forgive someone."

"I see, and I suppose you are having difficulty doing it."

"Yes ma'am."

"Did this person hurt you?"

"Disappointed me more than anything. They did something I didn't expect."

His mother sat back in her chair and collected her thoughts.

"I heard Adrian Rogers give a good definition of God's mercy and grace the other day on the radio. Do you realize how many Christians can't give anything better than a six-year-old's definition of God's grace? The common response is that we don't deserve grace but something God offers freely. But this definition doesn't tell you about the 'something,' does it?"

"No, it doesn't."

"Pastor Rogers explained it wonderfully. The first part is forgiveness. Most of us understand forgiveness, but some have a hard time with it."

She glanced at Michael, who nodded but remained silent.

"The pastor asked us to imagine a man who murdered a woman's son. When the trial concluded, and the judge was about to give his judgment, the mother of the dead son stood up and said, 'Judge, I forgive this man for killing my son. I want him to know I have no ill will toward him.'"

"That's tough to do," Michael said.

"Maybe so, but let's think about mercy. Same scenario, but this time the woman says, 'Judge, I forgive this man for killing my son, and I ask you to free him. That's mercy.

"This last part is God's grace. The woman continued, 'Your honor, this man can live in my home and stay in my son's room. I'll feed him, clothe him, and look after him.'

"That's exactly what Jesus does for each of us who accepts Him. We were lost in sin, but He took us in. To truly understand God's mercy and grace is to understand forgiveness. If you can't forgive, you might struggle with the other two."

"I understand Jesus said many times that we are to forgive. I know I should do it. I'm just having a hard time doing it," Michael said.

"Are you saved?"

"You know I am."

"Did you ask God to forgive you of your sins?"

"Yes, I did. I know not forgiving makes me look like a hypocrite, but …"

"But nothing. When we forgive, there's no but. It's over and put behind us."

"I'm not disagreeing with you," Michael said.

"Remember the story in John's Gospel where a woman was caught in adultery. The law said she should be stoned. Jesus told her accusers to chunk stones at her — but only those who were without sin. They all left, and He forgave her. Many forgive, but we keep a rock in our pockets. The rock is there because we say we forgive, but in our hearts, we haven't. John says God is light. Walking in the light as He is in the light, we have fellowship one with another, and the blood of Jesus Christ, His Son, cleans us from all sin."

Several seconds passed as Michael thought.

"Forgive her, son."

"I didn't say it was a she."

"No, you didn't, but a mother knows these things."

Michael seemed frustrated. "I know what I must do. I knew it before I headed home. I can't understand why I'm having such difficulty with this," he said.

"Son, God does not make us sin — that would be against everything He teaches. Sin comes from one place, and the devil is jumping up and down because he has you twisted up. Do you think she might be going through a rough time? She's probably praying for your forgiveness, but you are playing right into the devil's hand. Stop thinking of yourself; think of her a moment."

"That's why I've always enjoyed our talks, Mom. You don't sugarcoat it," Michael said, shaking his head.

His mother laughed. "You know what they say: If it walks like a duck, quacks like a duck, and swims like a duck, it's a duck. Maybe you need to ask for help with this. Take it to the Lord. He won't lead you astray."

On Sunday after church, Michael returned to Charlotte. He finally realized he had been wrong. Jesus would have forgiven Rachel, but Michael had kicked it up a notch. He wallowed in his past wrongs. Shutting Rachel out would not help him get over that. He saw his error. He knew he had responded wrongly to her when it happened, but he let his shield down, and the devil smacked him on the chin.

He pulled into Rachel's driveway. As he got out, she opened her door. She was anxious to talk. She had so much she wanted to explain, but Michael had not given her the opportunity.

He walked up and looked into her eyes. He could see she was hurt.

"Rachel, I forgive you for what you asked. I'm sorry I've taken so long to tell you."

She threw her arms around him and sobbed.

"I needed to hear you say that. I'm sorry for all the pain I've caused."

He wrapped his arms around her and consoled her.

"I'm sorry for the pain I've caused you."

"I don't know why I said what I did," Rachel said. "I guess my impatience got the better of me. I'm glad you forgive me. Now, I need to forgive myself."

"I feel like a hypocrite telling you this, but give it to the Lord and put it behind you."

"I will. Do you want to come in for a while?"

He agreed, and they walked in and sat on the couch.

"Would you like a sweet tea?"

"No, thank you. I can't stay long. I need to get home and get ready for work tomorrow. You know, boots to shine and uniforms to press."

"Oh, yes. I know that routine. Dad was in the army when I was born."

"I just wanted to assure you that I have put this behind us," Michael said. "It hasn't changed anything. I still want to move forward with our relationship."

"I do, too. I love you so much."

Michael was caught off guard. The two had expressed their love for each other in actions, but he had never heard her say she loved him, and he had never told her. He rubbed her back and confirmed her feelings.

"I love you, too."

"I've been waiting to hear you say that," Rachel said.

"I guess I have taken my time getting around to that."

"It's okay. You're teaching me patience."

"And you're teaching me forgiveness."

On Saturday at the Davidsons, Michael sat next to the general as they waited for the girls to arrive. Monica had announced she was bringing a guest.

"So, have you and Rachel kissed and made up?" the general asked.

"Yes sir. I think all is well."

"That's good."

"What do you know about Monica's guest?" Michael asked.

"The difference in my daughters is one tells everything while the other tells nothing. You know which is which.

"However, Monica has provided a lot of information. 'Guest' is her term used mildly. I think "boyfriend' would suffice. His name is Roman Kaminski. He's from Poland and served in their army."

"I wonder what he did in the Polish army?"

"He was in their special force's unit, JW GROM," the general said.

About that time, they looked up to see Monica and her guest walking out the back door and approaching them. Monica hugged her father and Michael.

"Daddy, Michael, I would like you to meet Roman."

Michael and the general stood and shook Roman's hand.

"It's good to meet you. Monica has told me a lot about both of you," Roman said.

"It's good to meet you, Roman. Welcome to our home," the general said.

"Yes, welcome. Have you been in the States long, Roman? Your English is good," Michael added.

"A few months, but I spoke English while in Poland."

"We hear you served in the military in the special forces unit," the general said.

"Yes sir. I was chosen in the late 1980s to begin training with the new unit. Your Special Operations soldiers instructed us in counter-terrorism tactics and urban warfare. We graduated in the middle of 1990. I was in the first class to wear the JW GROM patch. After that, I was asked to help start a school for training future candidates. When my time was up, I moved to North Carolina and started studying to take the real estate exam."

"No kidding. My oldest daughter is in real estate." He looked at his watch. "Speaking of Rachel, I wonder where she is?"

"She probably had a late showing. She's still behind from our trip," Michael said.

No sooner had the words left Michael's mouth than Sarah came running out the back door.

"Tom! Tom!"

The general stood and focused on his wife like a bird dog pointing out his quarry. Michael also stood, looking confused and concerned.

"Rachel's been in an accident!"

The general glanced at Michael, unsure and unwilling to believe what he had heard.

"Accident … Rachel?"

Michael bolted toward Sarah with the general hot on his heels. They grabbed Sarah, who was out of breath and sobbing loudly.

"Rachel was in a car accident. They just called."

"Which hospital did they take her to?" Michael asked.

"The one where Monica works."

Michael raced to his truck and peeled out of the driveway. A few minutes later, he arrived at the emergency room. Gen. Davidson and Sarah were not far behind. And soon, Roman and Monica followed.

"Are you a relative?" the nurse asked Michael.

The general stood beside Michael. "Yes, he is. And I'm her father."

"Rachel is here, and the doctors are with her now. If you want to sit, someone will be out shortly to update you."

The general turned, frustration on his face. He wanted to know her status … now. The general and Michael paced back and forth.

"Tom, will you please sit?" Sarah asked.

"Sorry, dear. I need to know something about our daughter."

Monica tried to calm him. "Dad, she's probably in X-ray. They will let us know something in a few minutes."

Michael said nothing but bent over with his head in his hands. He didn't want to lose Rachel. The accident had confirmed how much he loved her.

"Don't you worry, son. They'll give us an update momentarily," the general said. Then looking at Monica, he asked, "You work here. Do you think you can go back and find out anything?"

Monica nodded, got up, and entered a door just as a doctor exited.

"Hello, Monica. What brings you to the ER?"

"My sister was in a car accident."

"I was just coming to get the family. Gather them together, and we'll meet in the waiting room outside surgery."

The family followed Monica and the doctor into a smaller waiting room, where he offered them a seat.

"My name is Doctor Edwards. I wanted to give you an update. She broke a few ribs, and the lower part of her liver and one of her ovaries are bruised and slightly ruptured. Also, she had some head trauma, and she has some swelling."

"Is she going to be all right?"

"I feel certain she will. She is being prepped for surgery now. We will relieve the swelling in her head and flush her liver out."

"You mentioned an ovary?" Sarah said.

"Yes ma'am. We'll have to remove it."

Sarah sobbed loudly as she clutched her husband's arm. The general consoled her, holding back his tears.

"I'm going to get back in there, but as soon as we're done, I'll update you."

After the doctor left, Sarah looked at Michael and tried to calm herself enough to speak.

"She may not have children, Michael."

Michael only nodded as he felt a tear form. Rachel was going to be devastated. Having children was something she dearly wanted. He lowered his head and silently prayed.

For the next few minutes, no one spoke. Everyone was in deep thought, hoping and praying for the best. Michael smiled slightly. He looked at the clock on the wall and remembered his mother's advice: "Get quiet and listen to God."

"How long do you think she'll be in surgery?" the general asked Monica.

"Between one and two hours, possibly."

Michael and the general alternated between pacing and sitting for the next hour. The emergency room remained relatively quiet, except for the shuffling of the men's feet and the occasional squeak caused by their shoes on the waxed floor.

Michael remembered how Rachel had learned a lesson in patience, but now he was having his tested. The wait burdened him. Was Rachel going to have any associated problems in the future? Could she still have children? How long did they have to wait before knowing some of the answers?

Michael felt helpless. He wanted to do something to ease Rachel's discomfort. He finally sat and led the family — and Roman — in prayer.

"Father, we thank You for Rachel. We ask that You give the doctors and nurses the skill and alert attention she needs. We love her, Lord. We pray for You to comfort and heal her. In Jesus' name, amen."

Each person replied with an "Amen."

"Roman, I'm sorry that meeting the family went like this," Michael said to Roman.

"Don't think anything of it. I'm just hoping the best for her."

Monica squeezed his hand and smiled.

"Can you give us details about what they are doing?" the general asked Monica.

Monica was reluctant but knew her father would not relent. She tried to spare too many details, hoping the doctor would cover that for her.

"They will relieve the pressure and fluid in her head by drilling a small hole."

"Maybe not all the details, just yet," Sarah said.

The family fell silent again as each one imagined Rachel's surgical procedure.

After what seemed an eternity, Dr. Edwards walked in.

"Rachel's surgery went well. She's resting comfortably," he said.

"What did you have to do?" the general asked.

"Since she had swelling in her head, we drilled a small hole to relieve the pressure and fluid. And we flushed out her liver. The rupture isn't that large, but it will take time to heal."

"Can we see her?" the general asked.

"As soon as they get her settled in a room. I should mention, though, that she's still unconscious."

Sarah covered her mouth as she sobbed. The general hugged her.

"When will she wake up?" the general asked.

"With head injuries, it varies. I would suspect when the swelling goes down some."

"Can she still have children?" Sarah asked.

"Mathematically speaking, she only has a 50 percent chance by removing an ovary. However, the remaining ovary is healthy, so if she produces eggs, yes, she can."

Sarah exhaled deeply as she grabbed her husband's hand. They were both relieved to know grandchildren were not out of the question.

"If you have any further questions, I'll be happy to answer them. Just know we are going to take good care of Rachel."

"Thank you, doctor. Thanks for all you've done," Michael said.

After the doctor walked out, the nurse announced, "You can visit Rachel now, but only two at a time."

Gen. Davidson and Sarah followed the nurse as Michael waited his turn.

"They probably don't allow anyone to stay at night, do they?" he asked Monica.

"No, not in ICU. Are you considering staying with her?"

"Yes. I remember waking up in the hospital, not knowing where I was or how I got there. Maybe I can eliminate that fear for her."

"I don't think that's an unreasonable request. Let me ask someone."

Monica got up to find the answer to her question.

"Monica tells me you and Rachel are dating," Roman said.

"Yes, funny thing. I met her in a hospital."

"You were wounded in Kuwait, right?"

"Yep. Seems like a long time ago."

Monica walked back into the room. "I persuaded them to let you stay tonight, but there are some conditions. You must stay out of their way. They will be in and out all night."

"I can do that."

"My best friend, Janet, will be on duty tonight. She knows you will be staying."

"Thanks for asking. I appreciate it."

"You're welcome. The doctor was reluctant, but Janet spoke up for you."

"I'll have to thank her, too."

"You'll meet her."

The general and Sarah walked back into the room. Michael could tell some of their worries had been relieved.

"Michael, would you like to go next?" Monica asked.

"I'll go in after you."

Roman got up and walked out of the door with Monica.

"How does she look?" Michael asked the general.

"She has a few cuts and scrapes, but for the most part, she looks good."

"Monica cleared it for me to stay with her tonight," Michael said.

Sarah grabbed Michael's arm. "That's sweet."

"Good. You can call us when she wakes up," the general said.

"And it doesn't matter what time it is," Sarah added.

"Yes ma'am. I'll call you even if it's two in the morning."

Sarah glanced up at her husband and Michael.

"Seems we have been in hospitals a lot lately."

Both men nodded but said nothing. Then, Gen. Davidson changed the subject.

"Michael, after you see her, we can get something to eat."

A few minutes later, Monica and Roman walked back into the waiting room, and Michael got up to take his turn. He could see Rachel in a room surrounded by glass walls. He walked up to her and took her hand. She didn't respond to his touch. She looked as if she was in a peaceful sleep. The monitors hooked to her did not indicate alarm.

"Rachel, it's Michael," Michael said, clearing his throat. "I'm going to talk to you a little bit. The doctors believe there is evidence to say you may hear me. Just know you are safe. Your family and I are here with you."

He stood there, remembering Rachel at her finest. Memories of seeing her walk toward him on the pier, her in her apron when she opened the door, and the smile she always had when they sat together in the church came rushing back.

"Rachel, I haven't told you enough, but I love you. I think I fell in love with you when I was in the hospital. I feel certain God brought us together."

He began to pull his hand away, but for a second, he thought he felt the slightest movement. He paused, then decided he was imagining things.

"I'm going to grab a bite to eat, but I'll be back. I'm going to stay with you tonight."

He bent down, kissed her on the cheek, and whispered, "I love you and always have."

When Michael returned to the waiting room, he noticed Monica and Roman had left.

"Monica will be back after church in the morning. She will call the pastor and the Boones," the general explained.

"That's good. I haven't done that yet."

The three walked to the cafeteria, thankful that Rachel was doing well.

"I plan to take this week off, Michael. I'll let them know you are, too, if that's what you want to do."

"I would like to stay with her."

Sarah looked across the table and smiled. "Rachel would like that."

"I don't want to leave her alone. Also, I remember waking up in the hospital, confused and not knowing where I was or how I got there."

"Yes, I remember that as well," the general added. "It's considerate of you to relieve her from that burden."

After the Davidsons left, Michael moved a chair closer to Rachel's bed for the night. He focused on Rachel as she lay there motionless. Even in a hospital gown, she looked beautiful.

God had given him this gift. He felt sure of that. He had waited for the right woman for years, and God had steered him to Rachel. He thought about how the events, starting in Kuwait, had set him on the path to where he sat.

Only God could have thought this one up, he thought.

Michael remembered his doctor in the hospital and how God had put it on his heart to minister to the doctor. God had sent him to Maryland, all the way from the sands of Kuwait. *And I didn't even have to pay airfare.*

A nurse walked into the room to check on Rachel and smiled.

"You must be Michael. I'm Janet. Monica and I are friends. We work together sometimes. I'll be taking care of Miss Rachel tonight."

"It's good to meet you," Michael said, shaking her hand.

Janet walked to the bed and replaced an empty IV bag.

"She's going to be fine. She may have to stay in bed for a few days until her liver heals, but she will be fine."

"That's good news."

Janet changed the subject as she talked over her shoulder, attending to Rachel.

"Monica tells me that you two may be getting married soon."

"I hope. I haven't officially asked her yet."

"You don't have cold feet, do you?"

"No, just been waiting for the right time."

Janet finished with Rachel. "I'll be back in to check on her in a little while. If she wakes up, you can come to get me."

After Janet left, Michael searched for a Bible in the nightstand.

"Would you like me to read to you?" He looked up at Rachel, who didn't respond. "I'm going to take that as a yes."

He turned to Psalm 145 and read the first two verses: "I will extol thee, my God, O king; and I will bless thy name for ever and ever. Every day will I bless thee; and I will praise thy name for ever and ever."

Michael found comfort in David's song of praise and said, "I think I found my devotional for the morning."

He placed his finger inside to hold his place, shut the Bible, and prayed. "Father, I thank You for bringing Rachel through her trials. Thank You for everyone here at the hospital who had a hand in your mercy. I thank You for bringing me here and putting Rachel in my life. I ask that You would continue to comfort and heal her. In Jesus's name, amen."

As Michael opened his eyes, he heard a slight groan. Rachel was waking up.

He quickly took her hand. "Rachel, I'm here with you."

She groaned again and slowly opened her eyes.

"Michael, is that you?" she muttered, still groggy.

"Yes. I'm standing beside you."

She opened her eyes more and breathed deeper, trying to understand.

"What happened?"

"You were in an accident, but you're okay now. You're safe."

Rachel tried to recall what had happened.

"I remember getting thrown around and then getting loaded in an ambulance," she said.

"You've been knocked out for a few hours. Let me grab a nurse."

Michael hurried down the hall and found Janet.

"She's awake."

Janet rushed into the room with Michael close behind. A doctor followed, and Michael stepped out of the way, walked outside, and used the pay phone to call the Davidsons.

Sarah picked up on the first ring.

"She's awake," Michael said.

"Thank you, Jesus. We'll be right there."

Michael hung up, ran back to the room, and waited outside as the medical team finished.

"She's going to be fine. I'll come back in a few minutes and talk to her," the doctor said as he walked out.

Michael went back to Rachel's bedside and took her hand. She looked up at him.

"I'm glad you are here, Michael."

"I wouldn't be anywhere else."

She smiled and gripped his hand tighter.

"Where's Mom and Dad?"

"They are on the way. I called them."

"What happened to me?"

Michael assumed the doctor hadn't told her about her injuries, and he was reluctant to tell the whole story.

"You broke some ribs."

"That explains why my side hurts. Anything else?"

"You had some swelling in your head, so they had to relieve it."

"I'm not going to ask how they did that."

"Yeah, we don't want to ruin the doctor getting to use all of those big words."

She lightly giggled until her side hurt.

"Don't make me laugh. It hurts more."

Michael changed the subject, trying to get her mind off her injuries.

"Did you know about Monica's boyfriend?"

Rachel looked at him with a puzzled expression.

"Not hardly. Are you serious? How long was I out?"

"She brought him by the house to meet everyone. He seems like a nice guy."

"That's news to me. But it doesn't surprise me. Monica doesn't tell her business, so they could have been dating for months."

"I thought the same thing, although it did surprise me."

The doctor walked back in and stepped to the side of her bed.

"How are you feeling, Miss Davidson?"

"I suppose it could be worse. Mostly sore all over."

"That's understandable. Being in a car accident, you probably got banged around some. How is your pain?"

"I think it's okay for now."

"I wanted to explain the extent of your injuries and our corrections. You had some head trauma that caused some swelling, so we drilled a small hole and drained the fluid. We want to run another scan now that some swelling has gone down. You broke a few ribs, and the lower part of your liver was bruised and ruptured. We flushed it out, and with four or five days of bed rest, you should heal."

Sarah and the general walked in as the doctor continued.

"You also had a ruptured ovary that we had to remove."

Rachel gasped for air, covered her mouth with her hands, and cried. Sarah turned to her husband to hide her tears.

"However, your remaining ovary is healthy, so I see no reason you can't get pregnant."

Rachel looked up at Michael and held his hand even tighter. The lower probability caused her concern, but she tried to be positive and focus on the possibility.

Michael held her hand, thankful that she was alive. Removing an ovary didn't change his outlook. If children were in God's plan, then it would happen.

Sarah and the general stepped to the opposite side of the bed.

"Welcome back, Sunshine," Sarah said.

"Yes, welcome back. We've missed you," the general said.

"It's good to see you both," Rachel said.

After the doctor walked out, Michael quietly listened to Rachel and her parents' conversation. He was overjoyed to have his Rachel back. It was wonderful to hear her speak again.

Rachel's condition improved in the days that followed, but her demeanor didn't. Michael could tell she was depressed. He had attempted to lift her spirits, but making her laugh caused her pain. He felt as if he were between a rock and a hard place. But he never left her side except to run home for long enough to shower and grab a sandwich. He would doze off and on in the chair beside her bed each night. She seemed to rest easier with him there.

Around the middle of the week, the doctors moved Rachel to recovery. They put her on Monica's wing, which pleased everyone. Monica had brought a roll-away bed so Michael would be more comfortable at night.

As Michael sat beside Rachel one morning, sipping his coffee, he remembered when he was in the hospital and how he had grumbled and complained about being in bed for only a short time. Rachel had not been allowed to get up for days but never complained.

"Good morning," Michael said when Rachel awoke.

"Good morning. Did you sleep well?"

"Better than I did in that chair. I admire you, Rachel."

"Well, I admire you, too," Rachel said.

"No, I'm serious. You haven't complained about getting out of that bed once."

"They said I would be stuck here a few days, so why complain?"

"That's true, but you have a better attitude about it than I did."

"I wouldn't say that. They wanted you to get up. With me, they don't."

Monica walked in, smiling. "Morning, sis. Michael. How is everyone this morning?"

"I'm feeling better. Do you know when I can go home?" Rachel asked.

"Your liver needs to heal a little longer. I would say a couple more days. So far, though, everything looks good. The doctor will be in this morning to check on you. I'll be back in a few hours."

As Monica left, Michael glanced at Rachel, knowing he would lift her spirits today.

"Rachel, will you marry me?"

"Of course, I'll marry you, Michael."

He got up to kiss her.

"I will ask your father for your hand when they arrive."

"He'll give you both of them."

Michael saw an instant change in Rachel's mood. He saw the joy return. He sat there listening to her, excitedly giving the wedding details.

"Who do you want to be your best man?" Rachel asked.

Michael replied without a moment's hesitation. "Dutton."

Rachel raised an eyebrow. Heather had been her bridesmaid, and she assumed Michael would have chosen Chris as his best man. But after Michael explained his reason behind the choice, she agreed.

"We can let the Boones know our decision when they come by to visit," Michael said, "and you can tell them."

A few minutes later, the Davidsons walked in. Rachel tried to conceal her joy, but instead, she smiled like an opossum eating persimmons.

"Someone must feel a little better today," the general said, leaning down to kiss her on the cheek.

"I suppose I do."

Rachel glanced at Michael, giving him his cue.

"General Davidson, sir, I want your permission to marry your daughter."

The general glanced at Sarah, then sat down as his emotions poured out. He sobbed as Sarah smiled and rubbed his back to console him.

Rachel wept as Michael held her hand while the general regained his composure. He looked up at Michael, trying to speak but only nodded.

No one spoke for a moment until her father breathed deeply and replied, "You have our permission, son."

Rachel told them about Michael's choice of best man. The general nodded his approval.

"I think that's an excellent choice. Have you asked him yet?"

"No sir. He doesn't know yet, and Boone doesn't either. Rachel and I plan to break the news to Chris this evening when they come by."

"I see. I hope we're still here when you do."

"I do, too," Rachel said.

Their anticipation built as they waited hours for Heather and Chris to arrive. Shortly after the evening meal, they finally walked into the room. Monica had also been given the news and stood beside Rachel's bed as the Boones greeted everyone in the room.

Michael could no longer wait as he looked at his former gunner.

"Chris, I've asked Rachel to marry me."

Heather squealed with surprise.

"That's wonderful. Congratulations, Sergeant Logan."

"Thank you."

Rachel glanced at Michael again, waiting for him to give Chris the news.

"I wanted you to hear it from me. I'm going to ask Dutton to be my best man," Michael said.

Everyone remained silent, paying particular attention to Chris's reaction. He replied without showing any sign of disappointment.

"Dutton is a good choice. He's experienced at it."

Michael looked at Rachel for her to tell the last part of the news. She smiled as she got Chris's attention.

"Chris, Dutton has to be the best man. You can't do that and marry us."

"Marry you? You want me to marry you?"

Rachel looked at Heather and then Chris. "We do."

"I'd be glad to marry you."

Michael walked toward Boone and hugged him.

"Forgive me for leading you on, but I couldn't resist."

"You had me there for a minute," Chris said.

"So, have you decided on a date?" Heather asked.

"In the spring?" Rachel asked, looking at Michael.

"That's fine with me."

Rachel recovered fully, and when she wasn't working, she spent much time with Heather, planning the wedding. She never mentioned that children could be a challenge, but Michael knew it was in the back of her mind.

Rachel hired Roman to help grow her business. He was an immediate success, and she regretted not hiring someone sooner. She even considered hiring an additional agent after the wedding.

One Sunday after church, Michael sat at Rachel's dining room table, enjoying her prepared meal.

"I guess you will be moving into my apartment after we are married?"

"You know better than that. You will be giving up your bachelor pad and moving in here," Rachel said.

Michael changed the subject.

"How would you like to go to my mom's with me next weekend? You can sleep in my sister's old room."

"I'd like that. I've wanted to see where you grew up."

"It's just a little farm in the country. I'm not that far from retiring. Someday, I want to move back home and raise cattle. How would you feel about that?"

Rachel sat her fork down, realizing there had to be a compromise.

"My business is taking off. How soon are you talking about?"

"If I make First Sergeant, maybe in the next five to eight years."

"Well, by then, I may be able to step back and spend more time at home. I would still want to maintain the company, though." There was a moment's silence, and then Rachel giggled. "Cattle? I'm marrying a rancher?"

"No, just a farmer. Ranchers have a lot more land and a lot more cows."

"I've never been around cattle. Are they profitable?"

"Raising them takes a lot of work. Fences to keep up and hay to cut. You can make a little money selling them for beef, but you earn every penny."

"I don't understand. If you're retiring from the army, why do you want to do something so labor-intensive?"

"I can't sit on the porch and do nothing. It'll give me something to do. Dad raised cattle before he died but did it as a hobby. I want to do it full-time."

"I support what you want and am fine with living there, but I want you to support me in keeping my business going."

"I will. I know you aren't ready to retire just yet. How will your parents feel about your moving away?"

"I think they will be fine with it since I will work here a few days a week. I'll keep the house until I retire, and then we can sell it."

"Sounds like a plan."

Michael wondered how children could change everything. He didn't mention it to Rachel since he felt it would add to her grief. He remembered his childhood and how he was raised on the farm. He wanted his children to experience what both parents had to offer.

Michael left work at lunchtime on Friday, and Rachel crawled into the pickup with a small suitcase. She smiled, excited to make the trip and see what Michael had told her about.

"What does your family think about your marrying me?"

"They think it's about time. Mom met you at the awards ceremony and thought you were the one."

"Really? I guess I felt that way, too."

As they continued, the ground began to show signs of recent snow. Rachel paid close attention. The farther they went, the more snow she saw.

"How often does it snow here?"

"October through March. Four or five months is all," Michael said.

Rachel turned away and looked out the window. He could tell she didn't care for snow.

"Do you like to ski?" Michael asked.

"Not really."

He knew they would have to deal with the snow if they were to live in the mountains.

"Mom said they got about four inches last night, so we will see more of it."

"I'm just not used to it hanging around. In our part of North Carolina, we get snow, but usually, in a few days, it's gone."

When they pulled into the driveway, Rachel sat up and studied the scenery. The real estate agent in her was impressed.

"This is beautiful. I love the house and all the trees. How much land is here?"

"It's on forty acres."

"Forty acres? Wow, impressive."

"Forty acres in West Virginia that's level would be impressive. This has a fair number of hills and valleys."

"Hey there, Rachel. Come on in before you freeze," Janis said, stepping onto the porch to greet them.

"You have a beautiful place here, Mrs. Logan," Rachel said as she stepped onto the porch.

"Call me Janis, and thank you. It's home."

She turned to Michael, who carried their two bags.

"Welcome home, son. It's good to see you both. Come on in. Coffee's ready."

Michael took Rachel's suitcase to her room while Janis gave Rachel the tour. Michael put his bag in his room, returned to the kitchen, poured two cups of coffee, and sat at the kitchen table, waiting for the ladies to return. He could hear them talking and giggling as they moved throughout the house.

When Rachel walked into the kitchen, she looked at Michael and said, "This is beautiful. I love the country charm."

Michael nodded and offered Rachel her coffee. "It's home. Dad did all the renovations."

Janis sat at the table and glanced at Rachel. "Yes, he did. I wish you could have met him."

"I do, too. Michael has told me so much about him."

Janis changed the subject. "Congratulations on your engagement."

"Thank you."

"Michael has mentioned a spring wedding. Do you know where and when yet?"

"Yes, it will be at our church."

"I love church weddings. Since both of you are Christians, it will be good to include God in the celebration."

"Yes, God brought us together. He gets the glory," Rachel said.

Janis began to tear up.

"Are you okay?" Rachel asked.

"Yes, I'm fine, just overcome with God's goodness. It's been a long wait, but God is faithful. Michael has waited for a godly woman, and now the wait is over. Praise God."

The ladies continued to talk as Michael sat there, listening and occasionally commenting. He felt his mother was right, and he was thankful. He looked out the window and saw the snow begin to fall softly. He thought about how his journey had started in the heat of the desert. God had brought him a long way to fulfill his prayers. It seemed so long ago.

Rachel was included in his journey. She was everything he wanted in a woman. He sipped his coffee and smiled, thinking to himself, *Thank You, Lord.*

CHAPTER 9

A few weeks later, the general and CSM Samson entered Michael's office.

"Sergeant Logan, it appears we will have to get a new nameplate on this door," the general said.

Michael looked up and smiled. "How's that, sir?"

The general reached out his hand. "You made First Sergeant. Congratulations."

"Thank you, sir. Thank you, Sergeant Major," Michael said, shaking both men's hands.

"You deserve it," Samson said.

Michael had reached another goal in his life. His career was moving closer to his final goal: retirement. He thanked God. Everything seemed to be coming together nicely.

The general called a formation on the drill floor inside because of the cool weather. Michael made his way to the front where, once again, he was surprised to see his family, Rachel's family, Roman, Pastor Hatcher, the Boones, and Dutton.

The general gave a short speech, and then CS Samson, read the promotion orders.

"Attention to orders. The Secretary of the Army has reposed special trust and confidence in the patriotism, valor, fidelity, and professional excellence of Sergeant First Class, Michael Logan. Because of these qualities, demonstrated leadership potential, and dedicated service to the United States Army, he is promoted to First Sergeant."

The general and CSM Samson stood side-by-side in front of Michael as each prepared to pin the new rank on his lapels. CSM Samson removed the old rank and tossed it over his shoulder. He then pushed the sharp ends of the new rank into Michael's uniform, made a fist, and pounded it into Michael's chest.

Michael stood at attention, not reacting to the scene. He had experienced the tradition enlisted men receive when promoted. He knew it was coming. It symbolized, "Keep this rank and live up to the standards it requires."

The general pinned his side and shook Michael's hand.

"Congratulations, First Sergeant Logan."

The celebration moved to Rachel's house. She had prepared several hors d'oeuvres for her guests. Michael and the general were stationed close to the prepared table. Each one had a sampling of everything on their plates. Dutton approached to congratulate his old platoon sergeant.

"I will have to get used to calling you First Sergeant," Dutton said as he shook Michael's hand.

"I will have to get accustomed to hearing it, too. Thanks for coming, Dutton."

Dutton cleared his throat and changed the subject. "I wanted you to know that my leave got denied for your wedding."

Michael quickly glanced at the general. "Really? That's not good."

Dutton added, "We have a training exercise that will take place during that time."

The general looked at Michael and then Dutton with an unconcerned expression. "I'll make a call. I'm sure they can get by for one day without you." Dutton and Michael nodded. "But let's not say anything to Rachel about this. No need to give her something to worry about. I know your division commander, so let me see what I can do."

Michael and Dutton breathed a little easier, knowing the general would try to make his daughter's wedding successful.

As the general stepped away, Rachel walked up. "Where's Dad going?"

"I think he had to make a call. He'll be right back."

Michael turned the conversation, hoping not to reveal Dutton's news. "I hope you saved me some of these pigs in a blanket for later."

"I may have saved some for you and Dad. You know how he enjoys eating."

"Miss Rachel, have you decided what's on the menu for the wedding?" Dutton asked.

"Oh, yes. We are having BBQ or chicken with slaw, baked beans, and macaroni and cheese. We both agreed on simple country style."

"Sounds good."

After a few minutes, the general returned and gave Michael and Dutton a thumbs up. Dutton would be at the wedding, after all.

As spring arrived, the anticipation grew. The general and Sarah seemed as excited as Rachel. They both looked forward to grandchildren but tried to remain positive, knowing it might not happen.

Rachel had not spoken about children since she received the news in the hospital about her ovary removal. Michael didn't talk about it either. He was leaving it up to God. He would welcome children, but it wouldn't change how he felt about Rachel if they never had any.

Everyone gathered at the church early on the wedding day to begin their preparations. Rachel and Michael had asked Pastor Hatcher to orchestrate and manage the event. Chris was relieved to have him close at hand for questions.

Rachel had decided her father, Michael, and Dutton would wear their Class A uniforms. She had been brought up in a military home, and it only seemed fitting since she was marrying a military man. Chris was given the freedom to wear the suit of his choice. Michael appreciated her simplicity.

The men gathered in a Sunday school room, waiting to be called to their positions. Chris nervously read notes.

"My hands are sweating. Nerves, I suppose," the general said.

"Mine, too," Michael said.

Gen. Davidson put his hand on Michael's shoulder, revealing how humble he felt.

"Michael, I just want you to know that Sarah and I couldn't be prouder. The two of you complement each other nicely."

"Thank you, General."

"I agree, General. He's got him a good woman there," Dutton added.

Chris stood near the three men but hadn't commented or looked up. Michael understood; Chris was nervous — maybe more than he was. Michael glanced at the general and Dutton as he tried to ease Boone's anxiety.

"Boone, you have nothing to worry about. We all know you'll do a fine job."

"I'm a little nervous. I don't want to mess things up."

"You won't mess things up, son. That sermon you gave a while back is evidence of that," the general said.

Pastor Hatcher opened the door and stepped halfway in. "Gentlemen, you can take your places now."

As everyone began to file out, Chris quickly spoke up. "Hold on, everyone." He turned to Pastor Hatcher with a help me expression.

The pastor understood the look, stepped the rest of the way in, and shut the door. "Let us pray."

Everyone bowed their heads as the pastor laid his hand on Chris's shoulder. "Father, we come to You today with gladness in our hearts. We thank You for bringing these two children of God together. We thank You for leading Chris into the ministry and giving him the words to speak that bring glory and honor to You. We give You thanks and praise. In Jesus' name, amen."

Everyone said "Amen" and quickly moved out. Michael noticed Chris had a more confident appearance. The pastor had reminded him that God chose him and would give him the words he needed.

As the wedding march began to play, Michael and Dutton turned to watch the general and Rachel make their entrance, and the congregation stood. Michael glanced at Sarah and Monica, who were both sobbing.

As the father and daughter got closer, Michael could see the tears in the general's eyes. The general wanted the best for his daughters. He was amazed at how his little girl had grown up. He remembered teaching her "Itsy Bitsy Spider" as he held her on his lap. The years had flown by, and now he was walking down the aisle to give his daughter in marriage.

The general and Sarah had witnessed Michael's love for the Lord and knew he would also love Rachel. They had noticed the attraction almost immediately when Rachel had first met Michael in the hospital. Michael couldn't take his eyes off Rachel as she came closer. She was the type who could look beautiful in jeans and a t-shirt or a wedding dress and veil.

The general stopped just short of Michael.

"Who gives this woman to be wed?" Chris asked.

Gen. Davidson tried to speak, then glanced at Sarah with tears in his eyes. "Her mother and I."

Michael held out his arm for Rachel. She laid her head against his shoulder and wept as her father walked to his seat and sat down. Heather joined in with the sobbing, and for a moment, Chris nearly broke down as well.

"Dearly beloved, we are gathered here today in the sight of God and in the face of these witnesses to join together Michael and Rachel. Marriage is commended to be honorable among all men and, therefore, not to be entered into unadvisedly or lightly by any but reverently, discreetly, advisedly, and solemnly. Into this holy estate, these two people present now come to be joined. If any person can show just cause why they may not be joined together, let them speak now or forever hold their peace."

Chris paused and looked up at the congregation, thankful no one interrupted.

"Michael and Rachel, as you prepare to take these vows, give careful thought and prayer, for as you make them, you are making an exclusive commitment one to the other for as long as you both shall live. Your love for each other should never be diminished by difficult circumstances, and it is to endure until death parts you.

"As God's children, your marriage is strengthened by your obedience to your heavenly Father and His Word. As you let God control your marriage, He will cause your home to be a place of joy and a testimony to the world.

"Michael, repeat after me: I, Michael, take thee, Rachel, to be my wedded wife, to have and to hold, from this day forward, for better, for worse, for richer, for poorer, in sickness and in health, to love and to cherish, till death do us part, according to God's holy ordinance; and thereto I pledge thee my faith and myself to you."

Michael repeated the vows, and Chris turned to Rachel.

"Rachel, repeat after me: I, Rachel, take thee, Michael, to be my wedded husband, to have and to hold, from this day forward, for better, for worse, for richer, for poorer, in sickness and in health, to love and to cherish, till death do us part, according to God's holy ordinance; and thereto I pledge thee my faith and myself to you."

Rachel repeated the vows, trying to hold back her tears of joy. Rings were exchanged, and the couple looked into each other's eyes as if they were looking deeply into their hearts.

Chris looked up at the congregation. "Michael and Rachel, by their solemn promises, freely made before God and in the presence of this assembly, have joined themselves to one another for love and life. Those whom God has joined together, let no one separate. I now pronounce you man and wife, united in marriage. Michael, you may kiss the bride."

Michael held Rachel tightly as they kissed. Everyone stood and applauded.

"I present to you, Mr. and Mrs. Michael Logan," Chris said.

The couple held hands as they walked toward the opened doors in the rear of the church. The applause and congratulations continued until they walked down the steps.

Everyone moved to the fellowship hall as Michael and Rachel stood on the sidewalk, taking a moment to soak in what had just happened.

Michael held out his arm as he joked his best *Gone with the Wind* impersonation. "Mrs. Logan, would you care to join me for a refreshment?"

Rachel smiled and curtsied, adding her sense of humor to the question. "Why, yes, Mr. Logan. A refreshment would be most welcome."

They laughed as they walked around the sidewalk and entered the fellowship hall. Several mingled conversations were quickly muted as everyone turned their attention to the couple. Rachel's humor continued as she faced the crowd, holding Michael's elevated and outstretched hand. She curtsied again, like a proper southern lady, as everyone laughed.

They made their way to their table as Dutton reached the front.

"I am still active in the military, so excuse me if I address Michael as First Sergeant Logan. Actually, I feel uncomfortable calling him by his name. You know I've known First Sergeant Logan for several years and have a deep respect for him. So, knowing that, I want to turn my attention to the beautiful lady seated beside him. Rachel and the First Sergeant met at Walter Reed Hospital while Michael was a patient. Their attraction and fondness for each other became apparent almost immediately. I asked Rachel's parents a few questions as I was preparing for this speech, and they felt certain we would end up here. They witnessed Michael and Rachel's love for each other grow. I admit, the first time I met Rachel, I felt she was the one for Michael. God doesn't always give us our heart's desire, but in this case, I believe He did for Michael. Please join me in wishing the newlyweds a life filled with God's love and love for each other."

* * * * * * * * * *

In the weeks that passed, Michael and Rachel adjusted to married life. Michael still felt he should knock on the door before entering their home. And Rachel would look up surprised, wondering who was coming into her house.

Getting used to each other's company and new surroundings was expected. It didn't dampen the love they had for each other. They were both extremely happy to have found the mate missing from their lives. They felt sure God had blessed them.

Michael was humbled to know God had brought him through it all and to the godly woman he had waited for. They both had areas of spiritual weaknesses, but having been made aware of them, they each grew closer to God as they addressed their issues.

Rachel seemed to be fine, waiting for God's gift of a child, until it didn't happen. They had agreed to try to have children as soon as they were married, but by the end of the first month, Michael realized God was giving them a new test.

Rachel stood in the bathroom, reading the results of her pregnancy test.

"Negative. It says we're not pregnant," she said to Michael.

He stepped closer behind her, wrapping his arms around her waist. They looked at each other in the mirror.

"It's okay. I don't want you getting stressed out."

"You're right. This may be something that never happens. I need to trust God and the plan He has for us."

Michael was pleased with her response and felt Rachel was giving the issue to God. But after six months of negative results, she seemed to take it back from God. Heather had found out that she and Chris would soon be parents. Rachel tried to be happy for them, but her lack of patience and doubt began to creep in. She became irritable. Michael knew her every waking moment was focused on a baby.

One evening as they sat at the table eating, Rachel looked up and asked, "Michael, do you think we should get checked out?"

"The doctors said you are fine, so I guess you mean I should get checked?"

She said nothing but nodded. "Would you, please?"

"Sure. Make me an appointment."

Michael was almost disappointed to find out the results. The doctor told him he was normal. Rachel seemed disappointed as well. She would have taken the news better to find out Michael couldn't father children. Now, the burden fell back on her.

They gathered at Rachel's parents' house for a cookout one Saturday that fall. Michael sat outside next to the general and Roman as the ladies prepared. Gen. Davidson sipped his iced tea and offered Michael a few words of encouragement.

"Michael, I have always heard that Rome wasn't built in a day."

"Yes sir, but I believe it burned in one day."

"Valid point. Perhaps not the best example."

"I'm okay. Rachel is the one who's having a difficult time. She wants kids."

"Does that mean you don't want kids?" Roman asked.

"I'm okay if it happens or if it doesn't."

"So the outcome only affects her?" Roman asked.

Michael hadn't realized it, but Roman had made an interesting discovery.

"Do you want children right now?" the general asked.

Michael sat back, thinking before he spoke. "If it happens, yes."

"Michael, have you prayed for children?" Roman asked.

"My prayers are for my wife to accept God's will," Michael said.

"Accepting God's will is a good thing, but often we don't understand his will," Roman said. "The Bible tells us that a man and woman should unite. The two of you seem to have different thoughts on the subject."

"I suppose," Michael admitted.

"Remember, we are told that we receive not because we ask not. Maybe you and Rachel need to get on the same page and pray together. Accept God's will, but how can you truly know His will if you never ask?"

Michael sat back and reflected on Roman's words. Michael realized he had let his wife make her supplications for a family, but he had remained silent.

The men looked up to see Sarah, Rachel, and Monica approaching. Rachel sat on Michael's lap. Roman stood and took Monica's hand. Sarah sat beside her husband as everyone looked on questionably.

Roman kissed Monica on the cheek and then turned to the general. "Mr. Davidson, sir, I have come today to ask for your daughter's hand in marriage."

Gen. Davidson looked at Sarah, who smiled.

"You have our blessing, son."

The marriage proposal had come as a surprise, but Michael was thankful. It gave Rachel something else to occupy her thoughts other than having children. Monica and Rachel began discussing the details, and Rachel even volunteered to help with whatever was needed.

Monica knew it would be good for her sister to focus her attention elsewhere. She chose Janet as her bridesmaid but enlisted Rachel to help with the planning.

In the months that followed Roman and Monica's wedding, Rachel had endured endless negative pregnancy results. She seemed to accept the situation more than before, even after Monica announced she was pregnant.

Rachel smiled each time she held Heather and Monica's children.

Michael knew she still wanted children but realized it was up to God.

Michael thought back on the journey God had taken him on. Initially, it seemed to be a soul-saving task, but now he realized it was more than that. God wanted him to learn a few lessons about himself as well.

Everything that had happened was to bring glory and honor to God. Michael had a strong relationship with God but discovered that as he tried to be more righteous, he became more self-righteous. He had learned his willingness to forgive had a beginning and an end. God had shown him that forgiveness is endless, like God's love.

Rachel and Michael strengthened their relationship with God. They focused on what they had, not what they didn't have. God had brought them together, and they were thankful for that.

* * * * * * * * * *

Five years after the birth of Monica and Roman's child, Michael retired from the army and kept true to his plan. He and Rachel moved back to West Virginia and began raising Black Angus beef cows … and a family.

Early one crisp fall morning, Michael carried a hay bale to the corral where he had ten older cows and a bull waiting for shipment. A blonde-haired, four-year-old girl in cowboy boots and jeans began pulling the straw from the bale and tossing the handfuls to the cattle on the opposite side of the fence.

"I want to help, Daddy."

"Okay, you can help."

The bull walked up to the fence, inches from the young girl. She backed away a few steps. "Whoa, bull."

"The bull has to eat too, baby."

"I don't like the bull. He's mean."

Rachel walked up as the pair fed the cows. She had traded her business casual attire for work boots and jeans. Her ponytail was pulled out from the opening of her cap, which read, "Logan Angus." On her hip, she balanced a toddler. The young boy pointed at the cattle and tried his first words. "Cow."

Rachel smiled at him, "Yes, that's a cow."

Michael stepped back to Rachel as their daughter continued throwing hay through the fence from a greater distance than before. Some hay fell short, and the cows lowered their heads against the fence, sticking out their long tongues to retrieve it.

Rachel looked at Michael. "Breakfast is ready."

"Sounds good."

"I see you are taking the bull this morning."

"We need to rotate a new bloodline."

The little girl turned, hearing part of the conversation.

"Can I pet the calves? I like the calves."

"I like the calves, too. What about that bull? Do you like him?" Michael asked.

"No. He's mean."

"We need the bull to have calves. If we get rid of him, you won't have more calves to pet," Michael explained.

Rachel and Michael smiled at each other as they watched the wheels turning in their daughter's head. She didn't like the choices: keep the bull and pet calves, or get rid of the bull and have no calves.

Michael gave her a third option. "How about we take this bull to the auction, and you pick out a new one?"

She turned around quickly, eyes wide open. She threw her hands in the air and went through all the motions for jumping, but her feet stayed firmly on the ground.

"Yes. I'm going to pick one that's not mean."

Michael laughed as he tossed the rest of the hay over the fence.

"Good luck with that, baby doll."

He held out his hand for his daughter to take it.

"Come on, Violet. Let's go eat."